under the stars

Cottonwood Cove ~ Book 2

laura pavlov

To all the dreamers who beat to their own drum…
Keep dreaming my friends. We only get one chance at this life, so, dance in the closet, sing in the rain and embrace everything that makes you unique.
The brightest lights were never meant to be dimmed.
They were meant to light up the room.
Hugs & Love, Laura

copyright

Under the Stars
Cottonwood Cove, Book 2

Laura Pavlov
https://www.laurapavlov.com
Cover Design: Hang Le
Cover Photography: Madison Maltby

Message from the Author:
Under the Stars contains mature content that may not be suitable for all audiences. Click the link below for content warnings.
https://BookHip.com/HACZMZL

one

. . .

Georgia

NO MORE DIRTBAGS.

I'm officially closed for business.

Now and forever.

I made this silent promise to myself as my hands gripped the steering wheel, snowflakes falling from the sky and splattering across the windshield as I watched the road in front of me.

"I curse the ground you walk on, Dikota Smith," I hissed to myself.

He was the reason I was even in this current situation where I'd needed to lie to my family and borrow a car from my brother's fiancée.

My ex-boyfriend brought the term *douchebag* to an all-new low.

I was grateful that Lila had loaned me her car to take to my interview, as it was freezing in Cottonwood Cove today, and I did not want to walk.

I hadn't told my family the truth about my car because I knew my siblings would lose their minds, and my parents would be upset—I'd have to figure something out in the meantime.

I'd wait him out and hope that the morally challenged dickweasel would come to his senses and no one would be the wiser.

I'd put Dikota in my rearview, and that was exactly where I intended to keep him—just as soon as I got my car back.

Today was a fresh start. A new beginning.

And I was here for it.

My mom had taken me shopping for a new outfit for my interview, which she'd deemed a graduation gift, as I'd just walked at my commencement ceremony less than a week ago.

The town was so festive this time of year. I drove down Main Street, where lights were strung around every light post, and they zigzagged overhead down the length of the entire street. Daylight did not do them justice. I'd been downtown last night having dinner with friends, and it had been all lit up and looked like a winter wonderland. Cottonwood Cove was not only my home, it was my happy place.

Lancaster Press had moved into the large three-story brick building not far from my brother's restaurant, Reynolds', a few months ago. I was interviewing for a personal assistant position for Maddox Lancaster, who was the president of the company.

I'd heard that he was an intimidating rich guy, a bit of a playboy, and a recent resident of my hometown. Apparently, they'd moved the business out of the city, and he'd bought one of the large spec homes in town. Everyone was talking about it. Small-town gossip and all that. Yeah, it was a real thing.

Personally, I didn't know that this was the right career path for me, but I needed a job, seeing as I was temporarily homeless and carless.

Yes, I had a flair for the dramatics.

Obviously, I had a rock star family, and I could borrow a car from my parents or any of my four siblings, and I wasn't technically homeless, as I was currently living with my brother Hugh and his fiancée, Lila. But I wanted to prove that I could do things on my own. Being the youngest of five kids when all your older siblings were absolute winners wasn't always easy when you weren't sure what you wanted to do with your life.

So, first things first.

Get a job.

Get my own place.

And get my car back.

I'd already made it past the initial screening with human resources, which we'd done remotely via a Zoom meeting. But the final decision would be up to Maddox Lancaster.

I pulled in behind the building and glanced in the mirror one last time before dabbing on a little bit of pink lip gloss. I opened the car door and stepped outside, wishing I'd listened to my mother, who'd insisted I wear tights beneath my skirt. I'd refused because I was already wearing this winter-white suit with a pencil skirt and blazer with gold buttons. I loved it, but I wanted to keep things youthful. I was twenty-two years old, after all. So, I'd paired it with some tan heeled booties, which Lila thought looked adorable, even though my mother had insisted I wear my nude heels.

Listen, I was applying to be a personal assistant, not a rocket scientist. And the outfit was already pretty formal for me. So, the booties and all the bangles on my wrist made it feel more like me.

I'd call this look hipster-boss babe chic.

When I pulled the office door open, I immediately recognized the woman sitting behind the desk.

"Hi, Virginia. I didn't know you were working here."

She looked up, and a wide grin spread across her face. "I was thrilled to see you on the calendar, Georgia. I've been working here since they opened the doors. I hope you get the job because it's a little intense around here," she whispered. "If you know what I mean."

The entryway was pretty grand, with two black leather couches, and there were framed book covers hanging on the walls. Gray stained concrete covered the expansive floors, and exposed brick ran from the floor to the ceiling up the wall behind the front desk.

"Really? Did a lot of people move here from the city when the company relocated? Or are the employees mostly new hires?"

"Yes. It's a good mix of both. But lucky for me, the office manager did not want to move here from the city." She glanced around, making sure no one was listening before cupping her hands over her mouth and whisper-shouting. "The big guy can be a bit intimidating, and he's already gone through three PAs since we opened the doors. Apparently, he isn't easy to work for. But I interviewed with the man, and whew," she said, fanning her face. "He is a looker. He's kind of terrifying, and I haven't seen him smile yet, but as long as you do your job, he'll leave you alone. He's all business. And he's currently interviewing Joey Burns for the position that you're applying for right now."

You've got to love Cottonwood Cove if not just for the sheer fact that you can get the lowdown on everything going on in a matter of minutes.

"Joey Burns?" I asked. I grew up with the guy, who I often referred to as *Puff the Magic Dragon.* He was a pot-smoking skater.

"The one and only."

"Why would he want to be the assistant to the president of a publishing house?" I leaned over her tall desk, peering around the decorative brick, seeing people buzzing around. The office had a very cool vibe. Glass walls framed individual workspaces from the floor to the ceiling, with a desk and some shelves inside each one. There were iron stairs that ran along the side wall, leading up to the second level.

"Word on the street is that Joey was responsible for that

fire at his parents' house last month. Apparently, someone was too high to put out his own doobie, or fatty, or whatever you kids are calling a marijuana cigarette these days." She shook her head with disgust, and I tried not to laugh. She was in her mid-sixties, always dressed in colorful clothing, and her dark hair was cropped short, showing off her big hoop earrings. "His parents have kicked him out, and he's living with his brother now, so I guess it's time for him to put on his big-boy pants and get a job."

"Anyone else applying for the gig?" I asked, as I looked up to see feet descending from the stairs. There was one pair of Vans with some dark skinny jeans, and then there was a pair of black loafers with black dress slacks ending just at the ankle, exposing a sliver of fancy socks.

I felt confident that I could beat out Joey for this position, who had most likely greeted the man interviewing him by calling him *Dude*. The kid suffered from chronic red eyes, and his favorite word had always been, *whoa,* with *dude* following in a close second place.

"Alicia Rogers also applied for the position. She was here yesterday. That woman still has a stick up her ass, though, you know? I pray she doesn't beat you out."

Two sets of legs continued to appear in my peripheral. Joey's head was already making its way down the steps, but the other man must be tall because he was still all legs and torso.

I glanced back at Virginia with a groan. "That woman had me arrested for ding-dong ditching when I was in high school. She has a bad case of resting bitch face, and her frozen, unmoving eyebrows totally freak me out."

I mean, there was good Botox and then there was Botox gone bad. Alicia represented the latter.

"I remember that arrest scandal. But Bugs didn't hold you down at the station long, did he?"

I chuckled. Max Bugster, a.k.a. Bugs, had gone to school

with my oldest brother Cage, and he'd taken me in his squad car for ice cream as we laughed our butts off about a woman calling the cops because a teenager rang her doorbell and ran.

"Nope, he didn't. And just thinking about it kind of makes me want to ding-dong ditch her tonight," I said.

"Call me if you do it. I may be old, but I'd be happy to drive the getaway car."

I covered my mouth to keep from bellowing out in laughter. I loved Virginia Hawkson. She lived down the street from my parents and had always been a character, to say the least.

But my laughter halted as both men came into focus when they hit the ground floor and walked in my direction.

And holy hot president.

This man was something.

My mouth went dry as I took him in as he strode beside Joey, who was holding a skateboard under his arm.

Maddox Lancaster was impossible to look away from. He had to be somewhere around my brothers' height, and all three of them were fairly tall. I'd guess him to be a good six foot, three inches. His brown eyes locked with mine.

Dark.

Deep.

Mysterious.

His hair was dark and styled in a way that made it look effortless. Jaw chiseled, shoulders broad, and he didn't look pleased as he approached the desk.

"Whoa, Dude. Is that Georgia Reynolds?" Joey said with a big smile on his face.

"Hey, Joey. How are you?"

"Well, I just got scolded for coming to an interview high, so there's that. But, I am high, so there's that." He winked as his head fell back in laughter. "But I don't think the boss here was too impressed. I probs didn't get the gig, did I?"

He turned to look at the man beside him, who made no attempt to hide his annoyance, and Virginia broke out in a fit of giggles. I bit down hard on my bottom lip to keep from laughing when Bossman's gaze locked with mine.

"It's safe to say you won't be returning, Joey," he said, his voice deep and lacking any humor. "You must be Ms. Reynolds."

I nodded, but before I could extend my hand, he barked at me.

"I'm Maddox Lancaster. Follow me."

I widened my eyes as I glanced one last time at Virginia, giving a quick wave to Joey as I followed the man up the stairs. My feet clicked against each of the metal steps, and he looked over his shoulder, and his eyes moved down my legs to my booties in a disapproving scowl.

Damn. My mom was always right. I should have worn the heels.

When we got to the top of the stairs, he walked down the hallway, with me doing my best to keep up. The offices upstairs were not open with glass walls. There were five offices from what I could see on this level, and the only glass wall appeared to belong to a conference room with a table that looked like it had seating for fifteen to twenty people.

He came to a stop at the last door at the end of the long hallway, and he motioned for me to enter.

"Take a seat," he said, his tone as cold as his eyes, which were so dark, they almost looked black. He moved around the desk and sat in the leather chair across from me. He typed something into his computer and then looked up to meet my gaze. "I'm hoping you aren't going to offer me a gummy to take the edge off."

I chuckled, even though he wasn't smiling. "Nope. No gummies here. Just a résumé."

I reached into the briefcase that Lila had loaned me and pulled out the peach-colored paper that had light cream flowers in the background, and I handed it over to him.

He raised his brows. "Your résumé is floral?"

"So is my personality," I sang out, but grumpy Bossman did not smile or chuckle. I did notice his lips twitch a bit before he straightened.

"I'm not looking for a big personality, Ms. Reynolds. I'm looking for a person who can get the job done. I'm a busy man. I don't have time for ridiculous antics like coming stoned to an interview or the woman yesterday who bad-mouthed my employee who greeted her." He leaned back and folded his hands on the desk, his gaze boring into me. I crossed my arms over my chest. If he thought he was going to intimidate me, he was mistaken. I had three brothers, my oldest brother being a gigantic, grumpy thorn in my side, so I didn't scare easily. But I was pleased to hear that Alicia Rogers had shown her true colors so quickly. My competition was weak, and I was not sorry about it.

"Well, I'm certainly not high, and I won't be talking about Virginia, because I happen to be a big fan. I'm here to tell you why I'm the best person for the job, so prepare to be dazzled, Mr. Lancaster." I leaned forward in my chair and intertwined my fingers together, resting them on my lap.

I glanced around at how sterile his office was. There was a degree from Harvard hanging on the wall. *Shocker.* He reeked of Ivy League superiority. I may not have attended an Ivy League college, but I had more life experience than most. I lived that YOLO—you only live once—life better than anyone I knew.

"Not looking to be dazzled," he grumped as he glanced down at my résumé. "I see you recently graduated from college. You were an art major?"

"I majored in art history and minored in business. This is a publishing company, so I feel confident that I'd bring great value to this position with the combination of skills that my education afforded me."

He cleared his throat as he read further down my résumé, his brows furrowing when he got to the bottom. "How does being talented at *unusual sports* bring value to the position? How did that even make it as a bullet point on your résumé?"

I smiled. "Thank you for bringing that up. I'm happy to tell you. You know how most people shine at football or soccer or swimming?"

He raised a brow. "Okay…"

"I don't. I have four siblings that were all pretty amazing at every traditional sport. I could never beat them at anything back then because they were older and faster."

"Is there a point to this story?" he asked, his voice dry and lacking any humor.

"I know. You're anxious. I get it." I shrugged. "My point is… I had to be resourceful. I had to find something that I could be the best at. And go figure, I was a freaking rock star at unusual sports."

He ran a hand down his face and then looked up at me like he was torn between kicking me out of his office and asking me to tell him more. "What sports?"

"Badminton. Let's just say, my high school PE teacher said I could pursue playing collegiately, but I didn't feel a passion for it."

"Go figure. You didn't feel moved by the shuttlecock?" He raised a brow, and I swear his lips turned up in the corners just the slightest bit.

"Ah, you're familiar with it. Nope. It just wasn't something I wanted to pursue full time. So, in college, I joined a pickleball league, and I'm proud to say that I was the county champ last year."

"Pickleball? Who were you playing? Isn't that an elderly sport?"

I rolled my eyes. "Do your research before you offend me and the amazing sport you're referring to, please. Pickleball is open to all ages. And I won the gold, which leads me to my point."

So what if a few of the people I beat used canes on the

courts and had to chug an Ensure to have the energy to go one round with me?

A win is a win.

"Are you going to make said point today?" His gaze narrowed.

"I'm adaptable. I can figure anything out and make it work. I can find talent where no one else sees it."

"You aren't applying for a job as an editor. You're applying for a job to be my assistant. And the talent is sitting right in front of you."

"If you say so, Bossman." I smirked. He was used to intimidating people, and it was important that he knew it wouldn't work on me. Yes, I wanted the job. But I also had my dignity. "I'm a hard worker, I'm willing to learn, and I'll do whatever I need to do to get this job."

I leaned back in my chair and raised a brow.

The shuttlecock was in his court.

two

• • •

Maddox

WAS I in some sort of alternate universe? First, I get moved to this godforsaken town to open an office here a few months ago, per my grandfather's insistence. Many of our employees were now working remotely, so he didn't feel the need to have such a large office in the city. Financially, this was a wise move. San Francisco is outrageously expensive. So, with my brother off the rails at the moment, and my dickhead father vacationing in Europe while he pretended to run our real estate company, I was sent to Cottonwood Cove.

I'd just experienced a secondhand high from the stoner kid who'd asked me if I wanted to come over later to play video games with him and *get lit*.

His words, not mine.

I didn't mind leaving the city and the traffic behind, but I needed a good team around me to make this work. My father had failed at the helm these last few years, and my grandfather was looking to me to bring some life back into this publishing house. This company had been his baby, his pride and joy, and his passion. Sure, he was one of the largest real estate moguls in the country, but Lancaster Press had been one of the longest-standing pub houses in the world, even if our numbers were at an all-time low, and we hadn't signed a big author in quite a while. So, my grandfather shifted my father into the real estate business and put me at the helm to lead this company.

And I was determined to bring us back to the top of our game.

But I couldn't do it with a weak team, and not everyone had wanted to move to this small town. Luckily, I'd gotten a few good people on the marketing team to make the move, and our two top editors who lived in the city were willing to relocate immediately. Once they realized the cost-of-living advantages, they were all in.

But I needed more people, and so far, the pool of candidates in Cottonwood Cove wasn't very impressive.

"Okay. We've established your ability to dominate a geriatric sport and shine with a shuttlecock. What else do you have?" I raised a brow at the gorgeous woman sitting in front of me.

Her skin was tan, her hair was blonde, and her eyes were a rare sapphire blue. She was the quintessential California girl, with dimples and white teeth and the whole nine yards. A personality for days, which probably scored her points with most people. Unfortunately, I wasn't like most people. I needed a fucking personal assistant so I could stop wasting time setting appointments, ordering office supplies, and spinning my wheels. I'd grown up around assistants who managed both my grandfather's and my father's lives. And they sure as shit were not bragging about their badminton skills.

My last three assistants had been disasters. One had called in sick more often than she came to work. One had fucked up my calendar so badly, causing me to miss an important meeting, amongst a shit ton of other errors, which left me no choice but to fire her. And the last one had squeezed my thigh under the table at lunch with a client, moving her fingers dangerously close to my dick because she thought it would relax me.

She was wrong.

I'd sent her ass packing, as well.

I didn't mix business with pleasure, and I needed an assistant who could handle more than one task at a time—and threatening to grab my dick was not one of them.

"Well, I'm very organized. I handled the entire Reynolds family calendar growing up. And let me tell you, five teenagers and two adults going in seven different directions is not easy to manage. I was a teaching assistant for two of my professors, and they both sent over excellent recommendations." She reached into her bag again and handed me two letters that were also printed on peach floral paper.

Why in the world would she think this would impress me? It was distracting. Annoying even. I scanned the letters, and I would be lying if I said I wasn't relieved to see that they'd sung her praises. They raved about her work ethic, and one professor called her a ray of sunshine. I suppose that trumped the cloud of cannabis that I'd just interviewed and the woman from hell yesterday who'd bitched about everyone in town and tooted her own horn about being a social outcast.

My options were limited, and time was ticking, so I'd need to bite the bullet and hire someone already.

"You should have led with this. It's better than the gift for odd sports." I set the letters aside. "This is not a typical assistant job, Ms. Reynolds."

"I'm not a typical girl." She smirked.

"Do you need this job?" It was an important question because I wasn't here to play games.

"Absolutely." She cleared her throat and leaned forward. She met my gaze head-on. Most people didn't. "Listen, I don't have a lot of personal assistant experience, but I'm a really hard worker, and I'm a quick learner."

I didn't doubt it. She'd graduated magna cum laude, so that told me that she knew how to focus and push herself.

"This position goes beyond just office work. I need someone to run errands, handle things at my house, and, if needed, jump on a plane and travel at a moment's notice. You'd be in charge of scheduling my appointments, possibly sitting in on meetings and taking notes, and occasionally reading manuscripts. So, as you can see, you'd be wearing several hats."

"I love hats. I've yet to find one that I can't pull off." She smiled so big it was hard not to join her, aside from the fact that her answer made no sense.

"You won't actually be wearing hats. It's a metaphor."

"That was a little condescending, Bossman. I'm aware. I was being funny. Apparently, a sense of humor is not in the job description."

Smart-ass. Although I liked that she was witty and not some airhead. I'd have to set some ground rules if I gave her the job, which was looking very likely because there was no one else in the running.

"How about we lose the attitude and keep things professional?" I waited for her to nod, but for whatever reason, she continued smiling like this was all in good fun. It wasn't. I was fucking serious. "Are you a reader?"

"Of people?" she asked before she rubbed her hands together like she couldn't wait to tell me all about her skills.

"Of books, Ms. Reynolds. We're a publishing house."

"Oh. Yes. Of course." She looked off as if she were in deep thought, and just as I was about to speak, she continued. "I mean, I mainly read indie authors. No offense. I just tend to lean that way. But I'd be open to reading authors that you sign, of course."

Interesting that she knew the difference between a traditionally published author and a self-published author. Most people didn't. Self-pubbed authors were flooding the market, but understanding the market was not something I'd expected from my personal assistant.

"Why do you lean toward reading indie authors?"

"Well, I read predominantly romance. My cousin, Ashlan Thomas, is a traditionally published romance author, and I beta-read for her. She's fabulous. But otherwise, there are just so many authors to choose from in the self-published world of romance. Most are female, if I'm being honest, and I guess I appreciate a badass woman who is willing to make her dreams happen, right? That means they do it all. They write, they market, and they sell. It's hard not to respect it."

I'd never thought of it like that. But that wasn't what we did here at Lancaster Press, and she needed to remember that. I'd had no idea that Ashlan Thomas was her cousin, but I'd save that little sidenote for another time, as signing her would be great, seeing as she was a newer, but very popular author, and her name was getting a lot of praise.

"You do realize that we're a traditional publisher, right?" I raised a brow.

"Yes. But you hired me to manage *you,* not choose the talent."

"I haven't hired you yet, and if I do, it would be to *assist me,* not manage me."

"Tomato, tomahto. And I'm open to reading whatever you give me. You just asked what I read, and I was being honest."

I appreciated it, even if I wasn't sure I liked her answer.

"And how many books would you say that you read a year?" Why was I even asking that? She was my PA, not an editor or a cover designer. What she read was irrelevant, yet I was curious.

I found most people who had opinions on authors and the book world were usually all talk. When it came down to it, a lot of people that had these strong opinions only read two to three books a year, so their opinions were based on nothing at all.

"Hmmm…" She thought it over, and I wanted to chuckle. She'd just made this grand statement, and now she most likely couldn't back it up. "I think three hundred a year would be a conservative guess. I usually read a book a day, but sometimes it takes me a bit longer, so that's probably close to accurate."

I tried to hide my surprise with a slow nod. "I see. That could be useful if I need you to take a quick look at some submissions that my editors send for my approval."

"I'd be thrilled to do that. And trust me, I won't forget that picking up your dry cleaning and getting your coffee is also part of the job. I know I'll be wearing many hats."

"Shouldn't be too hard for the county pickleball champ," I said, keeping my tone even as I fought the urge to laugh. I wasn't normally much of a jokester, but I couldn't help myself.

I spent the next forty minutes going over the details of the position, the pay, and the benefits package.

"Does this mean I have the job?" she asked, doing some sort of little shimmy with her shoulders.

There was no doubt that she was charming and gorgeous and more intelligent than she let on at first glance.

But she was also unprofessional and a bit of a smart-ass. Of course, my brother and most of my tenured employees would say I was a stick in the mud, so there was that.

I'd have to make sure she understood that I was the boss and she worked for me. This was a job, and if she wasn't stepping up to the plate, I'd have no problem cutting her. It didn't matter how cute or sexy she was.

And goddamn, was she ever sexy.

"You have the job." I pushed to my feet. "Be here tomorrow morning at 8:00 a.m. sharp, and we'll get you all set up. I don't tolerate tardiness or excuses. I'm a busy man, and I need someone who can keep up."

She pushed to her feet and saluted me. "I will not let you down, Bossman."

"You can call me Mr. Lancaster," I grumped.

Once that was out of the way, I glanced at my watch, aware that I had a meeting in five minutes, so I walked to the door and held it open, extending my arm. "Welcome to the team. HR will have your paperwork ready to sign in the morning."

She squealed, and my eyes widened. "Thank you, *Mr. Lancaster.* I can't wait to dazzle you."

Once again, she was completely unprofessional.

But when her small hand landed in mine, I didn't want to let go.

And that had me yanking my hand away immediately. I held my arm out for her to leave, and when she turned around to say goodbye, I let the door shut.

We weren't girlfriends.

I didn't do small talk.

I needed to make that clear right off the bat.

And that was exactly what I intended to do.

three

• • •

Georgia

I WAS grateful that I'd worn pants this morning because it was bone-chillingly cold today. When I'd driven home from my interview yesterday, I'd passed the lot owned by one of my brother's best friends, Brax, where a lot of the locals had their cars for sale. Unfortunately, a car was well beyond my budget at the moment, but I did have some graduation money in the bank, so I'd purchased the cutest white scooter. It even came with a matching helmet, and the whole thing was only two hundred bucks. It was the temporary solution I was looking for. I didn't know how long I could pull off the excuse that my car was in the shop. My brother, Hugh, was already annoyed that I'd left it at an auto shop in the city when his good friend, Roddy, would have worked on it here in Cottonwood Cove and given me a deal.

No, duh.

I wasn't a dipshit.

I was a survivor.

I had a gift for buying time, and that was exactly what I was doing. My car was not in the shop. It had been stolen.

Well, stolen might be a bit harsh, seeing as I knew the thief all too well.

Dikota Smith, a.k.a. my insane ex-boyfriend, had taken my car and was holding it hostage. He'd refused to give it back to me until I agreed to start seeing him again.

I sure can pick 'em, right?

I loved finding broken things and trying to put them back together. The problem with Dikota was that he was broken beyond repair. The guy never acted like he was into me until another guy showed me any kind of attention, or when I'd finally called off the relationship.

Then he suddenly couldn't live without me.

So, he'd taken my keys the last time I saw him and had driven away in my car. He'd hidden it somewhere and wouldn't give it back.

And this wasn't even the worst thing that he'd done to me, but I wasn't going to ruin my good mood thinking about it.

Obviously, I could go to the police or ask my family for help, but the whole thing was embarrassing, and I was just hoping he'd come to his senses soon. Unfortunately, it had been several weeks, and he was still blowing up my phone about getting back together and acting like a lunatic.

Block him?

Sure. I'd love to. But the guy had my car, and I wanted it back.

I parked my scooter behind Lancaster Press and rubbed my hands together, thankful for the white furry gloves I'd grabbed this morning before I left. My nose was frozen, and I reached for my bag that was sitting in the basket behind my seat and hurried to the front door.

I was obviously the first one here because the door was locked. I'd come early, hoping to impress my grumpy boss on my first day on the job as well as sneak out of the house before Hugh or Lila discovered that I was driving a scooter. I'd been forced to park it a few blocks away from the house so they wouldn't see it.

Another downside to the scooter was the fact that it was freezing outside, and I couldn't turn on the heat and wait inside like I would if it were a car.

My phone vibrated, and I pulled it from my coat pocket and jogged in place as I read the messages in our never-ending sibling group chat. I had three older brothers and one older sister, and we were all very close.

BRINKLEY

Good luck today, Georgie! You're going to kill it.

HUGH

You left before breakfast? We wanted to feed you. I thought you started at 8:00 a.m.?

I wanted to make a good impression.

Had I known I'd be waiting outside, I'd have been less eager to be this early.

CAGE

That is a winning attitude. Early bird gets the worm.

FINN

Tequila drinkers also get the worm. I'm on set this morning, or I'd definitely still be in bed. You've got this, girl! Dazzle the billionaire.

BRINKLEY

Did you tell him that you were the county pickleball champ?

Yep. He didn't seem too dazzled.

HUGH

Did you share your ridiculous knowledge of seventies music?

Nope. I thought I'd pull that out at a later date.

I started jumping up and down because jogging in place was not working, and my eyes were watering. I feared my tears would freeze on my cheeks if I didn't start warming up.

CAGE

Just be yourself. You already have the job. And hey, if it doesn't work out, you can always come work for me. I've got an appointment with a sick pig and a duck with digestion issues this morning. Does it get any better than this?

FINN

A pig and a duck walked into a bar…

HUGH

And the duck said, "Be sure to give me the bill."

My head fell back in laughter as I continued sprinting in place as fast as I could.

"My god. How long have you been standing out here? It's freezing," Maddox Lancaster said, startling the hell out of me as I spun around. I gasped and dropped my phone before losing my balance and slamming my head into the brick wall and nearly falling to the ground.

Two strong hands found my shoulders and steadied me, and his dark brown eyes studied me with concern.

"Oh, hey," I said, trying to pull myself together as I moved to reach for my phone, but he stopped me as he bent down to grab it.

He handed me my phone and unlocked the door, holding it open for me to walk inside ahead of him. He flipped on the lights, and I pulled the gloves and hat off my head and quickly tried to pat my hair into place. My lips were still frozen, and my teeth were chattering. This was not the impression I was hoping to make.

He studied me for a few seconds, but it felt longer because he didn't smile, and he looked… annoyed? Angry? Concerned?

"Is your head okay?" he asked, his voice deep and growly.

"Yes. Of course. My hat has a lot of padding." I held it by the giant pom-pom on top and shook it in front of myself like a fool.

"Why didn't you wait in your car?"

"I didn't drive my car here. It's in the shop." I cleared my throat because the man had a way of making me feel like he could see through me. He narrowed his gaze like he wasn't buying it.

He didn't even know me.

How did he know I was lying?

Obviously, he was correct, but he didn't *know* that.

"Did you drive that white bicycle I saw parked in the lot here?" he asked, and it came off very condescending and rude, which I did not appreciate.

I squared my shoulders. He might be my new boss, but there was no reason to be an asshole. I'd come early and had frozen my ass off outside, and I didn't need to be treated like a child.

"It's a high-powered scooter, and yes, it's my temporary form of transportation. It also has nothing to do with my job, so I don't appreciate you acting like I've broken the rules when I was the first one to arrive today, on my *bicycle.*" I glared at him, and the feeling started to come back in my hands because they were fisted at my sides.

The corners of his lips turned up just the slightest bit, and he nodded. "Fair enough. I'm impressed you beat me because I'm always the first one here. How about we get you a key, so if you ever arrive before me, you'll be able to come inside?"

"Okay," I said, my anger starting to dissipate.

I followed him through the bottom floor, and he showed me where the employee break room was, and I gasped that it was stocked with protein bars, fruit, nuts, and energy drinks.

"I take it you like snacks?"

"Doesn't everyone?" I shrugged as I followed him down the hallway, and he pointed out different offices. There were two offices for editors, a whole area for the marketing team, and even a big space to brainstorm ideas with couches and bean bags.

"Ah… I'm a big fan of the bean bag. I had a huge hot pink bean bag in my room in high school, and I would sleep on it most nights," I said.

He paused and looked at me. "Interesting. You drive a *high-powered scooter* and sleep on a bean bag."

He was such a pompous ass sometimes. But damn, he was good-looking. He wore a black trench coat, a gray scarf, and he looked like he'd just stepped off a photo shoot for a fashion magazine. I had a feeling there was a more casual guy beneath this façade somewhere, and if anyone could dig him out, it would be me.

"What can I say? I'm a girl of many talents—" My words were cut off when we turned the corner, and I came to a screeching halt.

"What's wrong?" He shoved his hands into his coat pockets as he watched me.

"There is a ping-pong table here? I told you that I excel at unusual sports."

"Let me guess. You're the county champion of ping-pong?" He was trying to be sarcastic, but there was humor in his tone.

"I guess you'll just have to see for yourself. Do you play?"

"Ping-pong?" He raised a brow. "That's a hard no."

"Then why do you have a table at the office?"

"Because studies show that creative people need outlets. I had the team vote on what they wanted brought in, and this was the winner. But it's only used when there is something to celebrate, at lunchtime, or after working for several hours when the whole team takes a break. I don't micromanage my employees. I trust them. If they do their job, I'm happy. So, they have a space to have a little fun, and they appreciate it. This was similar to our setup in the city."

I glanced over to see a large whiteboard with names listed and numbered. I couldn't wait to jump in and get on that list.

He started walking again, and I followed him as we made our way up the stairs to the top floor.

"These are the administrative offices. This is your space here." He motioned to the desk outside his office. It was a large, white modern desk, L-shaped, with lots of drawers and storage cabinets on the wall behind it. It wasn't enclosed, so I'd be out in the open. I set my briefcase down and unzipped the top and pulled out the photo of my family and set it on the desk, before reaching back inside and finding the gold "G" that looked like a paperweight and setting it in the corner before pulling out my pad of inspirational sayings and setting it on the side of the desk. I liked to start the day with a positive mantra to kick things off.

He smirked. "You came prepared. Is that your family?"

"Yep. That's all of us."

"There's a lot of you."

"You can never have too many Reynolds," I said, biting down on my bottom lip.

"I don't know about that. One seems like plenty, so far."

Ouch. He really wasn't a fan of mine. I'd have to work on that.

"So, will I be working for everyone on this floor?"

"Absolutely not. You are *my* admin. If anyone starts tasking you, let me know. Grab a notebook—there are a few in the drawer—and meet me in my office. We'll go over everything you'll be doing for me."

I glanced in the drawer and saw the bland spiral notebooks and shut it immediately. I reached into my bag and pulled out my cheetah notebook, along with my pink pen. I slipped off my coat, dropped my keys in my top desk drawer, and hurried into his office.

He'd taken off his coat, and his fitted black dress shirt strained against his broad shoulders. He wore black pants, black expensive-looking loafers, and a black belt.

"Wow. Someone's channeling their inner Johnny Cash today."

"Is that a cheetah notebook?" He completely ignored me as his eyes scanned my face and then moved down to my waist. He slowly perused my pink silk blouse, and I nervously pressed the nonexistent wrinkles out of my cream dress pants.

"It is. Do you have something against the cheetah?"

"Are you always a smart-ass?" he asked, folding his hands together and resting them on his desk. He was an intimidating man in a way, but for whatever reason, he didn't scare me. I imagined most people squirmed under his death glare.

"Well, it depends on who you ask. Most of my family members would probably say yes. My friends would probably agree, too," I said, in a bit of a ramble.

He groaned and held up his hands. "You do understand that I'm your boss, correct?"

Obviously, I knew he was my boss, as he'd interviewed me, and he was the president of the company. Bossman really wanted to drive this one home.

"I do."

"Then let's leave the smart-ass comments at the door." He raised a brow, and I nodded.

Think of what Mom always says… You do not need to share every thought that runs through your mind.

"Got it, Mr. Lancaster," I said, plastering a wide smile on my face.

He leaned back in his chair and cleared his throat. "Good. Tell me why you're driving that ridiculous contraption in the cold."

"My car is in the shop." I'd already told him that, but I was trying not to be a smart-ass, so I wouldn't remind him that he already knew the answer to that question.

"When will it be ready?"

"Soon, I hope."

"And you can't borrow a car from one of your many family members?" he asked, and there was that condescending tone again. But I would not react.

"I don't want to ask them. I'm trying to prove that I can do things on my own. I just graduated from college, so it's time to be a grown-up."

His lips twitched the slightest bit, and if I was reading Maddox Lancaster correctly, I'd say that he liked my answer. But I had the feeling that he'd never admit it.

"I understand that. So, let's go over your duties."

I pulled the feather cap off my pink pen and slipped it onto the back, crossed my legs, and balanced the notebook on my lap.

He proceeded to spend the next thirty minutes giving me the most exhaustive list of duties. I would be doing everything from getting coffee, ordering lunch for the office, sitting in on his meetings and taking notes, to picking up his dry cleaning and setting dinner reservations. He would also occasionally have me read blurbs and give feedback, and we'd be adding in other things as *he saw fit.*

So, basically, I'd be a coffee and errand girl if I didn't prove that I was up for more.

But I planned to impress the hell out of him.

Odd sports may be my specialty, but difficult men were a close second.

Game on, Bossman.

four

. . .

Maddox

OUR TEAM WAS FINDING their rhythm here in Cottonwood Cove. My new assistant had two weeks under her belt and had started her third week with the same gusto. She'd surprised me with her work ethic several times already, although this was still a trial period.

I'd learned that many people come out of the gate strong with a new job, and then they'd fizzle out. Georgia Reynolds had handled everything I'd thrown at her with ease thus far, which was saying a lot because I'd been known to go through assistants faster than most people went through a cup of coffee. And I'd hit her with everything I had in my arsenal. Sending her on bullshit errands and giving her tasks I didn't think she'd finish; yet every single time, she'd come back with a smile on her face. I expected a lot from the people who worked for me, and I rewarded them well for it. I hadn't rewarded her yet because it was too soon. The jury was still out on whether she'd make it here.

If there was a popularity contest at Lancaster Press, Georgia would be the queen of the office. Everyone loved her already, and she'd only been here for a few weeks. She knew how to turn on the charm, and I admired people who knew their strengths and capitalized on them. Where most people made an effort to be friendly, there was a genuineness with her that was rare to find in people. Her name was at the top of the whiteboard for the ongoing ping-pong game that they all played every day on their lunch break, as she'd wasted no time taking part. She only took twenty minutes a day for lunch, which I noted, because I was prepared to call her out if she spent an hour in the break room with the staff playing games. She'd go down, play one game, apparently dominate, and then eat her lunch at her desk while she worked. She'd also brought donuts in the last two Fridays to celebrate her first week on the job, and this past week for Virginia's birthday, and that had won her big points. I believed in doing something special for employees that had been with you for five, ten, and even twenty years. But a party to celebrate a week on the job? Who the fuck did that?

Like most new employees, I was prepared for her to go at a slower pace at the start of week two and then again at the start of week three. It was common, and I had no intentions of easing up on her. But she'd upped her game last week and hadn't lost an ounce of steam.

I'd just arrived at the office, and I parked next to that goddamn white contraption that she drove to work, which pissed me off. It was cold as hell out, and she shouldn't be driving something that wasn't safe. And why the fuck did I care?

I'd come earlier today, an attempt to be first, but she'd beat me again. I didn't need to be here this early, but the fact that she had arrived before me every day since she'd started had me getting out of bed a little earlier than usual.

And how long does it take to fix a fucking car?

Was her family okay with her driving this death trap on wheels to work every day?

Why did it annoy me so much?

Maybe I was just in a mood because I'd woken up with a

raging boner after a dream about my assistant straddling me at my desk while wearing no panties.

It wasn't the first time I'd dreamt of her either. And that shit pissed me off.

I wasn't that guy.

I didn't fantasize about women I worked with.

When it came to women, I was always in control.

So, I had a bad case of blue balls, and it only added to my already irritable disposition.

I moseyed into the office, and I was immediately hit with seventies music, as I had been every day since she'd started. From Karen Carpenter's "Close to You" to the Knack's "My Sharona", the girl blared her music until I'd arrive every morning, and then she'd hustle and turn it off with no argument from me. I wasn't a fan of the seventies, so I'd just use my Shazam app that could tell me the name of a song right on my phone. That way, when I complained about it to her, I would act like I knew what I was complaining about. I did not need to Shazam today's song, as even I was able to recognize Abba's "Dancing Queen". I made my way up the stairs and found her in my office with her back to me as she stood at the filing cabinet, singing at the top of her lungs along with the music that was playing from her phone.

She sang like she was on an episode of *The Voice* and shimmied her hot little body down to the floor like it was her life's passion. It was sort of how she did everything from what I'd assessed over these last few weeks.

Everything with her was upbeat. Like a ray of sunshine all the fucking time—aside from the attitude that she gave me. However, she wasn't that way with anyone else at work from what I'd observed. She was too busy spreading pixie dust everywhere she went, like a modern-day fucking Tinker Bell. The problem was, I didn't care for pixie dust. Nor did I care for loud music booming through my office at seven thirty in the fucking morning. Or the fact that I couldn't take my eyes off her perfectly round, peach-shaped, tight little ass. I moved toward my desk and hit her phone with my fist to pause the music, and she jumped and turned before tripping over her own foot and flying across my desk.

Like I said… she was a fucking fairy.

But this Tinker Bell had just exposed her white lace thong, which did nothing to cover her gorgeous ass when her skirt flew up and she slid across my desk.

Her blonde hair fell all around her shoulders, and she blinked up at me, quickly adjusting her skirt and moving to her feet.

"Oh, hey. You scared me."

"Did I? How is that possible?" I hissed. Because for whatever reason, seeing her bare ass first thing in the morning had my dick going hard, *again,* and that shit pissed me off.

A. She worked for me.

B. I was always in control of how I reacted to others.

"How is what possible?" she asked, acting all offended as she reached for her phone.

"How did I scare you when you knew I was arriving? And didn't I ask you to stop with the annoying music?"

"I see we're in another fabulous mood," she said, raising a brow. She had a gift for insulting me with kindness, so I couldn't write her up because what she'd said was actually nice, even though we both knew she didn't mean it. "For your information, I set my alarm on my phone for 7:40 a.m., which is when you've arrived every day since I started here. You're early today. I had planned to stop spreading joy at 7:40. *On. The. Dot.* But now, I'll bring in the dark cloud at 7:30 a.m. instead. And for the record, there is nothing annoying about Abba. The *Mama Mia* fandom would not take too kindly to you insulting that song."

"I thought we were done being a smart-ass?" I moved around my desk, trying to adjust my raging boner without her noticing. It wasn't an easy task housing the beast when he was worked up.

"I *am* done being a smart-ass, Bossman. I was just telling you that I had a plan, and you sort of messed it up. Why are you here early today?"

"Once again, I'm the boss, and you're the employee. That is not a question you need to be asking." I sat in my chair and raised a brow. "Go flutter back to your desk, Tinker Bell. I've got work to do."

"I love Tinker Bell. She's my favorite fairy. Thank you." She slammed the drawer of the file cabinet and plastered a fake smile on her face.

"It wasn't meant as a compliment." I motioned with my head for her to leave. The girl was giving me a migraine, and I'd only been here for five minutes.

I did not appreciate starting the day with some fucked-up *Mama Mia* music.

A raging boner.

And a bad headache.

The phone rang, and I could hear her being all chipper to whoever was on the other line. She ended the call, and then my desk phone rang. Seeing as we were the only two people in the office, I squeezed my eyes closed for a minute, pinched the bridge of my nose with my finger and thumb, and let out a long breath before picking up the phone.

"You're sitting five feet from me; you don't need to use the phone. You could have just spoken from your desk."

"That wouldn't be very professional, would it?"

"What do you need?"

"Hilda called. She's sick," she chirped.

"Who the fuck is Hilda?"

"This is disappointing, Bossman. She's your housekeeper, and she said she works five days a week for you. She called you Maddy, so I assumed you were close."

I groaned. The woman had never called me Maddy, and I

knew my assistant was fucking with me. "I call her Mrs. Miller, and she calls me Mr. Lancaster. What's wrong with her?"

"She feels fine, but she has laryngitis, so she won't be coming to work today."

"I don't need her to sing. She's there to clean. If she feels fine, why can't she go to work?" I hissed, just as she started to speak, and I cut her off. "Never mind. My head is pounding. I'll take a cup of coffee."

"Please?"

"Please, what?" I asked.

"Can I please get a cup of coffee?" she said.

"Are you asking me to get you a cup of coffee?"

"I'm just reminding you that the word *please* goes a long way. Just a good thing to keep in mind. I'll be in with your coffee shortly, Boss." She hung up before I could respond.

What the fuck kind of mind game was this?

I didn't look up at her when she set the mug on the desk with a napkin and a banana, which was thoughtful, seeing as I hadn't asked for one, but I usually grabbed one when I first got here.

I glanced up just as she left my office. Her pencil skirt hugged her curves in all the right places, and I cursed myself for looking. Tan legs, fuck-me heels, and a body that could drop a man to his knees.

And damn, would I drop to my knees for that woman.

I picked up my cell phone and typed her contact info in. I'd been meaning to do it but hadn't gotten around to it yet. I didn't want to call her on the office phone after shaming her for calling me. But I didn't want to invite a new conversation either, because my dick was finally settling down, and I needed her to stay at her fucking desk for a while. She was my assistant, and I should have her number in my phone anyway.

Thank you for the coffee and the banana, Tink.

TINK

Who is this?

I chuckled because she was funny as hell, even if I wouldn't admit it to her.

Did you bring someone else coffee and a banana?

TINK

Bossman?

Obviously.

TINK

Is this your way of apologizing?

No. This is my way of thanking you for the coffee and the banana.

TINK

You're welcome. Now, if we can get you to say please, change your taste in music, soften the way you deliver your requests, and try smiling every now and then… it will be a win.

Don't hold your breath.

TINK

Ah... did you know that I had a brief stint with synchronized swimming? Holding my breath is another secret talent.

You're full of surprises. Get back to work.

TINK

<Thumbs Up Emoji>

I set my phone down just as voices started to fill the office. Georgia put a call from my grandfather through to me and held up her hand as she pulled my door closed so I could have privacy.

"Maddox, how are things going over there?" he asked, his voice always gruff from his early years as a smoker.

"Good. We've got a pile of new manuscripts to go through and a virtual meeting with Arthur Hobbs this afternoon."

"Great. Does he have new pages for you?" he asked. Arthur was a number one *New York Times* bestselling author, and we'd published more than two dozen books with him over the last decade. We were in talks with Paramount for a movie deal, and the man was one of our most important clients.

"He's working on it. He's in a bit of a slump, but we'll talk it through with him. Helena isn't concerned." I leaned back in my chair. Helena Rosewood was our chief editor and a brilliant woman. She'd been working at Lancaster Press since I'd been a kid, and the woman had an eye for talent.

"Well, if she isn't concerned, then I don't think we need to be." He paused as a deep cough bellowed from his lungs. I waited. Asking if he was okay would infuriate him. He was a tough old goat—his words, not mine. A real estate mogul, a brilliant businessman, and his most precious company was Lancaster Press. He cleared his throat. "How's the house? You settling in okay there?"

"The house is nice. The town is small. Things are slow here." I leaned back in my leather chair and crossed my arms over my chest. I'd fought the move here, but solely because I didn't want to leave the city. It was a wise move for the company. We didn't need to be located on the busiest street in San Francisco anymore. It served no purpose, and we could have a lot more space here. With so many things being remote now, there was no reason not to move. My grandfather had removed my father from his position as president of Lancaster Press, and with the shift of title to me, it was the perfect time to relocate. Start fresh.

"Slow isn't always a bad thing, my boy. And you are truly the only one that I trust to get this company back to where it was. Your father is still pissed at me."

"He'll get over it," I said, my voice harsher than I meant it to be.

My father was the devil. He just covered it well with his fake smiles and fancy suits for the press. The only plus to leaving the city was that I wouldn't have to see his face very often. We still had a ton of family obligations, and I wouldn't be getting out of those with a helicopter accessible to take me to and from the city at a moment's notice.

"Remember what I told you about anger," he said, and the way he paused afterward made it clear that he'd just lit his cigar and was puffing away.

The man had COPD and a chronic smoker's cough, yet he'd never gone a day without his cigar.

"Yeah, yeah. Anger only hurts the person carrying it. I got it." I reached for my coffee and took a sip. "How's semi-retirement treating you?"

"Really well. I emailed you something that caught my interest. Mara Skye is a self-published author who is making a real name for herself, and word on the street is she's shopping her next book and is interested in a traditional deal. I may or may not have gotten the first few chapters of the book, so we'd have first crack at her if you think it's worth it. But we were given a very short lead time, so we'd have to act quickly, as in—today." My grandfather knew every literary agent on the planet, so *word on the street* usually meant it was actually happening. "I thought you could find someone to take a look at it. She writes historical romance, not my thing, but I read the first few pages, and she's got a great voice. Maybe Nadia could take a look today, because if we want to make it happen, we should do it before they start shopping it."

"Sure. I'll have her look at it this morning. I'll let you know, and then perhaps you could stop beating around the bush and give me her agent's information so I can reach out directly," I said, shaking my head because the man was still finding ways to keep his nose in the business.

"Let me know what you think first, and I'll set up the meeting in the city for you and Ted Hagger, and maybe I'll just pop in for a scotch." He barked out a laugh.

"Ahhh, of course, she's with Ted Hagger." The dude was a total douchebag, but he somehow managed to sign every author we wanted. I couldn't stand the man. "I thought Grandmother was going to keep you in check with this retirement plan."

"She's trying. I can't have you rubbing Ted wrong. You're still learning how to control that temper of yours, and remember, we don't need to like the agent. It's the author we want. So, if that means bowing down to Ted Hagger to make that happen, that's what you do."

"I can play nice, Grandfather."

"Sure, you can," he said over his laughter that was mixed with a harsh cough. "You forget that you're me fifty years ago. You'll calm down with age. What you need is a good woman to keep you in check. None of this playboy shit. That's for kids."

I rolled my eyes. He was one of my favorite people on the planet, which was saying a lot since most people bugged the shit out of me. But he was old-school. His way was the right way, the only way, whether you agreed with him or not.

"I'm doing just fine. I'll get on this manuscript right away and keep you posted."

"All right. I'll speak to you later today."

We said our goodbyes, and I pulled up my email and forwarded the first three chapters to Nadia, and asked her to get on it immediately. She wasn't my favorite editor at the office because she tended to be a bit harsh and was quick to say no after many years in the business. But her forte was mainly historical romance, so this should go to her.

There was a light knock on the door, and I called out for whoever it was to come in. Georgia Reynolds strolled in with a mug in her hand and made her way over to me. Visions of bending her over my cherrywood desk filled my thoughts, and I internally cursed myself.

"I saw that you were off the phone, so I thought you might need a fresh cup of coffee." She set it down and picked up the empty mug. She was figuring out my habits quickly. I drank about four cups of coffee before lunch, and she seemed to know right when I'd need the next one.

"That was thoughtful of you," I said, my eyes roaming down her body before snapping back up to meet her sapphire eyes.

"What can I say, I'm a thoughtful girl." She smirked, heading for my door as I watched her ass sway back and forth in her black pencil skirt.

"Hey, have you ever heard of Mara Skye?"

She whipped around, her jaw falling open and accentuating her plump, pink lips.

And I wondered how they'd feel wrapped around my cock that was suddenly throbbing against my zipper.

Fucking Tink was going to be the death of me.

five

. . .

Georgia

I GASPED and gaped and made all sorts of dramatic sounds before I found my voice. "Have I heard of Mara Skye?"

"That's what I asked. Yes." He raised a brow, lips pursed as those dark brown eyes drilled into me.

"Is the sky blue? Is Mrs. Runither an old horndog?" I threw my free hand in the air, trying to think of an even better example. "Are you a stubborn, infuriating man?"

He barked out a laugh. An actual laugh. It was almost more shocking than the question he'd just asked me.

"Well, I don't know who the fuck Mrs. Runither is, but I'm guessing she's a horndog. What's your point, Tink?"

I liked the nickname that he called me. It was cute, and it meant he was getting comfortable with me, even if his moods were giving me whiplash.

"Mara Skye is the most brilliant author I've ever read. She's my unicorn. A definite one-click author for me."

"I don't know what any of that means, but it sounds good. How would you like to take a look at the first three chapters of an unread manuscript that was submitted to us?"

I started walking in circles and taking deep breaths because if you had told me three weeks ago that I'd be here, I would never have believed it. I was going to read the unread chapters of Mara Skye? What universe was I living in? It wasn't that long ago that I was in a bar fighting with my psychotic ex, who was singing there with his band, as he refused to tell me where my car was.

And now… I was working at Lancaster Press as the personal assistant to the sexiest, most annoying man on the planet, and he was going to let me read these secret chapters.

Hells to the yes.

"I would love to read them." I came to a stop, my legs a little wobbly from all the turning, but I let out a long sigh.

His lips turned up in the corners just the slightest bit, which I'd come to learn was as much of a smile from Maddox Lancaster as you'd ever get. "I just emailed it to you. But, this is for your eyes only. You can't share this with anyone. And Nadia is looking at it now, as well, and she won't be thrilled to know I let my admin see it, so you only report back to me. Got it?"

"Got it, Bossman. You won't regret this. I will give you detailed feedback." I saluted him with my free hand.

"I'm sure you will."

I hurried out of his office and raced over to my desk, setting his empty mug beside me. I pulled up the manuscript and started reading.

And just like that, I was in Ireland, and it was 1933.

This woman was the most captivating writer I'd ever read. I was enthralled. I wanted more.

And hello, Captain Jory Walker.

Her heroes were always a little bit alpha with a side of chivalry and a heavy splash of dirty talk.

I typed up my notes, reread them three times, and then sent them to Maddox.

The rest of the morning flew by, and I hurried downstairs for my twenty-minute championship ping-pong game. The defending champion always played the new contender each day, and so far, I'd stayed at the top of the list since my first day working here.

Thanks to my über-competitive siblings, I could handle the pressure. When we played games, we played to the death, and I didn't scare easily.

I went back and forth with Freddy, one of the marketing guys, for a very short time, and I beat him so quickly that everyone was giving him a hard time.

"Sorry, Freddy. I was just on my A game today." I winced.

"Don't apologize, Georgia. You swear you haven't played competitively?" he asked, and everyone laughed.

I loved the office environment. It was a lot of fun. Of course, you had your office buzzkills, as every company did. Nadia Wright being at the top of that list. She was in her mid-sixties, had a really wicked case of resting sourpuss face, and she wasn't a fan of the games or the laughter going on during our lunch break—or anything, really.

"Nope. But I do think the pickleball competitions prepared me for our ping-pong tournaments," I said over my laughter.

"Maybe you're just talented at everything," Craig purred. The man was a total flirt. He'd moved here from the city as part of the marketing team, as well. He was good-looking, and he knew it.

"Is that the best you can come up with?" Sydney rolled her eyes. She was my favorite new friend at the office. She was my age, had also moved here from the city, and was our social media expert. She worked on all the graphics and teasers for the company.

I glanced up to see grumpy Nadia coming down the stairs from her meeting with Maddox, and I glanced down at my phone to check the time.

"Got to go, guys. I'll see you on my next break." I waved and rushed away, and my booties clacked as I ran up the metal stairs before setting my phone on my desk.

"Tink, get in here!" my boss shouted from his office, and I hurried inside. The man was impatient and demanding, yet I kind of loved it. I could handle anything he threw at me.

"What's wrong?" I asked, and he motioned for me to close the door and come inside.

"Take a seat." He pulled something up on his monitor and then looked at me from the other side of his desk. "I read through your notes about the Mara Skye book. You really liked it that much?"

"Like is an understatement. I think it's going to be her best yet. Did you read it?"

"I did. I liked it, too. But Nadia didn't care for it, nor is she a fan of Mara's work."

My eyes bulged out of my head. The woman specialized in historical romance, and she didn't like Mara Skye? "I think Nadia Wright should change her name to Nadia Wrong."

He barked out a laugh, and the sound was so startling I couldn't help but laugh along with him. That was twice today that he'd laughed. I wanted to pat myself on the back for this enormous accomplishment.

"Nadia has an issue with self-published authors to begin with, so I have a hunch that might have more to do with it than the actual writing."

"Yeah. She seems pretty tough to please." I rolled my eyes. "Mara's writing is all-consuming. No one pulls me in quite like her, and this new book did it in spades. The only other person that can hook me that quickly is my cousin."

"I'd like to talk to her at some point, if you ever want to make that happen. We'd love to work with her on her next series, but her agent isn't a fan of my grandfather because he turned down a few submissions that she'd felt strongly about. But I'm here now, so maybe she'd reconsider?"

"I can get you a meeting, for sure. I can't promise you anything more than that, but she'd meet with you without question. She's the best."

"Aren't you just full of surprises?"

"I try to be," I said, pushing to my feet. "Trust me, you don't want someone else to get this book with Mara. She's the best of the best."

"I'll make the call now and inquire about taking the next step. But I've got an issue at the moment, and I need you to figure it out."

"What's wrong?"

"I have a Zoom meeting with the board of directors in an hour, and I left my sports coat at home this morning. Hilda's sick, so she's not there to run it over to me, and I have a call with Arthur Hobbs in five minutes, so I don't have time to leave."

"Give me your keys," I said, moving toward his desk. "I'll go pick it up. Just tell me where it is and what you want, and I'll be back before you know it."

He narrowed his gaze as he studied me. "How do you know where I live?"

"It's Cottonwood Cove, Bossman. You bought the largest house in town. Everyone knows where you live."

He squeezed the back of his neck and nodded. "All right. I'll text you the code to the gate to get onto the property and then the code for my keypad on the garage. Primary bedroom is downstairs, and my closet is off the bathroom."

"I think I'm capable of finding the closet." I placed my hands on my hips. "What am I bringing back?"

"My sports coats are all together on the far-left side of the closet. Get me the navy tweed coat. And don't be snooping around," he said, raising a brow, but his lips twitched again, which meant he was teasing me.

"I'll make a deal with you. Get me a few more chapters of Mara's book, and I'll be back with that jacket in no time."

"Oh, you're calling the shots now?"

"I think you know talent when you see it. That's all I'm saying," I said, walking backward toward the door.

The way his eyes roamed my body had me squeezing my thighs together. He unbuttoned his sleeves and rolled them up a few times, exposing his forearms, and the move was so sexy I nearly lost my balance, but I straightened quickly.

"Go. Get back before my meeting," he demanded, and I pulled the door closed behind me.

I grabbed my coat and hurried back downstairs and slipped onto Scooty. Yes, I'd named him. I grew attached to things easily. I pulled my helmet on over my hat and dropped my purse into the basket behind my seat. Luckily, it wasn't snowing anymore, and the sun was out. I slipped on my sunglasses and made my way to the big house on top of the hill. I glanced around a few times, making sure my siblings weren't on the road. I'd managed to keep Scooty hidden thus far. Hugh would have a fit if he found out I was riding a scooter to work. He thought the Lancasters were sending a car for me each morning, which was why I had to get out of the house so early before they caught me running down the street to my scooter.

Just another day in the life of a girl who had to hide the fact that her ex-boyfriend had stolen her car.

I approached the property and typed in the code to the iron gate that surrounded the estate. Once they opened, I rolled up the circular driveway, my mouth gaping open as I took it in. I'd seen the house from a distance, but I hadn't been this close to it before to notice all the stonework and detail. The positioning of the house allowed for what I could only imagine was an epic water view. The front door was a dark wood, and it looked grand and heavy. I parked my scooter in front of the garage, which was also a dark wood with black metal accents.

I reached for my phone and pulled off my gloves as I typed in the garage door code. Even his garage was grand. The flooring was a white shiny concrete with speckles of black and gold. There were rustic lights hanging above, and he had three sports cars parked in here, which I figured was the reason he'd offered me to borrow one of his cars, which I'd obviously refused.

I hurried inside, knowing I needed to be in and out of here and back on my scooter in twenty-five minutes to make it back to the office on time.

Dark wood floors ran throughout the house, and rustic beams similar in color hung on the ceiling above. I couldn't help but look in the kitchen really quick, and it was as breathtaking as the rest of the house. Dark wood cabinets with two grand black islands and white stone countertops throughout. Manly yet totally stylish.

The house was furnished like something out of a magazine, so he'd clearly had it professionally decorated.

I ran down the hallway to where I assumed his bedroom was, and I paused as I took it in. The entire back wall was covered in windows with views of the ocean. His house was set on a hill, so it would be a trek down to the water, but I imagined you could see it from every room in the house. Copper bedding covered the four-poster bed, and I was tempted to go jump on it just for shits and giggles, but I was a professional—I couldn't do anything so childish, could I?

I chuckled as I walked into his bathroom and took in the black lanterns that hung above the grand space. There was a walk-in shower that could hold twenty people along with an oversized freestanding tub.

I'd never seen anything like it. I'd never been very impressed by money, nor cared about things like this because I loved the home I grew up in, and I'd never wanted for anything.

Aside from the hope of getting my car back.

But this was… a whole different world.

I'd get lost in a place like this.

I immediately wondered if Maddox ever got lonely here. I think I'd be scared living in a place like this by myself, as a football team could be hiding out in a house of this size, and you wouldn't know it.

But for all I knew, he didn't spend his nights alone. Maybe he had a girlfriend. He hadn't shared his private life with me. Sure, we spent a lot of time together with him telling me what to do every second of the day, but it was never personal.

Maybe he had a woman.

Or lots of women.

I strolled into the closet and came to an abrupt halt. I didn't need to turn the lights on because they were on some sort of sensor, and the entire closet lit up when I stepped inside.

Holy hell.

This was not something I'd ever even seen in the movies or in a magazine. I quickly FaceTimed Brinkley, and she answered, but she was whispering.

"Why are you whispering?" I asked.

"I'm just heading into a meeting. Where the hell are you?" She kept her voice low when I turned the camera and scanned the closet.

"Bossman's house. He needs a coat for his meeting. Look at this place."

"Damn. He's even got an ottoman to sit on when you put on your shoes. My apartment is the size of a postage stamp, so I can barely find a place to sit in the family room." She chuckled, still keeping her voice low.

"Oh my gosh. There's a speaker for music. I think I might need to have a little fun. Go to your meeting. I'll call you later."

"Don't get in trouble," she said, using her normal voice now, which was well above a whisper, and I laughed before ending the call.

I connected my phone to his speaker and hit play on my favorite seventies playlist. My eyes caught on an entire section of baseball caps with lighting above each shelf. There was a section for suits, and even his jeans were pressed and hung perfectly in their own area. He had an entire shelf for cuff links and cologne and all the other manly stuff that wealthy people apparently had.

I found a very cool-looking brown suede cowboy hat sitting on a shelf by itself, and I popped it on my head and glanced in the mirror.

"You're right, Mom. I've yet to find a hat that doesn't work for me." I chuckled to myself as "I'm Coming Out" by Diana Ross played through the speaker. I paused when I found his navy sports coat, and then I hung it on the door before my gaze caught on the most luxurious black velvet suit jacket. I slipped my arms through the sleeves and moaned at how soft and warm it was, even if it completely engulfed me.

And then one of my all-time favorite songs came on… and I knew what that meant.

Dance party.

six

. . .

Maddox

THIS DAY HAD TURNED into a shit show. Arthur Hobbs had gotten on the call and then abruptly told me he was nauseous and proceeded to dry heave into the phone before violently vomiting while I was on speakerphone. I'd let him know we could reschedule and ended the call, not even certain he'd heard me.

I didn't do well with gagging and heaving, and I used that time to take a look at Georgia's notes again. I'd read the three chapters of Mara's work, and I agreed with my assistant. Even though that wasn't the genre I typically read, I knew good work when I read it. It was a gift I'd been given from my grandfather, who was an iconic man in the publishing world.

Nadia had torn apart the opening, which was near perfection in my opinion. So, I'd gotten on the phone with my grandfather and told him about my assistant being an avid reader and loving the submission and that I agreed with her.

He'd heard Ted was going to shop this story to other houses starting tomorrow, so he told me to reschedule the board meeting, and he'd booked a meeting with that dickhead Ted Hagger in the city for dinner. He told me to bring my assistant and take the helicopter and not to be late.

The problem was, my goddamn assistant wasn't answering her phone. I no longer needed the jacket she'd gone to get, but we'd both need to pack a bag and get our asses on the helicopter in an hour.

I jumped in my car and drove back to my house, finding her ridiculous scooter parked in my driveway. It infuriated me that she drove that thing, even after I'd offered her a temporary loaner, as I had multiple cars, and she'd turned me down. She was attached to the stupid thing she was driving, and she said she didn't need handouts.

Well, she needed a goddamn car, and I didn't care how she got it.

I jogged inside, and when I opened the door, music boomed through my entire house.

What the actual fuck?

Was she throwing a party?

I held up my phone and Shazamed the song and shook my head.

"Slow Ride" by Foghat.

Her taste in music was as bad as her taste in transportation.

I moved through my bedroom and into the bathroom, pausing as I stood against the wall with a view into my closet. She couldn't see me, but I could see her perfectly.

She was standing on top of my leather ottoman in her booties, which was an argument for another time, because I wouldn't care right now if she'd spray-painted the walls.

I was completely mesmerized.

She was wearing my black velvet jacket that covered the backs of her thighs, because all I could see was a set of gorgeous legs and her booties. Maybe she was naked beneath? That would be quite the fantasy. She had a cowboy hat on her head that I'd never worn, but it was my grandfather's, and he'd given it to me.

She belted out the lyrics to the song, which would now go down as my all-time favorite song forever. She danced and wiggled and shook her ass.

Fully invested in her performance.

A slower part to the song started to play, and she bent her knees and turned just enough for me to see her playing the air guitar, and I nearly blew my cover when I realized she was holding a can of shaving cream in her hand, which she was clearly using as her microphone, and she tossed it down on the ottoman.

She broke out into the chorus before doing some sort of rock star jump through the air and landing on the floor and then spinning in my direction when her gaze locked with mine.

She sang the words one more time, her voice much softer. "Oh, hey there, Bossman. Um, I was just heading back."

She hurried toward my speaker and turned it off, and the room fell silent, aside from the heavy panting coming from her mouth. I moved inside the closet. Her chest was rising and falling from her stadium-worthy performance, and she blinked up at me a few times.

"On a scale of one to ten, how much trouble am I in?"

Fuck. I wanted to lay her out on that ottoman and bury my face between her thighs.

Touch her and taste her and make her cry out my name.

My chest pressed against hers, and I tipped the hat back so I could see her eyes. "This looks good on you."

"I bet it would look much better on you," she whispered. The scent of orange blossom and cinnamon flooded my system. "I was just grabbing your coat, and I got a little distracted."

"I can see that."

"Are you mad?" Her tongue swiped out and ran along her

plump bottom lip, and my dick doubled in size as he raged against my zipper.

Back the fuck off, man.

She works for you.

She's too sweet. Too good. Too tempting.

Completely off-limits.

I backed away, reached for the hat on her head, and set it on the shelf where it belonged.

"Not exactly what I told you to do. But we don't have time to argue about it." I slipped my hand beneath the black velvet jacket to help her out of it, and my fingertips grazed the soft skin of her neck, and I abruptly tugged the coat off her. I moved across the closet and grabbed my overnight bag and tossed in a few items of clothing before grabbing a fresh suit that I'd wear tonight. I had a toiletry bag ready to go, as I traveled often, and my assistant stood there quietly for the first time since I'd met her.

"Let's go to your house. You need to pack a bag."

"I need to pack a bag?" She jogged to keep up with me as we made our way through the house. "You're forcing me out of Cottonwood Cove?"

I was glad I had my back to her because I could feel the smile spread across my face. She was cute as hell, and I enjoyed messing with her.

I pulled the front door open as she slipped into her coat and found her gloves and hat on my entry table. I motioned for her to step outside and walked toward my car before pulling the passenger door open.

"I have my own car here," she said, looking at me like I had three heads.

"You don't have a car."

"My actual car is in the shop, and this is my—" I cut her off before she could finish. I held my hands up to stop her.

"In the car. Now," I growled.

She didn't even have a smart-ass comeback. She just

climbed inside, and I raised a brow, waiting for her to buckle herself in.

"What are you? My father?"

"I'm your fucking boss. Buckle up. Now."

She glared at me and reached for her belt, and I slammed the door. She was the most infuriating woman I'd ever met. Arguing about driving a fucking motorized bicycle in the middle of winter. I knew her brother owned Reynolds', the most popular restaurant and bar in Cottonwood Cove because it was all anyone in this godforsaken town talked about. I'd be making a visit there this week and asking him how he was okay with his sister's current transportation situation.

Because I hardly knew her, and I wasn't okay with it.

I opened my trunk and walked over to her motorized piece of shit and removed the helmet from the handlebars before picking the whole thing up and maneuvering it into my trunk. It was definitely heavier than a bicycle, but still, it offered her no protection.

I closed the trunk and climbed into the driver's seat, starting the car up and pulling out of the driveway.

"Where do you live?"

"Why?" she asked, turning to face me. "It was just a freaking song. You're overreacting. Have you never performed in the closet or the shower or the privacy of your own home?"

"What the fuck are you talking about?" I hissed. "Do you ever just answer a simple question without asking one in return?"

"Are you really firing me because I danced in your over-the-top, fancy, pretentious closet? Newsflash, Genius: Not everyone has a closet like that. So, I had a little fun. Sue me. No, why don't you just fire me? I've done everything you've asked of me for the last two weeks. I've come early every single day. I've brought donuts and cookies, and I'm the most dominant ping-pong player in that goddamn office. I've been friendly with everyone who works there, and I've managed to ignore *Nadia Wrong's* condescending comments. I've made sure your coffee is fresh every two and a half hours because my sister Brinkley said that's the cutoff for stale coffee. I rushed out, in the cold, mind you, to get your stupid blazer, even though you bash my form of transportation constantly..." She was shouting, and then her words broke on a sob, and I swerved to the side of the road and put the car in park.

"Nadia Wrong, huh?" I said, trying to make light of it even though my goddamn chest squeezed at the sight of her with tears streaming down her face and her bottom lip trembling.

It physically pained me to see her upset.

I was not a man who reacted to the sight of a woman crying that way.

It was normally my cue to tap out.

Get the hell out of there.

But for whatever reason, I was fighting the urge to pull her close.

"That's what you took from all of that?" She swiped at her cheeks and shook her head.

"It's very fitting." I leaned forward, using the pad of my thumb to swipe beneath her eyes, one at a time. "Stop crying. Now."

"You can't tell me to stop crying." She threw her hands in the air.

"I can, and I just did. So, your argument is already flawed, per usual, Tink."

"I'm not giving you my address until you tell me why you're firing me." Her bottom lip trembled.

"For fuck's sake. I'm not firing you. We're going to the city. You need a bag because we're staying the night."

"I'm going to the city? With you?" Her eyes widened as she waited for an answer.

"Correct. We're meeting with Mara Skye's agent. He's an asshole, but we need to close this deal before he shops it. So, could you please tell me the address to your home so you can grab a bag? We'll discuss the rest of your insults on the helicopter."

She nodded. "Take this street down to the stop sign and make a right."

She proceeded to direct me to her house and then asked me to pull over.

"Is this it?" I asked, glancing out the window at the ranch house set on a large lot that was a good two hundred feet from where I'd stopped the car.

"Umm… you know how you asked me to answer a question and not ask one myself?"

"Yes. We need to get going, Tink. I don't have time for games."

She bit down on her bottom lip and fidgeted with her hands. "I need to take the scooter out here. My brother lives two blocks away, and I'm staying in his casita. It's like a guest room with its own entrance."

"I know what a casita is. Why the fuck are we taking out your hunk of junk two blocks from his house?"

"Because they don't know that I drive this. I don't want my family to worry about me. They think my car is in the shop."

I groaned. Everything was like a fucking riddle with this girl. "Where is your fucking car? No more stories. Just spit it out. You can tell me."

She let out a long breath and looked out the window before looking back at me. "My ex-boyfriend didn't take our breakup well, and he stole my car right before I graduated and came home. He won't give it back to me. So, everyone thinks it's in the shop. I bought the scooter to get me to and from work until I figure out what to do."

My hands fisted in my lap. I made an effort to calm myself down before I spoke. "How did he steal the car?"

"He took the keys, and he has it hidden somewhere. I went to the bar where he and his band perform in the city twice and tried to get him to tell me where it is, but he won't give it back until he gets what he wants."

"Who the fuck does that? What does he want?"

"He wants to get back together." She shrugged.

I ran a hand down my face. This was completely unacceptable. This dickhead was holding her car hostage, and that shit would not fly with me.

"What's his name? And what's the name of his band?"

"Why?"

"You just did it again. You answered my question with a question. If you want me to get that fucking glorified bike with a motor out of my car and leave it here, you need to tell me his name now."

"Dikota Smith. And his band is The Burnout."

"Was that so difficult?" I grumped before getting out of my car and yanking the piece of shit out of the trunk and parking it there.

We were silent as we drove to her brother's house, and I waited in the car as she ran inside to pack her overnight bag. I took that time to call Weston, a man who'd worked for my family for many years. He was sort of a private investigator slash bodyguard slash fix-it-man. A dude of many talents, I guess you could say. He was on my father's payroll at all times because my dad had a tendency to need a lot of cleanup in his life.

I filled him in on the situation and asked to see what he could find out. I'd be in the city tonight, and I had no problem going and having a chat with her shithead ex-boyfriend.

I'd be getting that car back if it was the last thing I did.

I was her boss, after all.

It was the least I could do.

seven

. . .

Georgia

I'D SPRINTED inside the house and packed my nicest black dress for dinner and grabbed a pair of heels. A meeting with an agent in the city was definitely not something I could wear booties to. I tossed in my pajamas and a change of clothes for tomorrow before gathering all my makeup and toiletries and tossing them into a bag before hurrying back outside.

This day had been exhausting, and now I was heading to the city on a helicopter to meet with my favorite author's agent.

I'd been caught by my boss dancing in his closet while wearing his coat and hat.

That had to go down as the world's most embarrassing moment to date.

Well, unless it was beat out by the fact that I'd just cried in front of him because I thought he'd fired me. And then I'd been forced to fill him in on my blackmailing ex-boyfriend.

If you looked up train wreck in the dictionary right now, there'd be a photo of me, holding a can of shaving cream and dancing in my grumpy boss's closet.

We'd driven back to the office in silence, and he'd hurried me up the stairs and through a side door I hadn't even known was there, which led to the rooftop of the building where he kept his helicopter.

I was getting a crash course in the lifestyle of the rich and famous today. Closets that were larger than my entire apartment back in the city and helicopter pads on top of buildings.

Maddox had both of our bags in his hand and rested his free hand on the small of my back as he led me toward the helicopter. A man who introduced himself as Benjamin stood outside and opened the door and nodded at me as I climbed inside.

Once we were in, the two men exchanged a few words, then we were up in the air and I'd yet to speak a word.

"You okay?" He leaned close, and his lips grazed my ear. I squeezed my legs together and glanced out the window before looking at him.

"Yeah. I didn't let my family know I was leaving."

He studied me for a moment as if the thought of my family not knowing my whereabouts was a foreign concept to him. "Why don't you send them a text."

I nodded. I sent my parents a quick text letting them know and then jumped into the sibling group chat.

Hey. I'm in a helicopter, heading to the city for work. I'll be home tomorrow.

BRINKLEY

Fancy closets and now you're in a helicopter? Go, Georgie, go.

FINN

Did I miss a conversation? What are we talking about?

CAGE

This is why you shouldn't get a dog. You can't just leave any time you want when you have a dog. #teachablemoment

HUGH

Stop being a #buzzkill, brother. Have fun in the city.

BRINKLEY

Where are you staying? I bet it's somewhere swanky!

"We're staying at the Four Seasons," Maddox's deep voice said as he leaned over my shoulder and read my texts.

I quickly put my phone down in my lap and shot him a look.

"It's not in good taste to read someone's texts over their shoulder."

"Says the woman who just danced around my closet. For all I know, you were sniffing my boxers," he said, his hand brushing against mine, and I didn't pull away. We were sitting awfully close in the back of the helicopter, and there was a sudden dip, which made me jump and squeal at the same time.

Benjamin glanced over his shoulder and apologized, and Maddox chuckled before his pointer finger stroked the back of my hand. "You're all right."

There were a few more dips, and I gasped a couple more times before I turned and buried my face in his chest until we were on the ground.

Let me tell you, sage and sandalwood had a way of soothing the nerves. The man smelled like strength and confidence and sexy man. And I was here for it.

Once we were on the ground, he tipped me back and cleared his throat, and I straightened.

"Sorry about that. I'm not used to this form of transportation." I reached for my purse and unbuckled myself.

"Says the woman who drives an unsafe, shitty piece of metal around town."

I rolled my eyes and stepped off when Benjamin opened

the door. "Thanks for the ride, Benjamin. Those little squeaks had nothing to do with you; they were all about me."

He chuckled. "I'll see you tomorrow. Have fun tonight."

There was a car waiting for us just a few feet away. "Wow. You've got all sorts of people waiting on you here, huh?"

"That's the one benefit to the move out of town. I can drive my own car. Have some privacy. No press in my business."

"Ahhh... the life of a wealthy socialite," I teased as we both slipped into the back of the car. Maddox introduced me to Jayden the driver, and we said a quick hello. "What's the downside to Cottonwood Cove? Not enough hot women?"

He glanced over at me and looked like he was going to say something, but he stopped himself. "I miss the food in the city. Meeting women has never been a problem for me."

I wanted to call him out for being cocky, but I knew it was the truth. The man smelled like sex on a stick, he was a good foot taller than me with broad shoulders and a hard body, a face that should be splayed across a men's fashion magazine, and he had a closet that most women would give a kidney for.

He was the whole damn package.

And he was clearly brilliant, because he'd listened to me about Mara Skye over his glass-half-empty editor who, was supposed to be a professional.

"How about I treat you to Reynolds' when we get home?" I said. He raised a brow, and I quickly explained that I wasn't meaning it as a date. "I mean, as a professional courtesy. You took my advice about the book, and I'm grateful. And a good slab of ribs will have you singing the praises of the food in Cottonwood Cove."

"First of all, you aren't treating. I'm your boss."

"Easy there, alpha dog. My brother owns the place. I was just being a show-off. I wouldn't actually be paying." I chuckled, and Jayden barked out a laugh from the front seat, earning him a warning look from Maddox.

"Glad we cleared that up. Secondly, I read the first three chapters, and I agreed with you. That's the reason we're going to this meeting. And lastly, I'm a bit of a food snob, so it'll be hard to sway me." He paused when the car pulled in front of the swanky hotel. "Okay, here's the plan. You have your own room, as do I. We'll go change clothes and then meet downstairs in an hour."

"You're staying here, too?"

"Would you prefer I didn't?" He rolled his eyes.

"No. I just assumed you had a home here. Or a condo or a penthouse or something like that."

Jayden opened the door, and Maddox motioned for me to get out. We said our goodbyes to the driver and then made our way inside. Maddox Lancaster was some sort of big shot here in the city, because from the moment we stepped inside the lobby, everyone hustled around us.

They gave him his keys, took our bags, and he led me to the elevators like he'd stayed here many times before.

Once we were on the elevator, he stood on the opposite wall from me. I leaned down to smell my pits to make sure I didn't stink because he sure was keeping his distance now that we weren't on the helicopter.

Nope.

I smelled like an orange creamsicle.

Everybody loves a creamsicle, right?

"I do have an apartment here, but we aren't staying long enough for me to go there. Our meeting is here, so I'll just stay the night at the hotel, as well."

"Hmmm... you must stay here often because the hotel staff sure seems to know you."

His mouth remained in a straight line. "My grandfather owns the place. I grew up coming here."

"Damn. My grandfather owns an apple orchard, which I thought was pretty cool, but a Four Seasons is impressive."

"Real estate developers own each individual property, and the Four Seasons operates them. My grandfather invests in things that he thinks will be profitable. So, if it was a good buy, he'd be the first to gobble up an apple orchard, too."

The doors opened, and he motioned for me to step off.

"Good to know. I thought you were going to say you bring all your ladies here. That you're one of those guys who doesn't take women to his home and just meets them at his swanky hotel room." I waggled my brows when he paused at the door and looked at me like I had three heads.

"You've been reading a lot of fiction, I see. And you seem a little consumed by who I spend time with outside of work," he said. It wasn't a question. It was a statement.

"Don't flatter yourself. I just figured a good-looking man like yourself who has access to the finest hotel in the city... it seems like a good place to..." I shrugged because I didn't know why I was saying this aloud.

He moved closer, crowding me as my back hit the door of what I assumed was my room, seeing as we'd stopped here. "Good-looking, huh?"

"I don't think it's a secret. The press has dubbed you the hottest bachelor in town." My tongue swiped out to wet my lips which were completely dry now, and I tried to play it cool with a shrug.

"Are you keeping tabs on me, Tink?"

"I work for you. It's my job to know what you do and who you... whatever."

"Who I fuck?" He raised a brow.

I sucked in a breath, a little shocked at his nearness and that we were speaking to one another like this.

He smirked and stepped back. "Cat got your tongue?"

"No. I'm fine. And I don't care who you... fuck."

"Good. Keep it that way. I don't date women who work for me."

A maniacal laugh escaped my lips as he sidestepped me and slipped the key into the door. "Please. You are most definitely *not* my type."

"That's right. You date guys who steal your car and blackmail you." He pushed the door open and handed me the key just as the guy with our bags came walking down the hall. Maddox leaned down close to my ear. "But for the record, Tink, I'm everyone's type."

Maddox stood there holding the door open, and I told the concierge which bag was mine and then followed him inside before he made his way across the hall to what looked like the corner suite.

"You can take the other bag across the hall." Maddox motioned to his door before turning back to me. "I'll see you in forty-five minutes. You'll be taking notes and observing."

I didn't say anything. I just let the door close behind me and moved across the room and fell onto my bed.

My boss was a bit of a conundrum.

Broody and mysterious, yet protective and thoughtful at the same time.

He clearly had a healthy ego.

My phone vibrated, and I pulled it out of my purse.

DIKOTA

You can't ignore me forever, baby. Eventually, you'll want your car back.

I groaned and tossed my phone onto the bed before making my way to the bathroom. Tonight was a big night.

I had a seat at the table in a meeting that could lead to something amazing.

I wasn't going to worry about my crazy ex, my current car situation, or the fact that my boss was consuming my every thought.

Both awake and asleep.

I'd had a dirty dream about the bastard last night.

Probably because we were spending so much time together and he had a way of getting under my skin.

Although in my dream, he wasn't under my skin. He was buried between my thighs.

I had a hunch Bossman knew how to please a woman.

But I'd be keeping those thoughts to myself.

eight

. . .

Maddox

I TEXTED Georgia to let her know I was heading down to the bar and to meet me there. She strolled in wearing a black dress and some hot-as-fuck nude heels.

No booties today.

Her hair was pulled back and tied in some sort of knot at the nape of her neck, and she looked fucking stunning.

Professional. Sexy.

Fucking breathtaking.

I'd kept my face neutral, not wanting to let her see that I was panting on the inside. For fuck's sake, this was my employee. My assistant.

I was not a cliché—that title had always belonged to my father.

"So, unless he directly asks you a question, just take notes and nod. When we're dealing with guys like Ted Hagger, the less we say, the better. Let him do the talking. Let him talk himself into a fucking corner. We just need a green light that we can sign Mara, and then we don't say another word. That's how deals get lost."

"Got it, Bossman. I'm ready. I'll be the perfect assistant.

You'll hardly know I'm there." She chuckled, and I rolled my eyes.

But the smell of orange blossoms and cinnamon was flooding my system, so there was no chance in hell I wouldn't know she was there.

"There's my boy." My grandfather's gruff voice pulled me from my unprofessional thoughts.

I pushed to my feet, and so did Georgia.

"Good to see you." I pulled him in for a hug. "This is my assistant, Georgia Reynolds. I told you that she was a big fan of Mara's work."

He clasped her hand in his, and he raised a brow as he took her in.

She was stunning, no doubt about it.

"Well, I think you'll be very pleased to know that Mara Skye is actually joining us tonight," he said.

Georgia's mouth fell open. Her plump, pink lips making a perfect O. Thoughts of filling that sweet mouth with—

Oh, for fuck's sake.

I needed to pull my shit together.

I wasn't that guy. Women didn't affect me. I was polite enough, a considerate lover who always pleased my women before myself, but I didn't gape or fantasize or think of anything beyond that moment.

A nice dinner, light conversation, and a great fucking romp in the hay.

That was me.

No attachments.

Ever.

"Mara Skye is coming to dinner tonight?" Georgia whispered and wrapped both her hands around my grandfather's hand, which he clearly found endearing because he beamed down at her.

"She is." He smiled before turning when someone called out

his name. Ted Hagger strolled into the bar wearing an expensive suit and waving his hands around, which was impossible to miss because the dude had rings on almost every finger and a fancy watch on his wrist, and he made sure everyone saw them.

He looked like a cheesedick trying to flaunt his money.

I leaned down close to Georgia's ear as my grandfather extended his hand to Ted.

"Keep your cool when she gets here, Tink."

She nodded and sighed before Grandfather introduced us. I couldn't stand the guy, but I'd be polite because we wanted to sign Mara, and we needed him to make that happen.

Of course, the asshole pressed his lips to the back of Georgia's hand, and it took everything in me not to yank him by his over-gelled, slicked-back hair and remind him this was a business deal.

I didn't need him panting all over my assistant, for fuck's sake.

"Maddox, what has it been? A year since I saw you last?"

I wished that were true. But we'd seen one another at a social event three months ago.

"Something like that. Thanks for meeting with us on such short notice."

"Of course. Mara's on her way, so we can head to the table and wait for her there. I'm assuming we'll be ordering the best bottle of wine they have, as I am representing the hottest author out there right now." His laugh was high-pitched, fake, and annoying as hell.

My grandfather chuckled, as he knew how to play the game better than I did. "Absolutely. Whatever you want is on us tonight. Thanks for giving me the first option to sign her."

We walked to the hostess stand, and she led us to the table in the back of the restaurant. The place was packed tonight, but it was quieter back here. This had always been my grandfather's favorite spot, and I'd grown up coming here.

We took our seats and the slimy jackass made sure to take

the seat beside Georgia, which pissed me off. I sat across from her, and my grandfather sat at the head of the table. We saved the spot beside me and across from Ted for his client.

"So, Georgia, you work for this guy, huh?" Ted smirked, his eyes roaming her face and chest so blatantly, I cleared my throat to remind him we were all watching.

"I do, yes." Her face was hard, not something I'd ever seen from her before now. She didn't like him, that much I could tell, but she remained professional, and that had the corners of my lips turning up just the slightest bit.

"Well, when you get tired of that hokey little town, just know we're always hiring at my firm here in the city. In fact, I'm in the market for a new assistant."

The bastard was trying to steal my employee while I was buying him dinner? The dude went through PAs faster than —well, faster than I did, but for different reasons. I was a workaholic who demanded perfection, which could be too much for people at times. He had a reputation for being a womanizer, and there were rumors of multiple women complaining to HR at his firm, but he'd always managed to buy his way out of it. I didn't like him sitting beside Georgia.

I didn't like him breathing the same air as her.

"Ted, I'll say this once, and I won't say it again. We'd love to work with Mara, but if you ever try to fucking poach my employee again, I will reach across this table and teach you some fucking manners. I don't give a shit if it costs us a deal. You got me?"

"Whoa, whoa, big guy, relax. It's just business, brother. But I can see you're very attached to your assistant." He chuckled.

My grandfather glanced at me before turning his attention back to Ted. "To make sure we're clear, we aren't desperate, Ted. We happen to be the biggest publishing house in the United States, and we already have some of the most influential authors on the planet working with us. Mara is talented, and we'd like to work with her, but you will not disrespect our employees. We'll walk so fast your head will spin."

"Ah, the apple doesn't fall far from the tree, I see." He shrugged, completely unfazed. The dude had fallouts with more people than not. This was nothing for him. "Georgia, you've got some loyal employers right here."

"Well, you know… being from a *hokey little town* and all, I consider myself lucky to be working with Lancaster Press. And us small-town girls are pretty loyal, too, Mr. Hagger." She smiled, but it wasn't genuine. She was trying to be professional while sticking it to him as much as she could.

And I fucking loved it.

He nodded. "There's just something about a small-town girl. Am I right, gentlemen?" He waggled his brows, like this was all just some fun banter, while everyone else at the table was on edge. And then he looked up and pushed to his feet. "Ah… here she is. Mara, thank you for joining us."

He made the introductions, and I watched as Georgia bit down on her bottom lip, trying to keep herself from reacting too much as she shook her hand. We all took our seats, and Ted ordered two bottles of the most expensive wine on the menu, and we placed our dinner orders, as well.

I got right down to business, telling Mara that we were beyond impressed with the sample that she'd sent over, and we were interested in making her an offer tonight.

"Well, this is fabulous news. I told Ted I only wanted to work with Lancaster Press on this one. Signing a deal with you all has been on my bucket list for a while now. I know you weren't interested in the last series, but I was hoping this one would pique your interest." She smiled and then glanced at her agent before turning back to me. "I told Ted if you passed on this one, I was going to drive to Cottonwood Cove myself and convince you of all the reasons why you should sign me."

We'd never received a submission from Mara Skye before,

at least not in the last decade that I'd been with the company. Professionally, throwing Ted under the bus might not be the wisest move, but the fact that he was licking his lips as he glanced over at my assistant left me with no choice.

"Well, I assure you, we would never turn you down. This is the first time we've received a submission, as far as I know, and we jumped at the chance to work with you."

My grandfather chuckled because he knew what I was doing. We weren't covering for this asshole. "I'm pretty ancient, so unless you submitted to us at a time that I wasn't running Lancaster Press, I'd know about it."

Mara's gaze narrowed as she looked between us and her agent in confusion.

"Well, no sense getting hung up on the past. We all know that paperwork can fall through the cracks. Let's focus on the here and now," Ted said.

He'd only submitted to us this time because she was going to go around him. This guy was a bigger dickhead than I'd given him credit for.

"That's fine. We can talk about it later, Ted." Mara's face did not hide her displeasure. "Tonight, I want to focus on the future. So, you really liked it?"

"We loved it," my grandfather said. "Georgia, here, is a big fan. She's read all of your work, and she gushed about this submission."

Mara clapped her hands together. "Stop. Really? That means the world to me, Georgia. Thank you."

"Are you kidding? Thank you. You are a one-click author for me. I literally stay up all night when your books release."

"Well, from now on, I'll be sending you an ARC for all of my books," Mara said with a big smile on her face. Advanced Reader Copies were popular in the book world.

"Oh, wow. That would mean so much to me. I beta-read for my cousin, and now I can be an ARC reader for you," Georgia said, raising her glass. "I will drink to that."

Everyone raised their glass, and Mara took a sip before turning her attention back to Georgia.

"Who is your cousin?"

"Ashlan Thomas. Her name is Ashlan King now, but she writes under her maiden name."

Mara's mouth fell open. "I'm a huge fan of Ashlan's work. I've read everything she's written."

They went back and forth as our food was set down in front of us. Georgia agreed to have Ashlan come to Cottonwood Cove when Mara came for a visit. We'd gotten off the professional track with the conversation, but with the way these two were bonding, it only worked in our favor.

Georgia glanced up at me and managed to steer the conversation back to the present. "So, Maddox doesn't normally read historical romance, but he admitted that he'd been pulled in by this one, too. I think you've got a new fan on your hands."

Mara turned her attention to me, and we discussed some of the strengths of her opening and where she planned to take the story. My grandfather was completely captivated by her as she walked us through the conflict and the way she planned to give them their happily ever after.

"Brilliant. When do you think you could have the next few chapters to us?"

"The book is done. I thought Ted told you that. We just didn't want to overwhelm you with the whole thing if you weren't interested."

I finished chewing and reached for my glass of wine. "We're more than interested. We can have a contract ready for you tomorrow if the numbers we discussed work for you?" We were offering her a four-book deal, which we didn't do often, but she'd felt passionate about the series, and we knew she was talented as hell.

"Yes. I'm ready to sign with you right now." She clasped her fingers together and chuckled.

"Consider it a done deal. We'll send something over to your office tomorrow, Ted." My grandfather did not look pleased when he turned his attention to her agent, who had clearly been lying about submitting to us in the past.

"Great. We'll look it over and get it back to you quickly." Ted glanced down at his phone as if he had something more important going on than the fact that we had verbally agreed to sign Mara.

She watched him for a long moment before turning back to the rest of us. "How about we keep in touch? Let's exchange numbers."

She handed her phone to Georgia, and she agreed to put her number and our office number in her contacts, and then she sent herself a text to ensure she had Mara's number, as well.

Ted's head snapped up. "That won't be necessary. I've got their information. Well, I don't have Georgia's number, and I should probably get that in case I can't reach the big guy over here."

I rolled my eyes. He had no reason to contact her. "If you call my direct line, Georgia will answer and patch you through. That should suffice."

Yeah, I shut that shit down fast and glanced at Georgia to make sure she didn't hand that asshole her phone.

"Well, I'll give you a call at the office tomorrow, Georgia." He smiled and slipped his phone into his coat pocket.

We finished dinner and celebrated with a few desserts as Mara and Georgia talked books. Ted told us he might have another client interested in signing with us, but I figured he was full of shit and just trying to kiss our asses after being caught in a lie tonight.

We all stood and said our goodbyes and my grandfather told me he'd call me in the morning. Ted walked Mara out, and from the looks of it, she was blasting him a little, as their conversation looked heated.

Georgia and I walked toward the elevators, not saying a word as we waited for the doors to open and stepped inside.

"You did well tonight," I said, standing on the opposite wall from her because I needed distance from this woman. Her scent. Her eyes. Her smile. It was doing crazy shit to me, and that didn't sit well.

"Thank you. I love her. She's amazing. Her agent is a real tool, though, huh?"

"Yeah. Unfortunately, he's got some of the biggest authors out there, and working with him is inevitable. But you handled him well."

"Thank you. Did you just compliment me twice in two minutes, Bossman?" Her voice was all tease as the door opened, and I motioned for her to step off first.

I was a gentleman, after all.

It had nothing to do with the fact that I had a perfect view of her ass swaying from side to side as she walked down the hall.

"Don't get cocky. I still think you drive a piece of shit, and you did dance around in my closet, so there are still those two things on the table." I chuckled as I paused in front of my door, and she stood across from me with her back against her door.

"I've got some moves, don't I?"

The best fucking moves I'd ever seen.

But I wouldn't say that.

I was her boss, after all.

"Goodnight, Tink."

And with that, I turned and slipped inside my room.

I'd gotten a text from Heather, a woman I'd seen on and off over the years, but for whatever reason, I wasn't in the mood for company.

Because I couldn't get my goddamn assistant out of my head.

nine

. . .

Georgia

I DROPPED onto my bed and picked up my phone to see the sibling group text and catch up on what I'd missed out on tonight.

FINN

I just had to do a sex scene with Jessica Carson, and she's even hotter in person. I think they are going to make her my new love interest. <panting face emoji>

CAGE

Well, that's a rough day at the office. You're getting naked with Jessica fucking Carson, and I'm checking the eyesight of the Wilsons' hamster. Where did I go wrong when choosing my career path?

BRINKLEY

Jessica Carson is so hot, but I saw her in an interview, and she was a little full of herself. I just had to go into the locker room with a bunch of sweaty NFL players, and I saw more asses than anyone should see at one given time. But wow, those are some good butts on those men.

HUGH

There's a lot happening here. Sex scenes, hamsters, and multiple asses? Georgie, anything you need to share?

BRINKLEY

She's in a meeting with Mara Skye right now. Although her boss is awfully sexy. Even if he's a broody bastard. But aren't those the best kind?

I'm here. The meeting was amazing. She is going to sign a four-book deal with Lancaster Press, and she talked to me the whole night. I think I've found my calling. Nobody was nude at the table, though.

CAGE

I knew you'd find your niche. And you were able to combine your business degree with your love for reading. Proud of you, Georgie.

FINN

Hey, I just had a sex scene with one of the hottest upcoming actresses on the planet. Are you proud of me, Cage?

HUGH

I'm guessing he's envious, for sure. You need a woman, Cage. Spending your days with pigs and chicks and hamsters isn't healthy. <laughing face emoji>

BRINKLEY

It's better than all the fancy boutique dogs you were seeing when you were in LA. Don't knock the small-town life.

CAGE

Says the girl living in the city.

I'm so glad you're raising Gracie in Cottonwood Cove and not in Los Angeles. I'll be home tomorrow. Let her know I'm going with you guys to see Santa this weekend like I promised. J.R. is the best Santa ever.

FINN

He is, but is Mr. Weber still running Santa's village and dressing as an elf? That man was three sheets to crazy town last Christmas. He burped in my face, and he reeked of Italian sausage and peppermint Schnapps. I can't eat a candy cane without having flashbacks now.

HUGH

He was at the restaurant last night, tipping back the whiskey sours and wearing a green jumpsuit and a hat. It's safe to say he's still a drunk elf.

CAGE

My god. That man was a drunk elf when we were kids. How is his liver still working?

BRINKLEY

Remember the year we did that Christmas photo with me and Georgie on Santa's lap and you guys standing around him for the family holiday card, and Mr. Weber photobombed us?

Yes. Mom was so mad when she ordered two hundred and fifty cards, only to see an elf with unusually red eyes jumping up in the background. <eyeroll emoji>

CAGE

Well, if he burps on my daughter, I'm going to have a word with him.

BRINKLEY

I would pay money to see you go all papa bear protective on Mr. Weber.

HUGH

Why don't you guys all come have dinner at the restaurant after taking Gracie to see Santa, and I'll have Mom and Dad come, too?

Perfect. Going to bed. I'll be home tomorrow.

I moved to the bathroom and ran a bubble bath in the fancy tub. I pinned up my hair and climbed in. I was deep into my beta read from my cousin, Ashlan. I often read on my Kindle app on my phone, and a text from Maddox appeared at the top of the screen.

BOSSMAN

I just emailed you a copy of the contract that we are sending to Mara tomorrow morning. Check it over for me, and then we will forward it to her and that douchedick agent of hers.

I laughed so hard I nearly dropped the phone in the tub.

I'm glad you're dealing with her and not just him. I don't get a good vibe from him.

BOSSMAN

Good. He's bad news. Tell me why you and your ex broke up.

That was random. Why was he asking about that now?

Nice segue. Why do you want to know?

BOSSMAN

You just answered another question with a question.

At least I'm consistent. Answer the question, please.

BOSSMAN

Because my employee drives a motorized bicycle in the snow due to the fact that her asshat ex-boyfriend stole her car. He's blackmailing you. So, I want to know why he's taking the breakup so hard.

I let out a long sigh.

It was a lot of things. We didn't have much in common. But the straw that broke the camel's back was when I went to one of his concerts. I was in the back room of the bar, waiting for him. A fire alarm got pulled, and I ran to try to find him when I could have just run out the back door.

My feet slipped as I texted, and the water sloshed over the side of the tub and bubbles covered my hands.

BOSSMAN

Are you going to tell me what happened? I'm guessing you didn't use the back door?

That's what she said! LOL. You set me up for that one. I wasn't done with the story, but I got bubbles on my hands, and I had to wipe them off.

BOSSMAN

Ridiculous sense of humor. Why are you playing with bubbles?

I'm in the tub. I added bubbles, and they got on my hand. Anyway…

BOSSMAN

Is it appropriate to be texting your boss when you're naked in the tub?

Is it appropriate for my boss to be texting me this late or inquiring about my ex?

BOSSMAN

Touché. Finish the story. You're in the back room. The fire alarm gets pulled.

I run to find him, right? Because if the place goes up in flames, you should make sure your partner is safe. There was an exit right next to the room I was in, and I didn't take it. I ran to the stage to find him. But he'd run out the front door. Not a care in the world about making sure I got out. And I found him talking with his bandmates and laughing afterward. He didn't come to find me. So, I knew I was done in that moment.

BOSSMAN

Who the fuck does that?

Dikota Smith.

BOSSMAN

It's a stupid name. So, you dumped him. And then he stole your car?

I wish it were that simple. I dumped him. He tried to get me back, and I ignored him. So, he slept with my roommate because he was having a temper tantrum.

BOSSMAN

You can't make this shit up. And then he stole your car after boning your roommate?

I found them naked in her room, and I was stunned. My roommate was crying and apologizing, and Dikota said it was my fault because I'd dumped him. Then he grabbed my keys off the counter and left before I realized it.

BOSSMAN

This wouldn't even work in fiction. I take it you and the roomie aren't friends anymore?

We are not. And she sat next to me at graduation, which was super awkward. She keeps calling, but there really isn't any way to come back after that.

BOSSMAN

And your family doesn't know he took your car?

They don't know any of it. They would be upset. My brothers would probably hurt him. Brinkley would give them both a verbal showdown. I've got it handled.

BOSSMAN

By driving a scooter in the snow.

Do you have siblings?

BOSSMAN

One younger brother. He'd most likely steal your car and sleep with your roommate, so if you meet him, stay away from him.

Got it. I really like your grandfather. Do your parents live here, too?

BOSSMAN

Show and share is over, Tink. Get some sleep.

Over and out, Bossman.

BOSSMAN

That's what she said. Night.

I laughed before setting my phone down and reaching for a towel and drying off. I pulled on my pajamas and climbed into bed.

And I fell asleep to thoughts of my boss telling off the man who offered me a job tonight.

Maddox Lancaster was full of surprises.

The week had flown by. I was hurrying to get out of the office because tonight I was going with my brother, Cage, to take my niece, Gracie, to see Santa. The whole family was meeting at Reynolds' after, and it had been a few weeks since we were all together.

Brinkley lived in the city.

Finn was away filming in a small town between Cottonwood Cove and San Francisco.

And Hugh and Cage had been busy with work.

I saw my parents often, but it had been a few days, and they were excited to hear about my trip and how my meeting went with Mara Skye.

We'd been swamped at the office, as Maddox kept his schedule pretty packed, and between the trips he had coming up and the contracts that were going out, I could barely catch my breath.

I'd somehow managed to stay at the top of the winner's circle in ping-pong at the office, and I really enjoyed my job.

It was busy and fun and challenging.

My boss was still exhausting and needy, but I didn't mind it because Mara had signed the contract, and Maddox had given me a copy of the manuscript to read. He wasn't giving this particular book to Nadia, who'd initially turned it down but then backtracked when she heard that Lancaster Press had signed her. He'd decided to have his chief editor, Helena, work on it. And he was letting me meet with her to discuss things since declaring me a *historical romance expert.*

I'd been staying up way too late at night to read. I'd just finished the manuscript last night, and it was definitely Mara's best work.

And we'd been texting nonstop about it.

Mara Skye and I were practically girlfriends.

My cousin, Ashlan, was over the moon that Mara knew who she was, and we'd set up a day to go to lunch in a couple weeks, after we got through the holidays, when they'd both agreed to come to town.

Life was good.

I'd just been in a two-hour meeting with Helena discussing the book, and Maddox buzzed her office looking for me.

"The boss needs you. Thanks for talking this through. You've got a good eye, Georgia. And I know I showed you the cover art we were considering for this one, but I think you might be right about it looking more like a fantasy book than a historical romance book. I have the team working on the concept that we discussed a few days ago."

In what world did anyone listen to me and my ideas about something so important?

I shook my head and smiled. "Wow. Thank you so much for letting me be a part of this."

The door swung open, and Maddox stood there, looking irritated. His jaw was set, shoulders stiff, and one eyebrow raised as his lips remained in a straight line when he looked at me. "I've called and texted. You're needed. Now."

Helena chuckled. "Sorry. It was my fault."

He held up his hand to her with a forced smile. "It's fine. Let's go, Tink."

He'd started openly calling me by the nickname in the office, and Sydney thought it was hilarious because it was so unexpected coming from him. But no one else commented about it. I think they all knew we worked closely together and we'd formed a friendship.

"Where is the fire? We were talking about the book," I whisper-hissed after saying goodbye to Helena.

We spent a lot of time together.

He texted me endlessly for things he needed.

Day and night.

He took the position of personal assistant to a whole new level. And patience was not his strong suit.

"Two hours is more than enough time. Come with me." He was so bossy and irritated most of the time, yet I loved it.

I woke up in a good mood every day.

I'd somehow found my purpose here.

He led me down the stairs, and a few people yelled out to me about the ping-pong massacre today, where I'd literally destroyed Craig as he'd beaten everyone all week and wanted to challenge me for the title once again.

"Get back to work. Ping-pong is over," Maddox growled.

"Says the man who never plays," I said, as I followed him out the door and around the building. It was freezing, and he seemed completely unfazed.

He turned and handed me a set of keys, and there sat my piece-of-crap car, looking like it had a massive makeover. Had he painted it? It used to be a faded gray, and now it was a matte black.

"Is that my car?"

"Yes."

"How'd you get it back?"

"I got it back when we were in the city. That night. But it was in terrible shape. Had he stripped the paint job? It was a horrible gray, and it looked like shit."

"No. That was the way I bought it. Don't be rude, *Money Bags*. We don't all have options about the color when purchasing our first car. But I see you went with black. The color of your cold, jaded heart?" I teased, as I moved around it and glanced inside. "It's amazing. Thank you. I don't know what to say."

"Well, this is thrilling. You've never been at a loss for words. Sometimes less is more, Tink."

"Says the man who publishes words for a living." I raised a brow and rubbed my hands together as the snow started to fall from above.

He surprised me when he pulled his suit coat off and wrapped it around my shoulders. He could be so grumpy one minute, but then he'd catch me off guard the next by doing something nice.

He'd gone to the city to get my car for me.

Maybe Bossman actually had a heart.

ten

. . .

Maddox

"SO, did he just give you the car when you asked for it?" Georgia asked me, as she tipped her head back to let the snow fall on her pretty face.

"He's pathetic. I could have snapped him in half if I wanted to. So, no, he didn't put up a fight. He whined and bitched, and I counted to three, and he handed over the keys. I told you… you've been dating boys, not men."

It had been all too easy. The bar that her dipshit ex had been performing at was a leased space owned by Lancaster Properties. I'd made a call and was taken into a back room, and the show was temporarily stopped until after our little meeting. The pussy had cried and said he still loved her. I told him to stop contacting her or I'd be paying him another visit, and I wouldn't be as friendly next time.

And I meant it.

"What are you? The dating expert now?" She smirked. I loved how salty she was with me when she was pure sunshine with everyone else. I brought something out of her, and I enjoyed it.

"I do very well. Thank you for asking."

"I haven't seen any dates on your calendar," she said, her gaze searching mine.

"I keep my personal life separate, Tink." I raised a brow, liking the way her little hands fisted before she shoved them into my suit coat pockets. The snow was starting to come down harder, and I didn't mind standing out here with her at all, even though I was freezing my balls off. It was worth it to have this moment with her without four hundred fucking people interrupting us with fires to put out.

"I would hear about it if you were dating anyone here in Cottonwood Cove. Virginia gets all the scoop in town," she said, her voice full of tease, but I could see in her eyes that she was anxious for me to answer.

She was right.

I hadn't been out.

Not once since the day she'd come to interview with me.

And I needed to blow off some steam. Stop fantasizing about my assistant.

"I actually have a date tonight. We're going to your brother's restaurant because, according to Yelp, it's the best in town. And I do like impressing my women."

I couldn't hide the smile on my face. Hell, I smiled all the time now. She brought out a softer side of me, which I'd normally despise, but I didn't mind it at the moment. She looked jealous, and I liked it so much that I couldn't stop smiling. How twisted was that?

"Really?"

"Not sure why that's surprising to you, but yes. Really."

"That's actually fabulous. My family is having dinner there tonight after we take my niece to see Santa. Can't wait to meet your girlfriend."

"I don't do girlfriends," I said, and she shivered, so I turned her toward the building and placed my hand on her lower back to lead her inside.

"So, what do you do? Just buy them dinner and have your

way with them?" she asked. Once we stepped inside, she looked up at me with her dark blue eyes wide and curious.

I leaned down close to her ear. "I buy them dinner and then I rock their fucking world."

She crossed her arms over her chest as we stood in the entryway, a few feet away from nosy Virginia Hawkson, who thankfully looked deep in conversation as she held the phone to her ear.

"A one and done?" She raised a brow.

"Nah. I get a lot of repeat customers." I chuckled because I knew I was infuriating her, and I enjoyed it. "Heather is a woman I've seen many times, and she's coming here tonight. *No pun intended.*" I winked. "She was pissed I didn't make time for her when I was in the city because I was busy dealing with your little fucker, and she insisted on driving here tonight to see me."

I didn't know what the hell was going on with me, but ever since our trip to the city—nah, scratch that, *ever since she was shaking her ass in the closet to "Slow Ride"*, I'd adjusted my boss-employee relationship with her. Georgia brought out a different side of me. She was easy to be with. I laughed more than I ever had, and I didn't mind it. Hell, even I'd noticed the stuffy aloofness that I'd perfected under the tutelage of my father had faded. Georgia was doing things to me physically and emotionally, and I liked it.

Her tongue swiped out to wet her lips. "Wow. Good for you, and good for her, if that works for you both. I'd never take part in that kind of deal."

Her claws were out, and I liked it.

"And why is that, Tink?"

"Because that means you're both allowed to do whatever you want when you aren't together."

"Correct."

"I'd never be with a man who was willing to share me with someone else. I want to be with a man who couldn't stand the thought of another man touching me," she said, one brow raised as if she'd just put me in my place.

"And is that how Dikota, the car thief, was? When he wasn't fucking your roommate?" I shouldn't have said it. It wasn't nice. But she was getting under my skin because even talking about another man touching her bothered me.

This conversation was completely unprofessional and inappropriate for a million reasons, and I didn't give a fuck. Georgia mattered to me more than I wanted to admit.

She cleared her throat and kept her face even, but I saw the hurt in her eyes.

I was an asshole.

She needed to know that.

"Thanks for throwing that in my face when you are one of the only people that I shared that with. But, if you must know, he was actually quite possessive, yes. And I was done with him long before he strayed, but that would have been a deal breaker for me either way. I don't share, Bossman."

"Good for you. You should hold out for Mr. Perfect. And I assure you, it's not that punk in the city."

"You think I'm going to take dating advice from you?" she said, glancing down at her phone when it vibrated. "It's getting late. I need to go send those emails and then get to my brother's house to go see Santa. I guess I'll see you and your *woman of the evening* at Reynolds'."

I barked out a laugh. "I guess you will, Tink."

She pulled my coat off her shoulders and chucked it at me before heading through the office and back upstairs. She got stopped several times because everyone loved her.

I took my time, watching the way she moved up the stairs. The way her lean legs elegantly took one step after the other. It was wrong, but I couldn't help myself. This woman was consuming my thoughts. And I was dreading dinner with Heather.

I'd agreed to her coming to town because she was relentless about getting together, and I knew I needed to get laid. It had been too long, and it was the only chance I had at getting Georgia Reynolds out of my head.

Heather Olivia was the daughter of a wealthy banker, and she was definitely looking for a wealthy husband. I'd been upfront with her from the moment we met when she'd pursued me hard. I was always clear with the women that I spent time with. I enjoyed dinner, a nice bottle of wine, and a show or the opera now and then. I liked having a date to take to events that I had to attend. But I didn't want anything deeper than that. I knew where that led, and I wasn't interested in it. I didn't open my life to the women that I spent time with. Everyone's version of the fairy tale was different. My mother had thought my father was her prince on a white horse, and though he'd set her up in a castle and given her the finest things in life, she'd soon learned that it came at a cost. That he didn't mean it when he said, "Till death do us part."

He was a selfish prick with a wandering eye and an ice-cold heart. He'd humiliated her at her lowest point, chipping away at her as her body deteriorated right before our eyes.

Love was overrated. It was bullshit. I wasn't here to say that it didn't work for some people. My grandparents were the rare couple that got it right. But I was more than aware that most of the women who had attempted to sink their nails into me were after two things.

The Lancaster name and the Lancaster money.

It came with the territory.

I was fairly certain that Heather wanted both.

But we'd been doing this sporadically for two years now, and it was clear that I wasn't going to change my mind. Yet she kept coming back.

She'd taken a car service here because the woman was a pampered princess. She didn't work or have any real ambitions beyond shopping and finding a husband who'd keep her living in the lap of luxury. That was why I wasn't sure why she hadn't moved on to someone else. Someone more likely to give her what she wanted.

She was gorgeous, no doubt about it.

I arrived at Reynolds' and was taken to a table in the back of the restaurant. The place was fairly busy, chatter and laughter surrounding me. Dark wood covered the floors, and stone accents on the walls offered a lot of character. It definitely had a rustic, cool vibe.

I looked up to see Heather walking my way. Her black hair was straight and shiny, and she wore a skintight red dress that clung to her and ended just below her knees. She wore a black fur coat that went almost to the ground, and sky-high fuck-me heels, per usual. Heads turned as she moved toward me because she stood out like a sore thumb in here, as most people were dressed in jeans and sweaters. I pushed to my feet and gave her a quick hug.

"Good to see you."

"Well, I had no choice but to come to you, obviously. I can't believe you're living in this godforsaken town. Is it just the worst living here?" she asked as I slipped her coat off her shoulders and set it on the empty chair beside us. I pulled out her chair, and she took a seat, and I settled across from her.

"Actually, it hasn't been so bad lately. It's growing on me. It's peaceful. There's no press snapping pictures every time you go to fucking dinner. No traffic. And the office is thriving, so I have no complaints."

"Well, why get all dressed up if no one is going to take photos of you and post them?" She chuckled. "I'm guessing the shopping is not great here. I'm sure there are some boutiques, but you know, I love my name brands. I'm hoping to see your new house while I'm here. I was disappointed you didn't have me meet you there."

Of course, she was. My plan to meet her here was intentional. I didn't bring women to my home often. I normally took them to the hotel in the city, even when I was living there. Georgia had been spot on when she'd made that statement, but I sure as shit wasn't going to admit it. I didn't like inviting people into my personal space, nor did I ever spend the night with a woman. I had my reasons, and I made that clear upfront. I knew Heather was hoping to come home with me, and I also knew that I needed to get laid.

But I hadn't decided how that would go down yet.

I'd probably take her to a hotel here in Cottonwood Cove, and then I could head home after.

Before I could answer, there was a ruckus a few feet away. A large group had entered, and for whatever reason, they were garnering a lot of attention.

Tinker Bell.

This must be the infamous Reynolds family. Georgia had her head tipped back in a full-bodied laugh as another woman with long, dark hair stood close, saying something to her with a big smile on her face. There was a big dude with long hair, and his arm was wrapped around another woman with dark hair. A taller dude held a little girl in his arms, and another guy huddled around them, telling a story with his arms flying all over the place. An older attractive couple held hands and stood there watching them with complete adoration.

Like something out of a goddamn movie. They were all unusually good-looking, and it was obvious they were all close and comfortable with one another. The hostess who'd seated us approached the big dude with the long hair and the woman beside him, and they both said something to the group before heading in the opposite direction. That must be the brother who owned the place. The rest of the group made their way to a table not far from mine.

Georgia was talking a mile a minute when her gaze found mine, and she halted. Her eyes moved to Heather, and she said something to her family as they took their seats, and she walked toward my table.

My dick reacted immediately at the sight of her, which pissed me off. He was supposed to be reacting to Heather, not to my employee.

She wore a pair of dark skinny jeans, boots that didn't have a heel, but came up her legs, ending just above her knees. It somehow managed to be sexy as shit. She wore a cream turtleneck sweater, and her hair fell in big, fat waves around her shoulders.

"Hey," she purred as she approached the table.

"Hey, Georgia, this is my friend, Heather. Heather, Georgia is my assistant at Lancaster Press." I motioned to my date. Heather's red lips formed a straight line as she glanced up at my assistant with the warmth of an iceberg.

"Hi, it's nice to meet you," Georgia said, extending a hand. Heather looked down at her hand for an awkward amount of time, before taking just the tips of Georgia's fingers in her grasp for all of two seconds before completely looking away and making it clear that she wasn't interested in chatting.

It pissed me the fuck off.

I knew she could be cold, but I'd never seen her behave like this.

"Nice to meet you," Heather said, but she was looking at me and not at the woman standing at our table.

"Hello? Yoo-hoo? I think you see me standing here," Georgia said, leaning her hand over the table and waving it up and down in front of my date's face as a loud laugh escaped my mouth.

The balls on this girl.

Heather startled and gasped, turning to look at her. "I see you."

"Ahhh… well, I see you, too." Georgia smirked. Her words had more meaning in them than the simple acknowledgement she'd made.

"Well, I think you're off the clock now, so…" Heather said, her lips turning up in the corners.

"I'm never really off the clock with Bossman." Georgia acted completely unfazed by how rude my date was behaving. I was not happy, and I would definitely let Heather know it. "You two have a nice evening."

She turned on her heels and marched over to her table. The older man, who I assumed was her father, saved a seat for her beside him, and the way he looked at her was the way a father who adored his child should look at them. I'd never been on the receiving end of that kind of adoration from my father.

Our server came to the table, and we ordered our drinks and dinner. I wanted to get things moving because I was already done with this date. After she stepped away, I looked at the woman sitting across from me.

"That was uncalled for. You were rude."

"She's your assistant, not a client. I didn't think I needed to try with her." She looked up at me, one eyebrow raised in challenge.

"So, you pick and choose who you make an effort with?" I hissed, as the waitress set our wine glasses down, and I took a sip.

"Of course. I don't waste energy on people who aren't important. And she's not important."

My blood boiled.

She couldn't be more wrong.

And I couldn't wait to send her on her way the minute we finished eating.

My dick would have to wait for my right hand once again tonight.

I'd rather get off thinking of my assistant for the millionth time this week than spend the night with this woman.

Check, please.

eleven

. . .

Georgia

MY FATHER WAS TALKING about our many trips to see Santa over the years, and Gracie was busy drawing a picture of her and Santa.

It had been adorable, and my phone was filled with pictures of Gracie sitting on his lap, giving him the long version of her wishes for Christmas. I snapped a few pics of Cage stewing as Mr. Weber followed him around, talking nonstop. Cage kept whispering in my ear that he was going to give a nasty Yelp review about being followed around by an elf that was three sheets to the wind.

As if anyone in Cottonwood Cove relied on those reviews. This was a small town. Everyone knew everything, so reviews weren't really necessary. But my stubborn older brother needed to take his aggression out somewhere, so I wouldn't point it out and ruin his fun.

My eyes kept moving to the table a few feet away, where my boss sat with the ice queen. The woman didn't even try to fake it.

She put the itch in bitch, no doubt about it.

My phone vibrated on the table as everyone continued

laughing and talking and telling stories as our food was placed in front of us.

BOSSMAN

Sorry about that. I let her know she was rude.

Rude is someone not saying thank you. Your date could give the devil a run for his money. Not sure what you see in someone who gives off major mean-girl vibes and has the warmth of an ice sculpture.

BOSSMAN

Didn't your last boyfriend steal your car?

Yes. He's not here, though, is he?

BOSSMAN

Fair enough. Would it be all right if I came over and met your family? I promise I won't insult you.

They'd like to meet you. I wouldn't let them come over for fear your date might pull the stick out of her ass and beat them with it.

BOSSMAN

Wise choice. I'll be over shortly.

Cage was ranting about Santa when Maddox approached the table, and everyone turned to look at him.

The man just had a way of drawing everyone's attention.

It was more than his height and his good looks. It was his demeanor.

"I'm sorry to interrupt. I just wanted to introduce myself," he said before my niece interrupted.

"You're Aunt Georgie's bossman?"

Everyone laughed, and Maddox's lips twitched in the corners before a smile took over his face.

"Yes. I'm Maddox Lancaster, and I just wanted to say you have raised an amazing young woman. She's done a fantastic job so far."

"She's the best. No doubt about it," my father said. "I'm Bradford Reynolds, and this is my wife, Alana." He went on to introduce everyone at the table, and Maddox made his way around, shaking everyone's hands. It was unexpected but appreciated.

When he got to Gracie, she held up her hand for a high-five. Maddox gently tapped it with his hand and bent down to meet her gaze. "Did you go see Santa tonight?"

She gasped. "Did he tell you?"

I used my hand to cover my mouth to keep from laughing, expecting Maddox to correct her and tell her that I had let him know where we were going. But instead, he shocked the shit out of me. "He did. I ran into him on my way in here, and he told me to look for the cutest girl in the place and tell her that she was at the top of his list."

Where the hell was Mr. Moody? Maybe he'd already had sex with his evil queen, and he was more relaxed now.

Everyone at the table smiled, including Cage, which said a lot.

"Thank you, Bossman. I told Daddy I was going to be the best girl this year."

Maddox pushed back to stand and smiled at her. "I think you did it. It was nice to meet you all. I'll let you get back to your dinner."

He sauntered back to the table, and Brinkley leaned in close to me. "Holy shitballs. My ovaries just exploded. He's so freaking hot. And sexy. He doesn't seem that mean… Not that I would care when he looks that good."

I licked my lips, trying to calm my racing heart because I felt the same way. "He was definitely being nicer to you guys than he normally is. He probably knows I've told you how rude he is, so he's trying to make me look like I'm being dramatic. But I guess I have seen the softer side of him a few times. He's just pretty intense at work." I couldn't tell her what he did for me regarding my car because I'd have to tell her the whole story and I didn't want to go there.

"Well, he definitely likes you."

"He can't stand me," I said with a chuckle because she was obviously misreading that.

"He hasn't taken his eyes off you since you walked in. I don't think his date is too pleased about it, nor do I think she'll be *getting any* tonight." She laughed.

"Don't be ridiculous. I work for him. He reminds me of that constantly. And he's a few years older than me anyway, so he dates women, not college grads."

"You are a woman. And so what if he's a few years older? Definitely not too old for you. You've been dating these losers, and that right there is a real man."

"What are we whispering about?" my mother asked.

"Nothing. Work stuff." I shrugged.

"Well, your boss seems very impressed with you," Mom said.

"He does seem impressed, doesn't he?" Brinkley teased.

"Well, he should be. She's amazing," Lila said as she winked at me. "She works such long hours. We hardly get to see her." I loved living with Hugh and Lila, but she was right. I usually got home so late they were already in bed. And I left early to avoid them seeing the scooter, but now that Maddox had gotten my car back, I could take my time in the mornings.

"Thank you. I got my car back today," I said proudly.

"Ahh… so your boss won't have to send a car to get you every morning, huh?" Hugh asked.

"Nope. I can drive myself." I hated that I'd lied to them, but sometimes, little white lies were necessary to spare everyone a lot of drama.

"Looks like our Georgie girl is growing up," Cage teased as he popped an onion ring into his mouth.

"I need to head back soon," Finn said, rubbing his belly. "I have to be on set early in the morning."

"I'll drop you off on my way to the city." Brinkley reached for her water and took a sip. "Glad we snuck in a family dinner this week."

"Well, it's a big day when our grand-girl gets to see Santa," my father said.

"And your grand-girl is at the top of the list. Bossman said so."

I glanced over to see Maddox and his date leaving the restaurant. Was he taking her home with him?

My stomach wrenched at the thought of her in that beautiful home.

The thought of her with him.

"You okay?" Finn asked, as he dropped an arm around my shoulder. "You look a little pale."

"No, I'm fine. Just tired."

"Your boss seems like a cool guy. Not what I expected," he said. "I thought he was going to be this rich, arrogant prick."

"Well, he is rich. He can be very arrogant. And he definitely has his prick-ish moments." But he'd taken me to that meeting and introduced me to my unicorn author. He let me read the entire manuscript. And he had gotten my car back for me. The man was full of surprises. "But he has a really decent side to him, too."

"Was that his wife?" Finn asked. "She was pretty hot."

"She is not his wife," I hissed.

"Ohhhh, down, girl. I struck a nerve."

We all stood from the table and made our way outside, and I turned to hug him goodbye. "Not at all. She just wasn't very nice. And she's not that pretty, is she?"

He laughed and shook his head. "No. I was mistaken. She's extremely unattractive."

"Who are we talking about?" Cage poked his head in. "The hottie with your boss? Is that his wife?"

"No." I rolled my eyes. "He's not married."

"I was just telling her how *unattractive* she was," Finn said, his voice all tease.

"The woman in the red dress?" Cage wasn't picking up on the social cues. "Big breasts, big ass, pretty face?"

"She had severe resting bitch face," I grumped.

"Bitches can still be hot," Cage said, and Finn shot him a look, as my three brothers had always been able to communicate without words. "But that woman was definitely not hot. Definitely not."

Now it was my turn to laugh as I turned to Cage and hugged him. "Good night, brother."

"Thanks for going with us to see Santa. Love you, Georgie."

"Love you, too. It was fun." I leaned forward and kissed Gracie goodbye as she patted Hugh's cheeks with her little hands as he held her.

"Love you," she said as Cage took her from our brother, and I hugged my parents goodbye.

I climbed into the truck with Hugh and Lila, and we headed home. We chatted about my boss on the short drive home, and they asked a ton of questions about him. When we got to the house, they asked if I wanted to watch a movie, but I was exhausted, so I turned them down and made my way to my room to curl up with a good book and forget about this night.

Why was I in a bad mood?

Bossman was allowed to date. Why did I care? He was my boss.

Nothing more.

The next week had been busier than ever as we were trying to get as much done before the holiday break as possible. Christmas was right around the corner, and I had just finished my holiday shopping this past weekend.

Maddox was running me ragged. We worked long hours, as I never left the office until he did. I'd taken care of ordering all the corporate gifts this year, and he'd also tasked me with shopping for everyone on his personal Christmas list. I was thrilled to see that Heather was not on the list, but maybe he'd shopped for her on his own… And instead of doing what he usually did, which was getting all of his gifts from one place for everyone in his family, I took the time to inquire about each person and their specific interests. It was a lot, but I'd gotten everything done.

And tonight, I had a date.

After seeing him out with that awful woman, he'd motivated me to put myself out there.

Or maybe I just wanted to tell him that I had a date.

I hadn't asked him about Heather after that night, and we continued on with business as usual this past week. He'd ordered dinner in for us most nights, and I ate in his office while we worked.

But tonight, I needed to leave early, and I'd let him know that a few days ago. I hadn't said why, just that I would need to leave at a normal hour. He hadn't asked any questions at the time, so maybe he didn't care.

My desk phone buzzed just as I shut my computer down.

"Yes?" I said, as I knew it was him. We were the last two people at the office.

"Did you order dinner? I feel like pasta. How about you?"

"I ordered you dinner, and I got you the pasta. It will be delivered in thirty minutes. But remember, I have to leave tonight, so I won't be eating here."

"Where are you going?"

Why was I so excited to tell him?

"I have a date."

Silence.

Crickets.

The sound of him typing on his keyboard halted.

"Are you there?" I asked.

"Yes. You aren't going out with that turdlicker that stole your car, are you? Because I will not go out of my way again to get your car back if you are. I don't believe in second chances, Tink, so it's a one and done for me," he growled.

I rolled my eyes, even though he couldn't see me sitting out here at my desk. "No. Not that it's any of your business, but I'm going out with a guy I went to high school with. Jake's great, and he will definitely not steal my car. But thank you for reminding me of my biggest mistake, once again."

"Hey, I can't help it if you have horrid taste in men."

"Well, after meeting your date, I'd say we have something in common."

"My dates don't steal from me," he hissed.

"No? They're just gold-digging ice queens with no personality?"

"Well, your whiny-ass ex cried like a little bitch when I confronted him. I think you still win for the worst pick of all time."

"I will not let you ruin my date tonight with your sour attitude. I'm leaving. You will have to answer your own phone and go downstairs and grab your dinner. I'm off the clock, Bossman," I hissed.

He appeared in the doorway so fast I jumped out of my chair. "Is that what you're wearing?"

"No. I'm going to wear something extra sexy," I said, plastering a big smile on my face as I slipped on my coat.

"Well, don't wear anything too revealing. We have that meeting tomorrow with Arthur Hobbs, and I can't have you in there if you're sick." He crossed his arms over his chest.

"I'm not sick. I'll be there."

"If you stay out late and you aren't here on time, that helicopter will leave without you," he said, his voice dark and angry as he moved closer to me and tugged my coat closed at the top.

"Have I ever been late?" I raised a brow. "Do you have a problem with me going on a date?"

His lips pursed, and he scoffed. "Why the fuck would I care if you went on a date?"

"I don't know, Bossman. You seem a little irritated." I glanced down at his hands on my coat.

He let go of me and took a step back. "I'm irritated when people don't do their job."

"And I'm irritated when people give me whiplash." I grabbed my purse and stormed away from him, heading for the door.

"That makes no sense. Remember, sometimes less is more, Tink!" he shouted, and I made my way down the stairs.

Less is more, my ass.

He was a pompous, arrogant jerk, and I was not going to let him ruin my night.

I got in my car and drove home quickly to change clothes and freshen my makeup.

I made it to the Cottonwood Café just thirty minutes later. The woman that owned the place, Mrs. Runither, was a real menace, and she constantly asked people way too many personal questions, but this is where Jake Pruit wanted to meet.

I was still fuming about my exchange with Maddox when I stepped inside, and Mrs. Runither greeted me.

"Georgia Reynolds. Look at you. Jake told me he's meeting you here, and I'm guessing you two will be bumping and grinding in no time," she purred. "But I want to know about that boss of yours. He's very easy on the eyes. Does he have a woman?"

I groaned. "I'm not a madam. I'm a personal assistant, for

god's sake. I don't manage his sex life. And shame on you for making everyone uncomfortable when they come here, and all they want is some freaking macaroni and cheese."

Her eyes widened. The woman had asked me about my sex life one too many times. She'd pestered me about my virginity for years and decided to announce to my parents at dinner one night that she could tell I was no longer a virgin when I'd come home from college my freshman year for a visit. I was obviously mortified, and we'd laughed it off and all agreed she was not playing with a full stack, but it hadn't been lost on me that she'd been correct. She had some sort of sex sniffer that could detect when someone was doing it.

And I was over it.

Because I hadn't done it in quite some time, and working for a man who happened to be every woman's wet dream was not helping my current situation.

I was horny and hangry.

It was a terrible combination.

"Well, then… let's get you some mac and cheese," she said, forcing a smile on her face before grumbling under her breath. "Clearly, someone isn't getting any."

I rolled my eyes and made my way to the table where Jake was sitting. He smiled and waved. I hadn't seen him in a while, as he'd gone to the East Coast for college, and he didn't seem to come home much. But he'd always been a good guy.

"Well, aren't you a sight for sore eyes, Georgia Reynolds," he said as he pushed to his feet and hugged me.

He was good-looking.

Smelled like a pine tree.

And he had a good job as an accountant.

But all I could think about was the sexy bastard who'd ruined my night.

twelve

. . .

Maddox

THE GODDAMNED pasta was not the same kind that I'd had the other night.

Was she purposely fucking with me?

I picked up my phone and texted her.

> They sent the spaghetti and meatballs, and you know I don't like red sauce.

TINK

> Well, sometimes, shit happens. I will call the place and have them send over the correct order, your highness. <crown emoji> <middle finger emoji>

> It's highly unprofessional to flip off your boss. Forget the pasta. I'm heading home. I'll eat something there.

TINK

> I'll send the correct pasta to your house, then.

I knew I was being a huge dick. I wasn't mad about the

pasta. There was hardly even any sauce on it. I was pissed that she was on a date, which made no sense at all.

Just skip it, Tink. They'll probably fuck it up again, and I'm not even that hungry. Just go have fun with your date.

TINK

Is that an apology?

Definitely not.

But kind of, yes. I didn't apologize often, but I knew I was in the wrong.

TINK

Why don't I go pick up the pasta and bring it to your house myself so I can make sure that it's the right one. Would that be better?

Now she had my attention.

Not having fun on your date?

I stared at my phone like a fucking teenager waiting to watch a porno.

TINK

No. My arrogant, ridiculous, grumpy, hot-headed boss put me in a bad mood. And my date has been talking about his ex-girlfriend for the last forty minutes, and he just finished crying about their breakup. A work emergency would come in handy right about now.

I smiled because I couldn't help myself.

I'm not ridiculous.

TINK

That's the only thing that offended you from that comment?

What can I say? You know me well. I'll order dinner for both of us from Reynolds'. Meet me at my house in twenty minutes. I've got some contracts to go over with you anyway.

I didn't. But I wanted her to come over.

Wanted it so bad I could barely see straight.

TINK

Good. I haven't eaten because I was too pissed off to eat.

Well, allow me to turn your mood around.

TINK

There's a first for everything.

Such a smart-ass.

I quickly called in dinner from Reynolds' because I knew she loved the food at her brother's restaurant. I ordered us both the ribs as I'd noticed her eating them the night I'd been there with Heather. I'd been fantasizing about the way Georgia had licked the sauce from her fingers ever since. I also ordered one of every single dessert on the menu as my way of apologizing.

And the fact that I was actually buzzing about grabbing dinner and meeting her at my house had me slightly freaked out.

But I didn't care.

That was how far gone I was for this girl.

I'd been pissed off since she'd left, and it was all because she'd told me that she was going on a date.

What kind of sick bastard has a hissy fit over a woman

that he hasn't even admitted he had feelings for going out with someone else?

In my defense, I didn't even know I was capable of having feelings for someone else until this woman fluttered her way into my life.

That was how long it had been.

I pulled into Reynolds' and jogged inside.

"Hey there, handsome," the hostess said, making me extremely uncomfortable, seeing as she was clearly a teenager.

"Hello. I have a pickup order for Maddox Lancaster." I didn't smile. I didn't need this child misreading me.

"Maddox, nice to see you," Hugh Reynolds said, coming around the hostess stand with a large bag of food. "Thanks for ordering."

"Of course." I wasn't about to tell him it was for his sister.

"Georgia called ahead to make sure they didn't mess up the order. She told me about the mix-up at the other place." He chuckled.

Wow. These were some close siblings. They talked a lot. I didn't have that kind of relationship with my brother because we weren't big on the emotional stuff in my family.

Clearly.

And now her brother probably thought I was a big pussy for complaining about the food.

It had nothing to do with the fucking red sauce.

"Yeah. I probably sound like an asshole. I was just in a mood." I shrugged.

He studied me for a long moment and then clapped me on the back. "Been there, man. No worries. Hopefully we got it right, and this is just a sign that you should be eating *all* your meals here."

I nodded and took the bag from him. "The food is damn good. Thank you."

"Hey, Maddox," he said, as I started to step away.

"Yeah?"

He moved closer, as we were standing off to the side from the hostess stand now, and the place was busy once again. Clearly, they had the best food in town. But no one was paying us any attention.

"Georgia is all sunshine and smiles, but she has a tender heart."

What the fuck did that mean? I knew she said their mom was a therapist, so maybe they were all very open about this type of shit.

"Well, she's pretty sweet to everyone at work aside from me, so I don't know what that's about," I said, trying to make light of whatever the fuck we were talking about.

He chuckled. "I think you know exactly what that's about, my friend."

I didn't. But I assumed he knew there was a bit of a gray area with us, because God forbid, she didn't tell her family everything.

"I think she hates me most of the time."

"Georgia doesn't have the capacity to hate. She's exactly what you think she is—all goodness, man. She's always been that way. Just… don't go there unless you really want to go there, all right? You got me?"

I now knew why she didn't tell her family about her car being stolen. This guy was my size and looked like a salt-of-the-earth dude, but he also gave off the vibe that he'd hunt me down and kill me slowly if I hurt his sister.

"I got you."

"Good. And nice move with all the desserts. That'll score you big points with her. She's got a sweet tooth. See you later, brother." He barked out a laugh before clapping me hard on the shoulder and turning around to walk toward the bar.

Why did I feel like I was leaving with a bag of food but also a warning?

Like, enjoy the ribs, buddy, but if you fuck up, you're going to find a horse's head in your bed tomorrow morning.

When I got to the house, I hurried inside and turned on the fireplace and set the food out on the table.

The doorbell rang, and I shook off whatever the fuck I was feeling.

Nervous.

Excited.

I wasn't that guy. This was dinner. With an employee.

So what if my right hand had been hard at work for weeks with thoughts of her?

I hadn't acted on anything.

Yet.

I didn't do relationships or feelings or any of that shit.

And Hugh Reynolds was right. His sister was all goodness. The kind of girl that deserved that fairy-tale bullshit.

I pulled the door open, and she stood there in a light blue trench coat.

"Hey, Bossman. I'm starving." She marched right past me toward the kitchen like she owned the place. Maybe after her over-the-top singing performance in my closet, she kind of did.

I poured us each a glass of wine and set hers in front of her before sitting down at the table across from her.

I picked up my fork to dive in, and she held up her glass and raised a brow. I dropped my fork and did the same.

"Cheers to you for acknowledging that you were wrong. Even if you couldn't really say it, you sort of did."

"I'll drink to that, but only because I'm thirsty." I smirked.

We clinked our glasses, and I took a sip, my gaze never leaving hers.

"How was the date?"

"Well, I think I got him back with his ex. We talked it through, and then I helped him send her a text message, and they're talking again. So, I guess it was successful." She smiled.

And my goddamn chest squeezed.

A smile from Georgia Reynolds was better than any gift I'd ever received. My family had a shit ton of money, and material things were the only way they knew how to show love, so that was saying something.

"Of course, you got them back together. Do all the Reynolds kids channel their inner therapist? Your brother seems like a pretty deep dude. I saw him at the restaurant."

"Hugh's got the biggest heart, but he pretends to be this big, tough guy. And Cage acts like a grump, but he'd give you the shirt off his back. Finn is a lover, and he doesn't try to hide it. Brinkley is tough as nails, but loyal to the core. So, I guess, yeah, they've all got magical qualities, you know?" She bit down on her bottom lip as she thought about it. "Tell me about your brother."

"My brother is… angry. He hates our father. Hates the pressure that comes with being a Lancaster. Wants nothing to do with the family business, aside from spending the money. And there's plenty of it, so no one really fights him on it."

"He sounds like he's just lost." Her dark blue eyes were filled with empathy. "Money can only buy you things. It can't buy you happiness or love. Why is he so angry?"

I finished eating my rib and dropped the bone onto the plate as I thought it over. I didn't do deep conversations —ever.

I liked to keep my private life private.

But I trusted Georgia Reynolds for reasons that I couldn't fully comprehend.

I let out a long breath. "Our father is an asshole. Not like the type of assholes that you know, or even like the last one you dated. He's a real dark fucker."

"Tell me."

"Do I need to have you sign an NDA first?" I teased, but it

wasn't really a joke. I protected our secrets just like everyone in our family did.

"If you tell me something and you say it's a secret, I will take it to the grave. I'm not going to sell you out. I don't need the money. I have everything I want already." She chuckled, but I could tell that she meant what she said. I found it fascinating that a woman who had been basically carless not so long ago, who also happened to live in a casita in her brother's house, claimed to have everything that she wanted. I'd been surrounded by people who had every material thing under the sun my entire life.

Big houses and fancy cars.

Vacations that most people couldn't even dream of.

Jewelry and purses and every luxury item one could want.

Yet they were all miserable in their own way.

And this girl really did have everything that she wanted. I admired it. I respected it.

A part of me longed for it.

"My father has been in the press over the years for being a bit of a douchebag. But that doesn't even scratch the surface. He was an absentee father, an absentee husband, and a selfish prick of a human being. But he has a ridiculous amount of money, so he gets excused for his actions constantly."

She forked a bite of mashed potatoes as she listened intently, like what I was saying was the most important thing she'd ever heard.

"And where is your mother?"

I startled a bit at her words, surprised that she didn't know. "You don't read the tabloids, huh? My mother passed away when I was a senior in high school. She fought Lou Gehrig's disease, also referred to as ALS, for two hard years."

She shook her head as her eyes filled with tears.

This girl had so much empathy and heart—she reminded me of my mother in a lot of ways.

"I'm so sorry, Maddox." Her voice was just a whisper.

"I'm surprised you didn't google me. Her fight with the disease was rampant on the internet. The billionaire's wife's life that came to a tragic end way too early," I hissed.

"I would never google you. I like to make assessments about people on my own. I'm really sorry about your mom. That must have been unbelievably hard."

Hard doesn't even begin to describe it.

When you have one parent who loves you unconditionally and then that's taken away... Well, it makes you a cold, ruthless bastard when it comes to personal relationships.

Just another reason that I should be staying far away from this woman.

But sometimes, all the reasons in the world just don't matter.

Because wanting her seemed to be trumping everything.

thirteen

• • •

Georgia

MY HEART ACHED. I'd come over here wanting to give him a piece of my mind, and instead, I wanted to wrap myself around him and make everything better.

I couldn't fathom that kind of loss. My cousins had lost their mom, my aunt, far too young, and it had been a horrible time for all of us.

Grief was a cruel beast.

"Are you and your brother close?" I asked, because after all they'd been through, I couldn't imagine not leaning on one another.

"We are in our own way. But he really shut down after my mother's death. Hell, I guess we all did. Wyle is a reckless and angry guy."

The heaviness in my chest made it hard to breathe.

"I'm guessing he's probably lonely. Did he live with your father after your mother passed?"

"No. He despises our father most of the time." He let out a long breath and stared at me for a moment as if he were deciding how much he would share. "ALS is a brutal disease. My father didn't handle it well, to say the least. He'd married a supermodel, and apparently, they'd been ridiculously in love at one point. At least, that was what she'd told us, and I do remember him being around a lot more before my mom got sick. But he checked out after she was diagnosed. Obviously, we had the money and the resources for the best care, so we had a nurse that lived with us full time that last year, on top of the staff that was usually around. My mother refused to go to a hospital, as she wanted to be in her home, surrounded by family. But my father was out being photographed with women, with not a care in the world about how that would make my mother feel, while she was losing control of her body and her speech every single day."

"Oh my gosh," I whispered, trying to speak over the lump in my throat that was so thick it was difficult to talk. "And you were there with her until the end?"

"Wyle and I were both with her. She was still mentally there, you know? And I learned to decipher her speech those last few weeks, even though most people couldn't understand what she was saying. I'd called our father and begged him to come home during that time, but he was off in Europe with some random woman. He wanted nothing to do with my mom once she was sick. So, I watched her suffer physically, but even more so emotionally."

"That's horrible. He never came back to say goodbye?"

"No. He hadn't been home in weeks, which is when things got really bad. He claims he couldn't watch it. He's a selfish asshole. He thought the nurses would handle everything. But my mom didn't want to die with a woman she barely knew at her bedside."

"So, what happened?"

"It was Christmas Eve, and we were all supposed to go to my grandparents' the next day. Apparently, my father was going to grace us all with his presence and return home the following morning like some sort of fucking Christmas miracle. Mom was in a wheelchair at that time, so she was no longer walking and hadn't been for a while. But I knew things were bad because she was choking all the time and had refused to be put on a ventilator. She didn't want to extend her life at that point because she didn't feel like she was really living, you know?"

"I can understand that."

He nodded before he looked away and then turned back to face me. "A gasping sound woke me from my sleep that night. I'd heard it before, but the nurse was always there trying to settle her. I didn't hear anyone talking to her, so I made my way down the hall and found her gasping for air in her bed. I called out for help, but there was no nurse, no staff. No one was there."

His shoulders were stiff, his eyes distant, and my chest squeezed at the sight of him. "Where were they?"

"We learned the next morning that she'd sent everyone home. I think she knew she was at the end. She didn't want them there. They respected her wishes. And I was fucking there with her. I saw her take her last breath."

"Maddox," I whispered, my bottom lip trembling. "Was Wyle with you?"

He shook his head. "I tried to shield him. Told him to go get his phone and call 911. I tried pounding on her back as she choked in my arms. And when she finally stopped coughing and choking, I attempted CPR. But she was already gone." Maddox had been there for his mother's last breath, on Christmas, no less. He'd stepped up for his brother. For his family. But who'd been there for him?

"Maddox, I'm so sorry."

"Yeah. It was a tough time. I tried to be there for my brother because he was drowning in grief. But he was never the same after she passed. And then I left for Harvard that following year, and we were all still grieving. We'd watched her suffer for so long, and then she was gone."

"And your father?"

"He stayed away for a while after our mother's death.

Obviously, he attended the funeral, but we didn't speak to him. I'm sure there has to be some shame there for the way he abandoned her during her dying days. I mean, one would hope he feels something, but I just don't know. So now, we do the family things we need to do together. He attends the press-worthy events—graduations, weddings for family members—and we all put on fake smiles and act like one united family. He said all the right things to the press to make himself look like the grieving husband after she passed away. Painted himself the victim. But the truth is, my mother loved a cold-blooded asshole, and he isn't capable of loving anyone back."

I moved to my feet, and his eyes widened when I walked over to him. I motioned for him to pull his chair back. He didn't fight it and did as I asked. I sat down on his lap, my arms wrapping around his neck, and I buried my face beneath his jaw.

He didn't move at first, but he didn't push me away either. After several minutes, his arms came around me, and one hand tangled in my hair.

We sat like that for several more minutes before he spoke.

"You're too good, Georgia Reynolds." He pulled back, and his dark brown gaze searched mine.

"You're too good, Maddox Lancaster. You just do everything you can to hide it."

He shook his head. "I'm not pretending to be someone that I'm not, Tink. This is who I am."

"And who is that?" I asked, my fingers gently tracing the scruff along his jaw.

I wanted this man so fiercely that my body ached for him.

Even when he made me angry, I still wanted him.

"I'm focused on work. And when I'm not working, I'm a pretty selfish guy. I demand a lot from the people around me." His hand moved to my jaw, and the pad of his thumb traced along my bottom lip. "I don't do relationships, Tink. You saw me with Heather. That's as deep as I go."

"I think you went pretty deep tonight. Tell me about your mom before she got sick. What was she like?" I ran my fingers through his hair, and he closed his eyes briefly, letting me know that he was enjoying it.

His dark eyes opened and found mine before he cleared his throat and let out a long breath. "My mom was an amazing person. The absolute best. But life wasn't fair to her. She got a horrible disease, and she had a piece-of-shit husband. And when Wyle and I would get mad and say shit about him, she would always stop us and say that she felt like their relationship brought her the two greatest gifts."

"You and your brother," I whispered.

He nodded. "Yep. The three of us were thick as thieves growing up. Dad was traveling for work most of the time. Her favorite thing to do was to go out on our balcony at night, under the stars and stare up at the sky. It was something she'd started with us when we were really young, and we'd do it every night before we'd go to bed. It was what she looked most forward to when she was sick. I'd push her out on the balcony in her wheelchair." His eyes were wet with emotion, and he cleared his throat.

"I love that. What would you look for?" I asked, watching as his face softened when he spoke of his mother.

"We'd look at the different sizes and shapes, and my mom would see patterns that Wyle and I didn't see. She'd claim that she could see a heart in the stars, or a fairy, and we'd both be desperate to see it, you know? But mainly, we'd point out the planets and she'd talk about how the heavens were shining down on us. My mother had an amazing imagination. She'd worked with my grandfather for several years at Lancaster Press before she got sick because reading was her passion."

"So, she was close with your grandparents?" I asked.

"Yes. They adored her. She'd arranged for Wyle to move in with them for his last two years of high school after she passed. She knew my father wouldn't be there, and she wanted me to go to college. I think she feared that if she had made it another year, I wouldn't have left."

"Was she right to worry about that?"

"Yes. I would have stayed with her until the end." Maddox shrugged. "She was loyal and kind and just—" He looked away for a minute. "She was good to the core. And everything fell apart after she was gone. I mean, with my father. The anger settled with Wyle and me, and we couldn't stand to be around him."

"It sounds like your mom was the glue that held you all together."

He nodded. "She was."

"Hey, I have an idea."

"You always do, Tink. Let's hear it."

"You got all these desserts, and you have this beautiful view. What if we go sit out back and eat them?"

"Under the stars," he said, his gaze searching mine.

"Yeah. I bet it's the place you feel closest to her."

He studied me for a long moment. "I never sit under the stars anymore, so I wouldn't know."

"Come on." I pushed to my feet, missing the feel of his arms around me the minute I pulled away.

"It's freezing outside," he said.

I moved to the couch and grabbed my coat and hat and started covering up. "We can bundle up, and you have a fireplace out there. Don't tell me you're afraid of the cold."

He was up now, shaking his head as he reached for his coat that was sitting on a barstool in the kitchen, and he slipped into it. He pulled a navy beanie over his head and grabbed the bags filled with desserts off the counter.

"There isn't much I'm afraid of, Tink. And I like the cold."

"Oh, yeah?"

"Yeah. Unlike you, I prefer traditional sports. You'd have a hard time keeping up with me on the slopes." He glanced over his shoulder and smirked.

Once my gloves were on, my hat secured on my head, and my coat zipped all the way up just beneath my chin, we made our way outside.

Maddox had the fire pit up and blazing within minutes, and we were settled on the cozy L-shaped couch. He handed me a plastic fork and started opening all the containers.

We sampled each one, both agreeing that the peach cobbler was the standout, although the butter cake was a close second. He told me about his family vacations to different ski resorts all over the country, and I could just picture him racing his brother down the mountain.

This side of Maddox was so vulnerable. So genuine and raw. I loved that he trusted me enough to share it with me.

"Show me how to stargaze," I said, as I tipped my head back to look up at the gorgeous sky. Twinkling lights sparkled overhead, and he shoved the desserts out of the way, placing the containers in a pile on a side table. He pulled me close, sliding my body along the couch until my thigh was touching his, and he wrapped an arm around me. I leaned my head on his shoulder as we both looked up.

"You see the ones that aren't twinkling?" he asked.

"Yes."

"Those are planets."

"And the twinkling ones are stars, right?"

"Yep."

"It's pretty peaceful under the stars, isn't it?"

"It is. It's been a while since I've done this."

I pointed up to the sky at the way the stars were clustered together in a cool pattern. "Look. It's a crown."

He chuckled. "I actually see it."

We sat in silence, staring up at the sky, just the sound of our breaths filling the air around us.

"Do you feel closer to her here?" I asked, keeping my voice low and soft.

He didn't answer for a few seconds. "I actually do. Thanks for bringing me out here."

"I'll meet you under the stars anytime, Bossman."

We sat there, staring at the sky for the longest time. He'd switched the conversation over to my family. Asking what it was like growing up with all those siblings and laughing his ass off at some of the stories I told him about the things we got into when we were young.

"It sounds like a pretty magical childhood, huh?"

"It was."

"It explains a lot about you," he said, turning to look at me. The light from the moon illuminating his handsome face.

"What does it explain?" I smiled up at him.

"Why you're such a little fairy, spreading all that joy wherever you go."

I laughed now. "I'm hardly a fairy all the time. But I try to live my best life, you know? But I can be salty, as you've seen."

"I've only seen it with me. And you have good reason to be cautious with me. That's your instincts warning you to put up your guard," he said, his hand moving around the back of my neck as I pushed up on my knees to face him.

"Or I just feel comfortable enough with you to be myself."

"I guess the feeling's mutual because I've never talked to anyone about my family. But apparently, I'm a sucker for a fairy." He smiled, his white teeth on full display, and I think it was the first real smile I'd ever received from Maddox.

"Apparently, I'm a sucker for the broody, mysterious type," I said, my face inching closer.

"What you see is what you get with me, Georgia." It was the first time he'd used my real name since the day we'd met.

"What if I like what I see?"

"Impossible." The pad of his thumb moved across my bottom lip slowly.

"Why?" I whispered.

"For starters, I'm your boss."

"So. We'll be a cliché. I've been called worse." I laughed, but his face was hard.

"I'm not that guy, Tink. I don't do relationships."

"Well, let's revisit how my last relationship went. He ended up in bed with my roommate and then held my car hostage. Maybe I shouldn't be a relationship girl anymore, anyway. Maybe I should switch things up." I raised a brow.

"I don't fuck my employees," he hissed, and I could see how conflicted he was when I searched his gaze.

"Well, relax, Bossman. I don't fuck people I'm not dating." I shrugged, but his face was so close, and I just wanted to press my mouth to his.

I could practically taste it.

His eyes widened at what I'd said before zoning in on my mouth again. "Then it's done. We keep things professional."

"Well, I mean, I was sitting on your lap in the kitchen, and now we're all tangled up, looking at the stars, so I'd say we've already kind of messed that up."

"How? We haven't crossed the line."

"We are friends, right?"

"I don't have female friends."

"You've also never talked to anyone about your mother, am I correct? And you got my car back for me, and we've shared a lot about our families. Have you done that with another woman?"

"No. Never. My last brief relationship was in college, and she was constantly crying because she said I was, and I quote, '*a cold, closed-off, cocky bastard.*'"

"I agree with all of it aside from the closed-off part," I said, and we both laughed.

"So, you're my first female friend, Tink."

"What did I tell you about being a pro at unusual things? Look at this. Another first."

"Yeah," he said, his thumb falling from my mouth, and I could feel him pulling away.

"But," I said, and his eyes locked with mine. "I don't think one kiss would hurt. We're curious. We're friends. Friends sometimes kiss, right?"

"Do they?" He smirked.

"Sure. I mean, we spend a lot of time together. We're both single. We're friends. We know it doesn't mean anything. It would just be scratching an itch."

"One time. One kiss," he said. It wasn't a question; it was a demand.

"Pucker up, Bossman."

He didn't hesitate. His mouth covered mine, and my lips parted with invitation. His tongue swooped in, and it slid slowly in and out with purpose. His hands were everywhere. On my face, my neck, my back. I didn't know when I'd moved onto his lap, straddling him, because everything was a blur.

I'd never been kissed like this.

And I knew that one time would never be enough.

fourteen

. . .

Maddox

HER LIPS WERE SOFT, and I instantly regretted that we were outside, because there were far too many articles of clothing between us.

One and done.

It wouldn't happen again.

But damn, if it wasn't the best fucking kiss of my life.

I'd torn her hat off, needing to run my hands through her silky hair.

She was grinding up against me, and my dick was so hard I thought it might burst through the zipper.

A little moan escaped her lips, and I continued to explore her mouth with my tongue, wanting more.

Needing more.

Had I ever wanted a woman the way that I wanted her?

This was dangerous. Reckless. She worked for me.

Thoughts of my father flooded my head, and I quickly reacted. The man was a walking cliché. I'd lost count of the assistants he had crossed the line with over the years.

I placed a hand on each cheek and pulled her back.

Her eyes were wild, and her lips swollen from where I'd kissed her.

I nipped at her bottom lip one last time.

"That's it. One time. We got it out of our systems."

Her gaze searched mine. And I saw it all there.

The hurt. The confusion.

And then she quickly rebounded, her face hard. "Yep. It wasn't even all that great anyway."

She slid off my lap, and I reached for her hat.

I didn't correct her because we both knew she was lying.

Hell, I got it. I was doing the same thing.

This shit was not going to happen. I wasn't that guy.

I pushed to my feet and turned off the fire.

She helped me gather up the desserts, and I glanced over my shoulder to see her looking up at the sky one last time.

And my fucking chest squeezed.

That was the kind of shit I avoided. This had been a massive fuck-up. Sharing so much. Crossing the line.

The pull was too strong, too much.

And it seriously scared the shit out of me.

We made our way inside, and she set down the few containers she'd brought in and reached for her purse and keys. "Thanks for dinner."

"Yep. Big day tomorrow. Don't be late."

She studied me for a minute before nodding. "Never. See you in the morning."

I walked her to the door and waited until she was in her car before stepping back inside. I thought about all that we'd shared tonight.

I liked hearing about her family, and I'd be lying if I didn't admit that it felt good to talk about my mother with someone that I wasn't worried was going to sell me out. The press loved getting any ounce of gossip about my family. We'd shielded my mother from the press those last few months, and though people knew that she'd lost her battle to ALS, they didn't know what she'd gone through.

I guess I'd find out real quick how trustworthy Georgia

Reynolds was. Because nothing that I'd told her was public knowledge.

The stargazing was something only Wyle and I knew about.

I picked up my phone. It had been too long. I hated the distance I felt with my brother. It made me resent my father even more. His destructive behavior had cost us all so much.

Hey. How are you doing?

I waited. He normally didn't respond right away, but the three little dots were moving on the screen, so I figured he was typing something.

WYLE

I'm actually doing well, brother. Looking forward to seeing you on Christmas.

We always spent Christmas at my grandparents' house. But it had never been the same since my mother's passing. Something about finding your mom without a pulse on Christmas Eve had a way of changing the holiday vibe. But our grandparents always did their best to make it a celebration. They were close to our mother, too, and we all grieved hard this time of year. Aside from my father, who acted as if it were just another day to open presents and eat a fancy meal. The man was heartless.

Me, too. Why don't you come stay with me in Cottonwood Cove for a few days after? I think you'd like it here.

WYLE

Are there any good-looking women there?

I thought of Georgia, and I growled, even though I was sitting here alone. My brother was a bit of a womanizer, and he'd be all over her. I'd just have to make sure that didn't happen.

Yes. There are plenty of beautiful women here. <eyeroll emoji>

WYLE

Dad has been calling me, but I haven't picked up. Have you seen him lately?

I was back in the city a few weeks ago, and we had lunch. Same shit. Different day. Yes, I've missed a few calls, too, but we'll see the bastard soon enough.

WYLE

Miss you, brother. I'll see you soon.

That was the most I'd gotten out of Wyle in a while. He was off traveling this past year, and I was hoping he'd eventually move back to the city or maybe even come work with me here or with my father at the real estate company.

I made my way to the bathroom and turned on the shower. My phone dinged, and I looked down to see a text from Georgia.

TINK

Thanks for trusting me enough to share your mom's story. I'm happy we're friends, Bossman.

I thought about bringing up the kiss. Asking if she thought it was as good as I did. But I wasn't going to play with fire. I'd been burned too many times in my life.

Me, too. Goodnight, Tink.

The next few days were busy as we had things in motion with Mara Skye. I'd just finished a Zoom call with Paramount and Arthur Hobbs, and things were moving forward there. Not only were my editors reading submissions, but my personal assistant, who now called herself my "bestie" and also happened to be the woman who starred in every fucking fantasy I had now, was also reading submissions for me.

I went downstairs for the holiday party that Georgia had organized for the office. It was the day before Christmas Eve, and we'd be closed until the day after New Year's. Normally, we just brought in lunch, but, of course, my assistant had decorated the whole place and had turned this into quite the celebration.

Personally, I fucking hated Christmas. It reminded me of sadness and darkness and death. I highly doubt Hallmark would be putting that sentiment on their cards, but it was how I felt. Somehow, though, when I came down the stairs and saw Georgia in a green fitted dress with red-and-white-striped tights and a green hat on her head, my hatred for the holidays dissipated a bit.

"What the hell is this?" I asked when I stopped in front of her, and my eyes scanned her gorgeous body. She'd been wearing a different outfit earlier.

"I'm the host, so I just changed into my elf costume."

If she was an elf, I was going to embrace fucking Christmas by the balls, because she looked like the sexiest bundle of holiday joy I'd ever seen.

"Since when do elves look this good?" I asked, leaning close to her ear before I could stop myself. I'd been really trying to keep my distance since the world's hottest kiss, but just one look at her in this tight little green number, and I couldn't see straight.

"Are you actually in a good mood?" she purred. "How about you try to take me out of the ping-pong championship? There's no one else left to challenge me."

"You sure you want to risk it? You're on top right now."

"I'd be okay with you being on top," she said as she waggled her brows. How the fuck did this just turn into a sexual conversation?

The pull was just so damn strong with her. I was exhausted from fighting it most days.

"Are you going to challenge her, boss?" Freddy asked as he held a glass of wine in his hand and walked over.

"Sure. I'm up for the challenge."

Georgia did some sort of little jump and hop and twirl, and everyone laughed as she made her way to her side of the table. I rubbed my hands together before picking up the paddle and tapping it against the table.

"Don't hold back on me, Bossman," she said, as everyone stood around the table eating the food from Reynolds' that she'd ordered and sipping their cocktails. Holiday music played through the speakers, and I glanced over at her.

"No mercy, Tink." Yes, I called her by her nickname in front of the staff. It was obvious that my relationship with Georgia was a bit different, but she was my personal assistant, so we worked closely together. They didn't seem fazed by it, nor did I give a fuck if they were.

Her head fell back in laughter just as she bounced the ball on the table and hit it over the net. Back and forth we went.

She'd surprised me with how skilled she was. But I'd grown up playing every sport under the sun, and I was pretty damn skilled at anything with a ball and a racket. Everyone watching kept gasping as we just went back and forth for what felt like far too long for a goddamn ping-pong match. So, I turned up the heat and scored a few points, and she did the same. It was a tie game, and everyone was far too invested, but I imagined it had a lot more to do with the fact that they were almost on vacation, so they were in a good mood and looking to have a little fun.

Game point.

I'd figured her game out fairly quickly. She was weak on the left side of the table. Every time I wanted to score a point, I just hit it to that side of the table, and she missed it.

Her smile was wide, and her eyes danced with mischief. "Game point, Bossman. One of us is a winner, and one of us is a loser after this one. Are you ready?"

Take her out. Hit it to the left side of the table, dickhead.

But when I looked up one last time and those sapphire eyes locked with mine, I didn't care about winning. I just wanted to see her smile.

It was just a goddamn ping-pong game. I'd had enough wins in my life.

So, I sent it to the right side, and she quickly responded. I made somewhat of an effort to look like I was trying to get to it just as the ball bounced, and I missed it.

The room erupted in cheers, and I glanced over at her watching me as she set her paddle down.

I walked around the table and extended my arm. "Good game, Tink. You're the champ."

She nodded as her small hand slid into mine, and she whispered, "Did you just give me that win?"

"Do I strike you as a man who would intentionally lose at anything?"

She studied me for a moment before someone pulled her away to cut the cake. I stood in the back of the room and took it all in. It looked like Mr. and Mrs. Claus took a big shit in my office space with all the red and green and white garland, but everyone was having a good time, and that was all that mattered.

"She's been good for this place," Helena Rosewood said as she saddled up beside me.

"Yeah. I think you're right."

"She might even be good for you. It's nice to see a smile on your face now and then, Maddox," she said. The woman had known me both before and after my mother's death. I was fairly certain that she knew there was a heaviness that had stayed with me all these years after her passing.

"It's a scowl, not a smile," I said, and she chuckled before hugging me goodbye.

"Merry Christmas. I'll see you after the holidays." She turned on her heels and walked out the door.

The place was thinning out, and everyone was saying their goodbyes. Georgia was gathering trash with Virginia, who was wearing some sort of red and green headband that had springs on it with little balls on top and looked absolutely ridiculous, but it also made me like her more that she'd wear it because I knew who'd convinced her to do so.

I made my way back upstairs to finish up some emails before calling it a day. It had grown completely quiet downstairs, so I figured everyone had left, but I knew Tink would never leave without saying goodbye. I had a gift for her that I wasn't going to give her in front of everyone.

The office line rang, and I heard her voice right outside my office. She didn't sound enthusiastic, so I wondered if it was someone calling to sell us something. She put the caller on hold and appeared in my doorway.

"Hey. It's your father. He said he'd called your cell phone several times and hasn't been able to reach you. He said it's urgent."

Fear coursed through my veins as I thought of my grandparents, but I'd spoken to my grandmother this morning, and she'd seemed fine. However, my father had never tried this hard to reach me.

I nodded. "I got it. You can close the door and head home. Merry Christmas, Tink."

Her mouth opened like she was going to say something, but instead, she nodded and pulled the door closed.

"What's so urgent?" I asked, my voice lacking any sign of emotion when I picked up the phone.

"Merry Christmas to you, too. I've been trying to reach you and Wyle for a few days. You can't return a phone call?"

"I've been busy." I never returned his calls this time of year. It was a reminder of how much I despised him, and I didn't want to hear about his fancy trips to Europe or any of his bullshit.

"Well, so have I, Maddox. I've got news."

"Let me guess. People have discovered who you really are, and you need me to lie for you?"

He chuckled. "You're hilarious. Nope. I got married, son. And she's having a baby. You're going to have a new little brother or sister. If that isn't the best news to make this holiday even more special, I don't know what is."

"Are you fucking kidding me? You ditched your first wife when she was dying. Do you really think marriage is a good idea for you?" My father hadn't changed since my mother's passing. It hadn't been a wake-up call or a rock-bottom moment—he'd just continued on, going through women at a rapid rate, making promises he never kept, and using his money to make ugly situations go away.

"You repeat that again, and I'll have your grandfather strip you of every title he's given to you, you pretentious prick. You have the life that you have because you are *my son*. You don't know what it's like to watch the woman you love die right in front of your eyes. Do you hear me?"

"You're shouting, so of course, I hear you," I growled. "And I do know what it's like to watch someone *I love* die right in front of my eyes, because I was fucking there. Wyle was fucking there. You were off doing God knows what with God knows who."

"We are not doing this right now. We will be there for Christmas dinner, and there will be a photographer there to take family photos. We want to make it official before news of the baby breaks. We'll have a reception on New Year's Eve. It's a small event that we'll host at the hotel. There will be a red carpet and photographers, so you best make sure you and Wyle are both there. And you'll put on a friendly face tomorrow night. Are we clear?"

"Do you have any fucking remorse for the shit you've done?"

"Maddox, you're my son. I love you. I understand that you're angry. And yes, I have made a lot of mistakes in my life. But your mother is not dead because I'm an asshole. She's dead because she got an awful disease, and it took her from us. When you and Wyle can finally admit that and stop blaming me, maybe we can all move forward. I'll see you tomorrow. I expect you to be there, as do your grandparents. It'll be like old times. We'll have a family dinner, and you'll be polite to my wife and pose for pictures and all that shit that we've all done a million times. So, stop pouting and get on board."

It always shocked me how much my grandparents tolerated from my father. But he was an only child, and even though they didn't agree with the way he lived his life, they loved him unconditionally.

The way a parent should.

The way my mother loved my brother and me.

I ended the call and sent a text to Wyle before seeing the group text from our grandfather, letting us both know that we were expected to be there tomorrow night and on New Year's Eve.

The message was clear.

Our family would be supporting my father and his wife.

And Wyle and I were no exception.

I walked over to my minibar and reached for the bottle of whiskey, pouring a double and tipping my head back as the cool liquid ran down my throat.

And then I filled it again.

And again.

fifteen

. . .

Georgia

I HEARD a glass shatter against the wall, and I paced outside his office door. I'd heard shouting earlier, and then I'd seen the light on the phone go off, so I knew he was no longer on the call with his father. And it had been an hour. His door hadn't opened. He'd told me to leave, but I couldn't leave him knowing that he was upset.

Plus, I had a gift for him out in my car that I hoped to give him before Christmas. I knocked on the door, and he didn't answer, so I pushed it open.

Maddox sat behind his desk, his hair a disheveled mess, coat flung on the floor, and his shirt was unbuttoned a bit, the sleeves rolled up, exposing his muscled forearms. A bottle of whiskey sat on his desk and broken glass pooled on the floor a few feet away.

"I thought I told you to go home," he said, his words slurred.

"I didn't want to leave you if you were upset."

He studied me for the longest time, and I suddenly felt very self-conscious in my elf costume.

"Why are you so fucking good, Tink?"

I moved toward him just as he tipped his head back and downed more booze.

"Tell me what happened."

"Why? You've got this perfect fucking family, and goddamn, you deserve it. I don't have that. And I don't need to bring you into my shit. Do you get that?"

He was angry, and he poured another drink before I tried to take the bottle from him, but he set it back down in front of himself.

"We're friends. This is what friends do." I reached for his glass, but he jerked it away and downed the liquid before I could stop him.

He wiped his mouth with the back of his hand. "Yeah? You think so?"

"I do." I moved closer.

"Well, I'm a friend who wants to fuck you, Georgia Reynolds. How about that?" He raised a brow, pushing to stand before falling back into his chair and laughing. "Yeah. That's what a good friend I am. I think about bending you over my desk every fucking day. About kissing you and tasting you and—" He shook his head, and then his gaze locked with mine. "I'm an asshole, Tink. You best run for the hills."

Holy wowsers.

I bent down in front of him. "Stop it. I'm taking you home."

He poured another drink and tipped his head back again. I'd only ever seen him have a glass of wine or two. I'd never seen him out of control or sloppy.

"He's fucking married. My dad," he whispered as his hands found each side of my face, and he looked at me. His eyes were wet with emotion, and all the air left my lungs at the sadness I saw in that beautiful, dark gaze. "He's having another fucking child, Tink. And she's gone. It's like she was never here."

"So, talk about her. Celebrate her. Don't hide your memories of her from the world. From yourself."

He shook his head and took another drink. "I'm so fucking tired. Go home, Georgia Reynolds."

"I'm not leaving you here."

He groaned, and his head fell back against his leather chair, and his eyes closed. I tried to lean forward and get him to his feet, but he was deadweight. He grumbled something I couldn't make out, and I pushed to stand, pacing around, trying to figure out what to do. I couldn't move him; he was too heavy. I hurried to the lounge and made him a cup of coffee while chewing on my thumbnail as I tried to decide what to do.

I was not leaving him.

That wasn't an option.

I picked up my phone and sent a text to Hugh, not in the family group chat, because I didn't need everyone knowing what was going on.

My boss is upset about something, and he drank too much. I can't pick him up to drive him home because he's too heavy, and I can't leave him here.

HUGH

I'm on my way. Get some coffee in him if you can. Be there in five.

I smiled as I stared down at my phone. There wasn't one sibling that wouldn't have responded the same way. I was lucky to have a family who was always there for me.

Maddox didn't have that.

He had jets and helicopters and fancy houses with closets that were bigger than my bedroom.

But family and love were not something that you could buy.

I made my way back to the office, and he looked pretty peaceful with his eyes closed as he leaned back in his chair, and his breaths were the only audible sound in the room.

His dress shirt was unbuttoned, and a little bit of dark chest hair was showing. I gently touched his forearm, and his eyes sprung open. The veins were bulging against his golden skin.

"Tink," he whispered.

"Hey, can you try to drink a few sips of this coffee for me?"

"Why are you here?" His lips parted when I put the mug to his lips, and he took a sip.

"I'm not leaving you, so stop wasting your energy."

He nodded, and we sat in silence as I got a few more sips into him.

"You're too fucking good," he grumbled, just as a loud ruckus had me turning, and all three of my brothers walked through the doorway.

So much for keeping this quiet.

"You brought everyone?" I hissed, setting the mug on his desk.

"We were together. Lila and Brinks are waiting for you at my house for your girls' night thing, and we were heading to Reynolds' for some food and beers." Hugh was already pushing me aside and looking at Maddox. "You okay, brother?"

"And why did you call him and not me?" Cage asked as he came around the other side of Maddox's desk with Finn on his heels.

"Because I figured you'd give me a lecture about staying here after hours." I shrugged.

"Well, you shouldn't be here when there's no one to walk you to your car, and it's dark outside," Cage grumped.

"I would have walked her to her car," Maddox said with slurred words.

Finn barked out a laugh. "I don't think that was going to happen tonight. And why was I not your first call?"

"Because you weren't supposed to get into town until late tonight," I said, shaking my head. The fact that they were all upset that I hadn't called them first was comical.

"Hey. Who gives a shit who she called? We're here." Hugh tried to pull Maddox to his feet, but he fell back into the chair.

"Just leave me here. I'll sleep it off."

"We're not leaving you here!" I shouted, because I was tired of him saying that.

My brothers all turned and gaped at me before Hugh bent down and got close to my boss's face. "I'm going to pick you up. Do not fight me because we'll both fall if you do."

"I'm too tired to fight you," Maddox grunted. Hugh pulled him over his shoulder, and seeing as they were both about the same size, it looked kind of hilarious. Hugh pushed to stand with Maddox draped over his shoulder. "Your sister is so fucking pretty, isn't she?"

"Oh. Yes. Okay." Cage raised a brow at me.

"All right. Let's do this." Finn laughed.

We hurried out to the car, and I asked my brother to put Maddox in my car, but he refused to do that. He set him in the front seat of his truck, and Cage and Finn hopped in my car, with Cage in the driver's seat, of course, insisting that I ride with them, and Hugh followed us as we all drove to Maddox's house.

"So, what's the story there?" Cage asked.

"No story. He's my boss, and I just didn't feel right leaving him alone when he'd had so much to drink."

"You did the right thing, Georgie. He seems like a pretty cool dude. You like working for him, right?" Finn asked.

"Yeah. It's a great job. I'm getting to do a lot more than I thought I would. Maddox has me reading submissions now, and I've gotten to meet a few authors, which has been amazing, and he's just so smart, you know? He's really good at his job," I said, and looked up to see Cage watching me in the rearview mirror.

"You like him." He raised a brow before turning the corner and pausing in front of the large iron gates. I gave him the code and he typed it in before driving up the long driveway leading to Maddox's house. "Has something happened between you two?"

"Of course not," I said with a gasp. I shared a lot of things with my siblings, but some things were off-limits. And my kiss with Maddox was just for me.

"Well, it's interesting that he gushed about how pretty you are." Cage put the car in park.

"He's drunk. He told me that the coffee mug was pretty before you walked in." I rolled my eyes because he hadn't said that, but I didn't need Cage getting in my business.

"He does seem to like you a lot, Georgie." Finn glanced over from the front passenger seat and waggled his brows at me.

"You're ridiculous." I pushed out of the car.

They both knew there was something going on. But was there? Nothing had happened aside from one kiss.

One glorious, sexy kiss.

I hurried across the driveway and typed in the code to the garage keypad, and we all made our way inside. Maddox was walking now with one arm around Hugh.

I went to the kitchen and put on a pot of coffee, and we all sat there for the next hour as we watched this beautiful, big, broody man sober up. He was quiet, and I knew he was mortified that I'd called my brothers. But he sipped his coffee and listened as Hugh, Cage, and Finn all made small talk.

Maddox sat forward and ran a hand down his face. "Thanks for getting me home. I'm sorry about that. I got some news from my father, and I lost my shit for a minute. I'm sorry for involving your sister. I honestly thought she'd gone home."

"You don't need to apologize, man. We've all been there. You're a friend of Georgie's, which makes you a friend of ours." Hugh clapped him on the shoulder.

"She didn't know we were all coming, so don't be too hard on her," Cage said, as he turned and winked at me. He could be sweet when he wanted to be.

"I'm not going to be hard on her. I shouldn't have put her in this situation. That's on me. You guys can head out. I've taken enough of your time. I'm fine now."

"You got plans for the holidays?" Hugh asked.

"Yep. I'm heading to the city tomorrow."

"Well, if anything changes, there's always room for more at the Reynolds' house when it comes to food. Our mother makes enough for a small army, and everyone is welcome." Cage extended a hand to Maddox.

"Thank you. I think my grandmother would lose her shit if I didn't show up, but I appreciate the invite."

"Here. Unlock your phone for me," Finn said as he pushed to his feet and handed Maddox his phone. Maddox handed it back to my brother, who quickly typed into the device. "I just put my number into your phone in case you need anything."

"You have a nice Christmas, all right?" he said as he wobbled a bit when he pushed to his feet. "Thanks again for cleaning up my mess."

Hugh did that half-dude hug, and Finn did the same before they all three made their way to the front door.

I stood in front of him. "Have a safe trip home, okay?"

"Yeah. Sorry for ruining your night." He leaned forward and kissed my cheek. "Merry Christmas, Tink."

"You didn't ruin my night," I said, reaching for his hand as we stood there staring at one another. "You can call me if you want to talk."

He cleared his throat, and his gaze moved beyond me,

where my brothers had all just walked out the front door. "You've done enough for me. I'll see you in a week."

My chest ached when he pulled his hand away. I hadn't gone more than a day without seeing him since I'd started this job. He'd always found things that we needed to do at least one day on the weekend, and we spoke several times a day. But the way he was talking sounded like he wouldn't be in touch for a while. I still hadn't given him his gift. It was in my trunk, but my brothers were waiting outside, and I could tell Maddox was ready for me to leave, so I'd give it to him when he got back.

"Okay, safe travels." I held up a hand awkwardly because I wanted to wrap my arms around him and make him talk to me.

I wanted him to beg me to stay.

But I knew better. Maddox wasn't going to do that.

I made my way outside, fighting the lump that had settled in the back of my throat.

Because somewhere along the way, Maddox Lancaster's pain had become my pain.

I knew that he was hurting because I felt it.

I felt all of it.

sixteen

. . .

Maddox

I WOKE up with a pounding headache and made my way to the kitchen for a large glass of water, two Tylenol, and a hot cup of strong coffee. What a fucking shit show yesterday had turned into. I was embarrassed that I'd been sloppy in front of Georgia and her brothers.

I wasn't that guy.

I was never not in control.

I knew better, and I'd slipped.

I'd let my father's shit affect me, which was something I was working hard not to allow to happen anymore.

I pushed to my feet and headed for my closet. I'd slept half the day away, and I needed to pack a bag as I'd be staying two nights with my grandparents. Georgia had done all my shopping for me, refusing to get everyone in my family the same thing. She'd claimed that just because it was an expensive gift, it did not make it a good one. She thought that everyone should receive a gift that was personal to them. So, she'd asked eighteen million fucking questions about everyone in my family, and she'd shopped and wrapped all the gifts for me. They were in a large shopping bag by my front door so that I wouldn't forget them.

She'd taken care of all the corporate gifts as well as the employee gifts. The girl didn't miss a beat. I hadn't had to buy one gift this year, aside from the one that I'd gotten for her. It was the least I could do after she'd done all my shopping for me and organized the office party. So, I'd taken her advice and gotten her something personal that I thought she would like.

I hadn't given it to her because I'd gotten ridiculously drunk and left it sitting in my desk drawer.

I didn't want to give it to her late. I wanted to give it to her now. She'd been there for me last night when I'd acted like a drunk asshole.

I tossed my things in my bag and took a quick shower. The hot water beat down on my back, and I pressed my head against the wall as thoughts of Georgia leaning down in front of me, one hand on each side of my face, flooded me.

Those eyes.

Those lips.

I gripped my dick as memories of our kiss invaded my every thought.

What it would feel like to touch her.

And I let myself go there.

Find my release.

I wasn't proud that I was basically getting off daily to thoughts of my assistant. I hadn't been with a woman since the day she'd started working for me.

This had never happened to me before, and I was still trying to wrap my head around it.

She'd put some sort of fucking curse on me because I thought of no one but her.

I cleaned myself up, turned off the water, and got dressed quickly.

I sent a quick text to my pilot, Benjamin, to let him know we'd be leaving a bit later than I'd originally planned.

I needed to stop by the office, grab her gift, and figure out where the fuck her family lived because she'd told me that she'd be staying at her parents' house the next few days with everyone home for the holidays. I couldn't go to her family's home without a gift, so I'd need to stop and grab something for them, as well.

I wasn't a complete asshole.

I never showed up somewhere empty-handed, especially on Christmas Eve.

But there were a lot of fucking Reynolds, and I wasn't a big shopper, so I'd have to figure something out.

After four stops in the cheeriest fucking town on the planet, I'd stopped for a bite to eat at Cottonwood Café. Tink had warned me about this place, and she was not kidding. The woman who owned the restaurant was odd, to say the least. She'd slowly perused my body and paused when her eyes moved below my waist, making me incredibly uncomfortable.

"Excuse me. I just wanted to grab a sandwich to go. I'm in a hurry."

"Are you always in a hurry, Mr. Lancaster?" the older woman with too-plump lips and a shit ton of cleavage hanging out of her dress, and not the good kind of cleavage, purred. "Are you in a hurry when you're with a woman?"

First, I'd battled crowds at the bakery and then again at the gourmet grocery store that was willing to put together a nice gift basket of wine, crackers, and chocolate for Georgia's parents. I'd gotten her brothers each a bottle of good whiskey, because she'd mentioned that they liked that, and I'd gotten her sister and her brother's fiancée a nice bottle of wine, and I still had to figure out what to get that little niece of hers because I knew nothing about kids. And now, I was dealing with a horny old bird who looked like she wanted to climb me like a tree.

I also had a raging hangover and felt like shit.

"I don't know what's happening here, but I would like a sandwich to go." I gave her a pointed look, hoping she'd get the message.

"Georgia Reynolds works for you, doesn't she?"

Maybe this woman could help me after all. "Yes. She does. I need to drop something off to her, but it's sort of a surprise. Would you happen to know where the Reynolds live? I am fairly certain she's at her parents' house today."

A loud, boisterous laugh escaped before she pulled herself together. "Everyone knows where the Reynoldses live."

"Well, not everyone, because I don't. Would you mind jotting down that address when you grab me my turkey on rye?" I handed her my card because the woman had yet to take my order, and I was done waiting.

"Of course. Let me get that for you, handsome." She chuckled and did some sort of awkward-as-fuck shimmy, and I looked away.

A woman in her mid-thirties stood a few feet from me holding the hand of a little girl who looked to be about the same age as Georgia's niece, so I walked over.

"Excuse me," I said, and the woman turned and smiled at me.

"Hi. Do we know one another?"

"No, no. I, uh, this is a bit awkward. I need to get a gift for a little girl who looks about your daughter's age, and I've never shopped for a kid before. Can you tell me where I should go?"

She chuckled. "Ahhh… no worries at all. The Tipsy Tea is the cutest little boutique in town for kids. They have all sorts of gifts, and it's a party place, too. They'll help you out there for sure."

"Thank you. I appreciate it." I nodded and sent my pilot a quick text that I'd be ready in an hour.

"Here you go, darlin'. The Reynolds' address is inside the bag, along with my phone number, just in case you need anything. Anytime. Day or night. Now you come back and see Mrs. Runither real soon, okay?" the crazy-ass horndog said. People who referred to themselves in the third person freaked me the fuck out.

"Thank you, I think," I grumbled before tucking my sandwich under my arm and hurrying to the drunken tea place the woman told me about.

The Tipsy Tea.

I pulled the door open, and there was a set of identical twin girls in the corner having absolute meltdowns while they stomped and shouted at their mother.

I shivered.

I knew nothing about kids, just that I normally stayed away from them.

But Georgia's niece seemed like the real deal.

"Hello, can I help you?" a woman said, with a big smile on her face.

"Yes. I need a gift for a little girl about this tall," I said, holding my hand up to just below my waist. "She's a good one from what I can tell, and I need to bring something for her with it being Christmas Eve."

"Okay, I'm Matilda, and I own this shop. Do you know the little girl's name?" she asked. Only in a small town would they ask the name of the person you're gifting to or give you the address of the home you're looking for. There were definitely perks to small-town living.

"Her name is Gracie Reynolds. Do you know her?"

She clapped her hands together once. "Ahhh… she's the sweetest little girl in town. How much would you like to spend?"

"However much it costs to get her something good." I

shrugged. I didn't have a fucking clue how much a kid's gift would cost.

She chuckled. "Well, it's hard to know what her father has gotten her for Christmas, but I know something that would probably be real fun for her."

"What is it?" And did it get me the hell out of this place soon? Because one of the devil twins had just bit her mother's shin, and I was getting twitchy to get the fuck out of here.

"Well, you could get her an experience." She clapped her hands together again as if this were the best idea anyone had ever thought of.

"An experience? Can you put that in a gift bag so I can take it to her?"

She chuckled. "Of course. We could do a tea party for up to eight people. I mean, if you're willing to spend the money. All the girls in town want to come and have a tea party here, and she's never had one. That way, she could bring her grandmother and her aunts and a few friends if she wants."

"She'd like that?" I asked, digging out my wallet from my back pocket.

"Oh, yes. We do little sandwiches and cookies and tea, and the girls dress up. It's really something."

I handed her my card. "Perfect. And you can wrap that up?"

"Yes. This is so sweet of you," she said as she pulled out some sort of certificate, charged me three hundred bucks, and tied a fancy bow on the bag just as something hit me hard in the back.

I turned around to see Satan's spawn smirking and noticed some sort of blonde doll at my feet. The thing had pegged me in the back, and it was clear that she'd thrown it. I looked down at the little redhead with freckles and wild eyes before bending down and picking up the doll. "Did you just throw this at me?"

"I sure did. What are you going to do about it, mister?"

I turned back and looked at Matilda as she rang me up. Her eyes were wide, and her face was flushed.

"What are my options here? I'm guessing I can't do much, am I right?" I asked the store owner.

She laughed a little and glared at the mother, who was standing several feet away and talking on her phone, while the other twin was tearing things off hangers and dropping them on the floor. But the little she-devil was standing right beside me with her arms crossed over her chest as she waited for an answer.

Like she was a fucking mob boss, and I was her little bitch.

"Unfortunately, this is just how they are every time they come in here," Matilda whispered.

Fuck that. This woman was running a business, and she was kind enough to sell me some sort of *experience*. She didn't deserve this. Nor did I deserve to be assaulted by a goddamn child. I signed the credit card receipt and placed my card in my wallet, which I slipped into the back pocket of my jeans.

I bent down. "I'll tell you what I'm going to do about it, Red. I'm real good friends with Santa, and I'll be sure to let him know that you just pegged an innocent man in the back with a rubber Barbie. How about that?"

Matilda laughed. The little demon ran away, screaming at her mother, and I nodded as I made my way out the door.

I had a car full of gifts, and I quickly took a few bites of my sandwich as I pulled the address from the bag. Of course, she'd written her phone number on the note, and there were big orange lips over the number, like she'd kissed the piece of paper.

I shivered, dropped the rest of the sandwich back into the bag, and drove down the snow-covered streets to the Reynolds' house. It was lit up like some sort of Christmas wonderland. There were lights on every inch of their house, just as the sun was starting to go down. At this rate, I would just barely make it on time for dinner at my grandparents'.

I parked, pulled out all the bags and the gift basket, and I made my way up to the door. It was cold as hell outside, and I startled when multiple blowups shot up and sprung to life as air filled them when I passed by. There was a large Santa Claus, a pack of reindeer, and a train. These people went all out. They were obviously on timers, and I'd arrived at the right moment for the big show.

I knocked on the door, and Hugh opened it with a smirk. "Well, well, well… this is a surprise."

"Yeah. Tell me about it. I had something to drop off to your sister, but then I didn't want to look like an asshole and come empty-handed on Christmas Eve," I said.

He laughed and reached for the large gift basket to help me out. "Dude. You've got nothing to worry about here. Come in."

Music flowed from the next room, and it was a song I recognized. "I Will Survive", another Georgia favorite.

"Do you all listen to the same unusual music?" I asked as he took a few bags from me.

A wide grin spread across his face. "Nope. You're just in time for the big moment. Cage has won our family backgammon tournament every year for the last decade, and Georgie is about to beat him. So, she and Brinks play this song whenever they accomplish anything big, and apparently, she's already got it blaring through the speakers, ready for her celebration."

When we came around the corner, the whole family was gathered around a large farmhouse-style table in the kitchen. It smelled like turkey and apples and cinnamon, and my stomach started grumbling. I'd barely eaten much of my sandwich because I'd lost my appetite from being pissed off that I'd been attacked by a child.

No one noticed us standing against the wall, and Hugh smirked, like we had the best seats in the house for what was about to go down. He set the basket on the floor, and I placed the bags down beside it.

Tink shook the dice and rolled, and before I even knew what was happening, she jumped to her feet and shouted. Her sister was on her feet, jumping up and down with her. Everyone was laughing, and Georgia and Brinkley turned to their older brother, who was sitting there across the table, rolling his eyes.

They started shouting along with the music.

Singing out something about him getting up and walking out the door.

They were laughing hysterically, and Cage joined in.

Gracie started dancing with her aunts. "Aunt Georgie beat Daddy. He gots to get out the door, right?"

More laughter.

Jesus. This was like a goddamn Hallmark movie over here.

Just genuine happiness. It would be impossible to miss it.

"Right, baby girl," Cage said, pushing to his feet as his sisters continued to sing ridiculously loud, and Hugh's fiancée joined in, dancing with them. "And your aunties are terrible winners."

Gracie gasped, put both hands over her mouth, and everyone looked at her. She pointed right at me. "Daddy! Santa sent the bossman here to see me!"

I barked out a laugh because she was probably the cutest thing I'd ever seen.

Someone turned the music off, and the whole room fell silent.

"Way to make a guy feel welcome. Why are you all so quiet?" Hugh said over his laughter as Lila walked into his arms.

They all shrugged and then rushed over to say hello, and Gracie moved in front of me and reached her arms out. I just stared at her, confused about what she was doing.

"Hugs, Bossman." I looked at her father, who nodded with a smirk, and I pulled her into my arms.

She wrapped her hands around my neck and laid her head on my shoulder, and I nearly stopped breathing, unsure about what to do. She smelled like pumpkin spice and pineapple, which seemed like an odd mix, but on little Gracie Reynolds, it just smelled like… sweetness.

"Thank you," I whispered as her curls tickled my nose.

She pulled back. "Who are all those presents for?"

"Gracie Reynolds, we don't ask that," Cage said, taking her from my arms.

Georgia was just staring at me, her mouth gaping open.

Those dark blue eyes locked on mine.

Just like they always were.

seventeen

. . .

Gerogia

I WAS COMING off an epic backgammon win and was completely stunned to see Maddox Lancaster standing in our kitchen. How did he even know where my parents lived? He hadn't texted me today, so I'd assumed he'd already left for the city, but now the sexiest man on the planet was standing in our kitchen, with gifts for my family.

"Hey. This is a nice surprise. What are you doing here?" I asked, moving closer to him.

"I had something to drop off to you, and I just wanted to wish you all a Merry Christmas." He bent down and picked up the large basket and handed it to my father, just as my mother wrapped her arms around him.

"That was so kind of you, Maddox. Thank you."

"Yeah, no problem." He cleared his throat, and I thought my chest was going to explode as I watched him fumble as he handed out all the bags. He'd gotten something for everyone. And then he bent down to meet Gracie's eyes after Cage set her on the floor. "And this one is for you."

She looked at the bag, and when she saw The Tipsy Tea logo, her entire face lit up.

"Bossman," she whispered, and the entire room erupted in

laughter. Gracie was crazy for that store. It was where I took her whenever we had a little date day, and we'd go pick out some stickers or a little treat.

"It's her favorite store," I said.

She pulled out what looked like a gift certificate, which made me laugh, because I couldn't even imagine Maddox inside that cute little store. She studied it for a minute before throwing her little body into his arms and wrapping her chubby little hands around his neck again.

"What is it?" Cage asked.

Gracie pulled back and looked at it again. "I don't know, but it's from my Bossman."

My sister, Brinkley, glanced over at me and waggled her brows. Everyone was smitten with the tall drink of water who'd just walked in unexpectedly, including my niece.

"Let me see, baby girl," Cage said, leaning down and taking it from her hand. "Oh, wow. A tea party for eight."

Gracie started jumping up and down and cheering.

"That was really kind of you," Cage said as he clapped Maddox on the back when he pushed to stand again.

"Glad you like it. Merry Christmas. I need to head out before my grandmother calls again to make sure I'm on my way." He looked over at me, the only one not holding a package, as everyone else tore into their bags and thanked him.

In typical Reynolds fashion, there were endless hugs and gushing, and it took everything in me not to laugh because he looked so uncomfortable as he wasn't a big hugger. But I could tell he liked it because the corners of his lips turned up each time someone approached him.

I grabbed my car keys from my purse. "I'll walk you out."

We made our way through the house and paused in the entryway so I could grab my coat and put it on.

"You don't need to walk me outside," he said, reaching into his coat pocket for a small blue box.

Tiffany blue.

"I have a gift for you in my car, but with everything that happened yesterday, I never got to give it to you."

"I was an asshole, and I'm sorry. I had something for you, as well, and I didn't want to leave town without giving it to you." He held out the box, and my heart raced so fast I was certain it would explode from my chest.

I took off the white satin bow and lifted the lid, staring down with absolute surprise at the stunning diamond star on a gold chain.

He cleared his throat. "I'm not much of a shopper, as you know from doing all my holiday shopping for me. But you said gifts should be something the other person would like. I saw this, and it reminded me of you. Thanks for showing me that I can sit under the stars again."

My vision blurred as my eyes were wet with emotion, and I pulled the necklace out and studied it. "It's stunning."

"Yeah? So are you, Tink. I'm sorry for the things that I said to you last night. They were inappropriate."

"I didn't mind it." I waggled my brows. "I think about it, too, you know?"

He moved closer. "What do you think about?"

"Us."

He scrubbed a hand over his face as if he didn't know how to respond. I handed him the necklace and turned around, lifting my hair for him to help me put it on.

His fingers grazed the sensitive skin behind my neck, and I wished we could freeze this moment right here.

"There you go," he said, his voice deep and gravelly.

I turned around and walked to the mirror hanging above the entry table by the front door and admired it.

"I love it. Thank you. Come on, I want to give you your gift."

He moved closer to me, tracing his fingers over the pendant resting between my collarbones, before finding my zipper and pulling it up just below my chin.

I rolled my eyes. "You know I can zip my own coat, right?"

"Maybe I like doing things for you."

I was good with that response, so I pulled open the front door, and he followed me outside to my car, which was a few feet from his. I popped the trunk and pulled out the large box covered in cute snowman wrapping paper with a white and red tulle bow. He undid the bow and tore off the paper, which I tossed in my trunk before slamming it so we could lean against the car. He looked down at the box with a picture of a telescope on the outside.

"I love this. Thank you. My mom always had one on our deck."

"Now when you sit under the stars, you'll have a better view," I said, biting down on my bottom lip.

"What if I like this view best?" he said, his hand cupping one side of my face, and I couldn't move.

"Maybe you should stop being afraid of taking what you want."

"What do you want, Tink?"

"I want you to kiss me. No strings attached. Just a kiss so I can have that to hold me over for another week."

He chuckled and moved closer. My butt rested against my car, and his mouth covered mine. His hands tangled in my hair, and he kissed me with a desperation that I felt. Before I realized what was happening, he lifted me off the ground, and my legs came around his waist. My hands wrapped around his neck before running my nails through his hair, and he groaned. His tongue tangled with mine. I could kiss this man forever, and it still wouldn't be long enough.

His phone startled us both when the alarm went off, and he pulled back. His eyes searched mine as he turned the alarm off on his phone.

"I've got to go." His forehead fell against mine. "I've postponed Benjamin twice already, and he needs to get to the city so he can celebrate with his family, as well."

His head pulled away from mine, but he continued holding me there. My hands found each side of his face as I smiled at him. "Thanks for today. I can't believe you did all this. And you even went to The Tipsy Tea."

"Never again. That place is dangerous. I got attacked there." He raised a brow, but I could hear the humor in his voice, even if he was trying to hide it.

"What happened?"

"Some fucking little devil with red hair and freckles chucked a doll at my back. That was after she and her doppelgänger destroyed the store, and one of them bit their mother in the leg. And then the little hellion squared her shoulders in challenge. Like I was just some pussy that she could intimidate."

My head fell back in hysterical laughter, but I groaned when I felt his erection poke me in the bottom. This man had me so turned on, yet so entertained, my body didn't know what to do with that.

"Those are the Warren twins. Kressa and Katelyn. They're pretty famous in town for being hellions. The mom has long, blonde hair and is always on her phone?"

"Yep. She didn't do anything to intervene, so I pulled out the Santa card and told the kid I was going to report back to him about her behavior. The little shit didn't like that, but I'm sure she's still over there torturing Matilda, who was far too nice to put up with that."

"I love Matilda. I worked at that store one summer when I was in high school. She's the best." I sighed when he slid me down onto my feet. "Look at you, Maddox Lancaster. You're practically a local now."

"Yeah? Well, I got sexually harassed by the old lady at Cottonwood Café. And then I was assaulted at the fucking drunk tea party store. So, the locals have not been all that welcoming."

I covered my mouth with my hand to muffle my laughter. "I promise, it's a very friendly town."

"There's only one resident I really give a shit about." His hand found the side of my neck. "But you know I'm no good at this, Tink. I don't date. And obviously, you work for me, so we've got that issue, too."

"How about we don't get ahead of ourselves right now? You wanted to kiss me, and I wanted to kiss you. I think we'd both like for it to happen again, and it's no one's business but ours." I rested my hands on his chest.

"I like the sound of that," he said as he nipped at my bottom lip and growled. "I'll call you later. Merry Christmas."

He picked up the telescope and walked backward toward his car.

"Merry Christmas, Bossman."

He placed the package in his trunk before climbing into his car, turning it on, and rolling the window down. "I'm not leaving until you're inside. Go."

I laughed. "So bossy. This is Cottonwood Cove. You don't need to worry."

"Well, I got attacked by a five-year-old today. I'm fairly certain it's not safe anywhere."

I laughed as I walked up the walkway and waved before pushing inside. When the door opened, I heard a loud crash, followed by muffled laughter, and turned to see Hugh, Lila, Brinkley, Finn, and Cage all running from the big window in the living room as the lamp on the side table lay on the floor with the shade half off of it.

"Seriously? You're spying on me?" I threw my hands in the air.

"That was some kiss. Somebody call the fire department because this bitch is about to go up in flames." Brinkley put an arm around my waist and bellowed out in laughter.

"I was trying to stop them and insist they give you some privacy, but then when he pulled you up, I couldn't look away." Lila was on my other side now, smiling at me.

"I feel like someone poured acid in my eyes. You can't be making out in the driveway on Christmas Eve, Georgie," Cage hissed. "It's just… wrong."

"Wrong? You spying on me is wrong, you big hypocrite."

"If it's any consolation… Finn, Cage, and I all covered our eyes when he kissed you. We don't want to see that. We were just curious if there was more going on than you were saying because it sure seemed like there was," Hugh said as he righted the lamp on the side table.

"And clearly, we were correct. And Cage is traumatized because he didn't realize what was happening and covered his face a little too late." Finn barked out a laugh.

"Serves you right. It's none of your business." I tugged off my coat and hung it on the coat rack before walking into the dining room with everyone following, just as my mother and father started putting platters down on the table.

There were white and gold plates, and white flowers ran down the length of the large table with green branches in between. My mother loved a theme, and she enjoyed decorating. She was a therapist by day, but she could give Martha Stewart a run for her money when it came to entertaining.

"I agree with Georgie," my mother said, looking up and smiling at me. "I told you to leave her alone. She's a grown woman who can handle herself just fine." My chest squeezed. There were times that being the youngest of five siblings was exhausting because everyone treated me like a baby. And my parents were guilty of it more than anyone. But hearing my mom support me meant the world to me. I was working hard to find my way as I had landed my first real job, and I was looking for my own place to live now that I had income coming in.

"Auntie Georgie is a big girl," Gracie said as she sat at the table watching my parents set the food down. She had a little piece of paper and some crayons, and she was drawing something colorful.

"It doesn't matter how old she is. We just wanted to make sure she was okay," Cage said, leaning down and kissing me on the cheek.

"Well, I like him. Show us what he gave you, seeing as he didn't gift you in front of us, even though we all got to see that kiss, which was smoking hot." Brinkley smirked.

My brothers laughed, my father scowled, and my mother rolled her eyes. Lila tried to hide her smile, and Gracie looked at everyone with confusion.

"He gave me this beautiful necklace," I said, twirling the star between my fingers.

Mom walked over with her mouth hanging open as she looked at it. "Wow. That's stunning. It seems like you two have a very special… friendship."

"Uh, I don't kiss my friends or give them diamond necklaces for Christmas," Cage said.

"You don't have any female friends." Finn raised a brow, and everyone laughed.

"Is Bossman your boyfriend, Auntie Georgie?" Gracie asked.

"No. He doesn't really date, so that's not going to happen. But he's a good friend."

Who I'd like to have endless sex with.

"Sure, he is." Brinkley laughed as she took her seat.

Everyone moved around the table, and the conversation and laughter flowed. But my hand kept moving to my neck, and I couldn't stop thinking about that kiss.

About him.

eighteen

. . .

Maddox

I ARRIVED JUST in time for dinner and jogged up the walkway with bags in my hands. I didn't even know what Georgia had ended up getting everyone. I'd given her ideas for my family members and told her my father might be bringing a random woman with him, although I hadn't known at the time that it was going to be his new wife, who I'd yet to meet. But I couldn't really be expected to bring a gift for a woman I'd found out about yesterday.

Bentley opened the door and greeted me, as he'd been working for my grandparents since I was born. Their home was massive, with a large crystal chandelier hanging over the grand foyer. White and black marble covered the floors throughout the space.

"Maddox, it's so nice to see you," the older man said as he reached for my bags.

"Thank you. It's great to see you, too. Merry Christmas." I slipped off my coat, and he traded me the bags for my black trench coat. I leaned close and whispered, "Any drama yet?"

He chuckled. "No. They're in the parlor having cocktails and appetizers, and the newlyweds seem very happy."

"Wyle's here, right?"

"Yes. And the first thing he asked when he walked in a few minutes ago was if you were here yet. I think he's anxiously waiting for his—" He paused as he thought it over.

"Wingman?" I teased. We'd always said that when we were young.

"Yes. That's it. Would you like me to bring the packages in for you?" he asked, as he slung my coat over his arm.

"I've got it, but thank you. I'll see you in a little bit."

He nodded, and I made my way down the long hallway. Their home was very formal, but it was the one place that felt like home to me because I'd spent so much time here when I was growing up. My father had sold the home I grew up in shortly after my mother passed away, as none of us wanted to be there. This had become home base. Wyle had lived here during his last two years of high school, and this was where I came when I visited during college.

When I walked into the parlor, my grandparents were talking with my brother, and there was no sign of my father or his… new wife.

"Maddox!" my grandmother shrieked when she saw me and pushed to her feet. She had gray hair that was always in some sort of stiff hairstyle ending at the nape of her neck, and she wore her trademark black skirt that ended below her knees and a white silk blouse. I dropped the bags beside me on the floor just before she wrapped her arms around me and hugged me tight. She was the closest thing that I had to a mother now, and I loved her fiercely. The only thing we ever disagreed about was my father.

Her only child.

She loved him despite all he'd done, and she desperately wanted Wyle and me to repair our relationship with him.

I would do almost anything for this woman.

I'd walk through fire. Take a bullet.

But being close to my father was not something I would consider.

I didn't trust him. I didn't like him.

Hell, I held him partially responsible for my mother's death. Because even though ALS had claimed her body and sucked the life from her day after day—her broken heart also contributed to that brutal experience.

There was no coming back from that.

After hugging her, my grandfather was next, followed by Wyle, who hugged me so tight it was bordering on painful and then leaned close to my ear and whispered, "Buckle up. You aren't going to believe this shit."

Here we go.

Mrs. Winters, who'd been working for my grandparents for the last decade, came around with a glass of champagne and handed it to me.

"Thank you," I said, noting that everyone had a glass sitting on the table in front of the couch as they all returned to their seats and reached for their drinks. I sat on the blue velvet chair beside the couch and took a sip of the bubbly when my father walked into the room from the other entry on the far side of the room, with Claire Strauss beside him. "Maddox, my boy. I figured you'd be delighted to see your new stepmother is a dear friend of the family."

I spewed champagne from my lips, and my brother barked out a laugh. Claire was the daughter of John Strauss, who was my father's closest friend. We'd practically grown up together, and my mom had always pushed for me to date her. But Claire had always felt more like family than a possible girlfriend, and I'd never considered crossing that line.

Obviously, my father's moral line in the sand was nonexistent.

But I did not see this coming. She was my age, for starters, and I highly doubted John would be okay with this.

I pushed to my feet as Mrs. Winters hurried over to hand

me a few napkins and helped me clean up. "Excuse me. You caught me off guard."

I cleared my throat and reluctantly took his hand when he extended it to me. Because that was as close as our relationship went. A handshake was a struggle.

"Hi, Maddox. Nice to see you," Claire said as she walked in for a hug. I patted her on the back, trying to figure out why in the hell she would be with my father. "It's been a while. We've got a lot of catching up to do."

Obviously. You're boning my father and carrying his evil spawn.

"Nice to see you, too." I stepped back and forced a smile.

Wyle had a big grin on his face when my eyes found his. He thought this was hilarious. He despised my father, but he didn't take shit as seriously as I did. He laughed most things off, even when he was angry.

And my grandparents were acting like this wasn't the strangest fucking thing on the planet.

"Isn't this wonderful news?" my grandmother said.

I don't know if wonderful is the right word.

I wouldn't bring up the fact that Wyle and I had actually taken bubble baths when we were kids with our new stepmother.

"Yes, it really is. Right, brother?" Wyle asked, and he couldn't hide the mischievous grin on his face.

"It's definitely… very unexpected. How have your parents taken the news?" I asked as I sipped my champagne.

"They were, um, surprised at first. But now that we're expecting our first baby, I think they are more open to it." She smiled and reached for my father's hand. Claire was smart and kind and confident, always had been. So, this was baffling. She wasn't doing it for the money, as she came from a very wealthy family. I didn't have a fucking clue what she was thinking.

I had to give it to my father, he was putting on a good show. Like this was the happiest moment of his life.

I had a brief flash of a moment when my mother and father were laughing when Wyle and I were young. I occasionally remembered happy moments when love and laughter had filled our home. But I also remembered him demanding my mother travel with him often while we stayed with the nannies or with my grandparents. My father was a controlling man, and he expected a lot of the people in his life.

And after his wife got sick, he pulled away more and more each day. He'd be gone for weeks at a time. And life was easier when he wasn't home, so we'd settled into our new normal during those years.

"They'll come around. We've always been family, and now it's official," Dad said.

I didn't know that he grasped the severity of knocking up and marrying his best friend's daughter. It certainly wasn't the best way to officially become family.

"Dinner is ready," Mrs. Winters said, and I'd never been so grateful to end a conversation.

There was a tall Christmas tree in the parlor, and there was usually one in the formal living room, as well. I hadn't been in there yet. Otherwise, my grandmother kept things simple this time of year, knowing that Wyle and I struggled.

It hit me in the moment that today was Christmas Eve, and normally, I wouldn't be thinking of anything other than the loss of my mother. But I'd been so distracted in Cottonwood Cove, shopping for Georgia's family and then making out with her like a fucking teenager in her parents' driveway. I was almost in too good a mood to be bothered by the fact that my father had married my childhood friend. Nor was I feeling the darkness that usually overwhelmed me on this day.

We settled around the dark cherrywood table, set with

sterling silver, linen napkins, and my grandmother's fancy plates. My phone vibrated in my back pocket, and I pulled it into my lap and turned off the ringer, knowing my grandmother would blast me if she saw it. She had a strict rule about not using phones at the table.

However, knocking up your best friend's daughter, who's half your age, wasn't a hard line for her.

The rules were always bent for my father. My grandparents tolerated him, and my mother loved him until she took her last breath. She never said a bad word about him, even though he'd been terrible to her. I'd never understand why he was the only one who didn't have to live by any rules.

I looked down to see a selfie of Georgia. It was the bottom half of her gorgeous face with her slender neck and the necklace on display.

TINK

I love it so much. I hope you made it there safely. My family can't stop gushing about you. And Gracie expects you to attend the tea party now. #anothertriptothetipsytea

I need to see your face.

That was all I could think to say, because it was true. Something about her face, her eyes, her smile—it calmed me.

Comforted me.

The photo came through, and she was clearly laughing because her mouth was wide open, and even her eyes were smiling. And my heart rate slowed. My anger dissipated.

She was better than a shot of whiskey.

I tucked my phone back into my pocket as servers filled our wine glasses and plates with silver domes were placed in front of us. My brother leaned close as he sat beside me. My father was deep in conversation with my grandfather, and my grandmother was asking Claire all sorts of questions about the baby.

"I've got to give it to the old dude. He's not as predictable as I thought he was," Wyle said.

"You couldn't have given me a heads-up before they walked in?" I hissed and nodded at Mrs. Winters when she set the plate with the silver dome in front of me.

"And miss out on you spewing Cristal all over the velvet chair? Hells to the no, brother. That was priceless. Maybe the best gift you've given me in a while."

"Nice." I shook my head and lifted my wine glass to my lips. The bubbly was not going to be enough to get me through this dinner.

"How long do we need to stay?"

I now understood why our father needed our support. John Strauss was a wealthy banker in the city, and Claire was a well-known socialite who'd been in the press a lot after she'd dated an actor a few years ago, and people became fascinated with her. It was mainly due to her lavish lifestyle, but this would definitely be big news that she'd married the much older best friend of her father, who was best known for being a selfish playboy and traveling to exotic places.

"I planned to stay two nights, but I think we should head back tomorrow night." The truth was, I wanted to finish my conversation with Georgia. I hadn't been laid in months, and for whatever reason, it wasn't going to happen as long as she was on my mind and invading my every fucking thought. She'd told me not to overthink it. She knew who I was, and if she was okay with it… I wasn't going to fight it.

"I met someone. I'm going to fly her to meet me in the city for a few days, and then I'll meet you in Crystal Cove," he said.

"It's *Cottonwood* Cove. And I thought you asked me if there were any women there because you were single. When did you meet someone?"

"Last night. I was in New York, and she's a friend of a friend, and we hit it off. At least for right now." He smirked.

"All right," Mrs. Winters said, and everyone stopped talking. "Dinner is served." The ridiculously formal domes were lifted from our plates, and the smell of beef tenderloin and rosemary potatoes flooded my senses.

My grandfather raised a glass and waited for us all to do the same. Claire held her water glass up and glanced over at me with a smile. The whole thing was awkward. We'd been friends for as long as I could remember. We'd even spent family vacations together. Now she was carrying my sibling?

"Cheers to another great year together. To this new adventure for Davis and Claire and their new baby, and to my grandsons, who are both amazing, and to my beautiful bride, who I love endlessly. Let's eat."

My grandmother blushed. She actually blushed. They'd been married for over fifty years, and they still had that spark. I knew it existed. I'd just seen the other side of it. The ugly side of love. The one that erodes and destroys and eventually sucks the life from you.

I shook it off as we listened to Wyle tell us about his travels, and Claire shared her plans for the nursery in the new home they were closing on next week. We ate, we drank, and then we moved into the formal living room to open gifts.

We always did it on Christmas Eve now, as Christmas morning was no longer what it used to be, and no one was pretending that it was.

I received more gifts than I needed from my grandparents, from clothing and shoes to cologne to fancy cuff links and a new watch. My father gifted us cash, which was typical for him. It wasn't really something any of us needed, but I didn't normally put thought into gifts, so who was I to judge about that?

The surprise of the evening was watching everyone open their gifts from me. My grandmother gasped when she unwrapped the gorgeous charm bracelet with charms representing my grandfather, my father, me, and Wyle. All her boys. Her eyes were wet with emotion, and her hand clasped her heart.

"Thank you. I love this," she said softly, almost at a loss for words.

"You always were a kiss-ass. Apparently, you've upped your game," Wyle whisper-hissed in my ear as my grandparents opened the wine and cheese basket from him.

I smirked as my grandfather tugged off the bow of the large box sitting on his lap. When he pulled off the lid, he just stared down, not saying a word.

What the fuck did she get him?

"Maddox," he said, his voice wobbly. "Very thoughtful, my boy."

A first edition of The *Great Gatsby* for his library. Georgia had asked me what his favorite book was in passing a few weeks ago, but I hadn't known why. I thought she was just curious, because she asked a lot of questions all the time.

But Georgia Reynolds really was a fucking rock star.

Wyle groaned as he leaned close to me. "Next year, we're going in on gifts together, you dickmonger."

I laughed, and the rest of the night was uneventful. My father was surprised that I'd gotten him a pair of super fancy black velvet slippers with his initials monogrammed on them.

I was just as surprised as he was.

And Claire appeared overjoyed with the soft, oversized white blanket that I'd gotten her.

But the most surprising had been Wyle's gift. A framed photo of me and Wyle when we were young sat beside a more recent one of the two of us. She'd obviously gone on to Facebook to find these, and my brother gaped as he took in the photographs. And then he reached inside the box and pulled out a super fancy camera. I'd shared with Georgia that my brother had recently found a love for photography during his travels, and it had annoyed me that he'd taken all these great photos from his phone.

She clearly listened.

"Damn, brother. I need to step up my game next year," he said, clapping me on the shoulder. "Thank you so much."

He spent the next hour looking at his camera and all the different components that it came with, and we ate dessert and talked, and there were no fireworks.

No blowups.

No drama.

And most importantly, I'd survived the night. Christmas was usually the worst time of year for me, but if I could get through tomorrow as easily as today, I would be heading home unscathed.

I didn't know when it happened, but Cottonwood Cove had started to feel like home.

And I knew the reason for it.

Tink.

nineteen

. . .

Georgia

I WAS IN MY ROOM, and Hugh and Lila had gone down to the cove to hang out. It was freezing outside, so I didn't know what those two did down there, nor did I want to know. I was deep into a new book that Mara had sent me.

Christmas morning had been great. We'd all been at my parents', and there were too many gifts, too much food, and an abundance of laughter.

It was my kind of Christmas.

I was charging my new Kindle that Brinkley had gotten me, and my parents had given me a bunch of new clothes that I could wear to work. Of course, Cage got me a subscription to Kindle Unlimited, just as he did every year, because he said it was the best bang for my buck. Finn had gotten me pajamas and slippers which I couldn't wait to slip into, and Hugh and Lila had surprised me with the most gorgeous cashmere sweater.

The highlight had been watching Gracie open her gifts. The girl gasped over every little thing, and she was thrilled that I had given her a pair of little earrings, which meant I was taking her to get her ears pierced. It had taken some work to get Cage to agree, but he'd finally given me the thumbs-up.

Maddox had been texting me all morning, shocked by the gifts that I'd purchased for his family. He was very impressed by how thoughtful they were, but it was easy once he'd answered a few simple questions, and it didn't hurt that he'd told me to spend "whatever it costs." With a budget like that, I'd had a lot of fun.

It was amazing what you could find out on Google when you searched gifts for the wealthiest of people.

My phone vibrated, and I jumped.

BOSSMAN

What are you wearing?

That was random. Long underwear. We went tobogganing earlier. How about you?

BOSSMAN

Nice. Do you still want me to kiss you again?

I chuckled. It was all I thought about. My finger and thumb found the star charm at the base of my neck.

I'm not one to waver. Absolutely. You?

BOSSMAN

Yes. How would that work with me being your boss?

I'd be your boss in the bedroom.

I fell back in laughter, knowing that was going to get a response.

BOSSMAN

Georgia. That's most definitely not going to happen.

Fine. You can be the boss in both. No one has to know at work. You've made it clear that you don't do relationships, so why complicate things? It'll be a fling, and we'll go back to being friends after.

BOSSMAN

You're fine with that?

Yes. Stop overthinking everything.

BOSSMAN

I can't.

For a guy who doesn't do relationships, you sure think about it a lot.

BOSSMAN

Only with you.

Why?

BOSSMAN

Because it's you, Tink. And you're kind of my favorite person right now. Which is saying a lot because I don't like most people.

My eyes watered, and my chest squeezed.

I love you, too.

You're my favorite, too, Maddox Lancaster. Even when you're stubborn and grumpy… you're still my favorite.

BOSSMAN

Open your door.

Did he send me something?

I jumped to my feet and opened the door leading outside, and there stood the sexiest man in the world. Dark jeans. Black trench coat. Tall. Broad. Intense stare.

I threw myself into him. "What are you doing here? You told me you weren't coming back until tomorrow."

"I don't want to wait anymore. I can't stop thinking about you, so here I am."

"Wow. You really want me, don't you?" I teased as I walked backward and dropped to sit on my bed.

He stormed past me toward the closet, as if he knew where he was going. "You've never been here. How do you know where the closet is?"

He came out holding a hot pink duffle bag. "This place is unusually small, so it's not too challenging to find a closet. And I did go to Harvard, remember?"

I barked out a laugh and hurried to the closet. "What are we doing?"

"Pack your things for a few days. You're staying with me."

I eyed him as I reached for my turtleneck sweater and pulled it on over my head because it was cold outside. And he started pulling sweaters off the hangers and tossing them into the bag.

"A few days? You weren't sure you could even handle more than a kiss. Now you're kidnapping me?" I laughed.

He tugged me against his body. "Do you want this, Tink? Because it's all I fucking think about."

"For someone who doesn't do relationships, you're awfully bossy about how this all works."

"We'll figure it out as we go. But right now, I want to take you home," he said, his voice deep and commanding.

You don't have to ask me twice. I'd fantasized about this man for weeks.

"Sounds fair. I need to tell my brother and Lila something, and this is sort of a secret, right? Isn't that how flings work?"

He groaned. "Are they going to report us to human

resources? Not that it really matters, seeing as I own the company."

"Of course not. They're already suspicious because they can't mind their own business. But they would never tell anyone. They know it's not anything big. But why is it a secret if you own the company anyway?" I rolled my eyes as I stared up at him. I wasn't about to tell him that they fully spied on us when we were outside and I climbed him like a spider monkey. The man would probably freak out. I moved to the bathroom to pack up my toiletries, and he followed.

"There's no sense involving people when it's temporary, right? We've got a few days off work, so aren't you the one who said we should take it one day at a time?" He stood behind me, and I looked up at the mirror to see his brows furrowed as he studied me. It was obvious that this was not something he was used to discussing.

"Yes. However, you just packed a bag for me to come stay with you for a couple of days. So, you've already changed the rules."

"Fuck the rules. We can make up our own as we go."

"I like the way you think, Bossman." I moved back out to the room, and he took my toiletries and dropped them into the pink bag. I typed out a quick text to Lila, asking her to find the right way to let my brother know I'd be gone for a few days with my boss.

She sent back a bunch of head exploding and fire emojis, which made me laugh.

"You ready?" he asked, as he shoved his hands into his pockets.

"I was born ready." I chuckled because this was really happening. And I wasn't nervous or anxious or even letting myself overthink the fact that I was about to have sex with my boss.

Who also happened to be the sexiest man I'd ever met.

Plus, I figured he was probably experienced, so he'd know

his way around a woman's body, unlike the other guys I'd dated over the years.

He slung my duffle bag over his shoulder and opened the door. I turned around to lock the door, and the snow was still falling. He surprised me by wrapping an arm around my shoulder and pulling me close as he hurried me to his car like I was going to freeze if I stayed out here one more minute.

Maddox Lancaster was full of surprises. He could be very thoughtful when he wanted to be.

He helped me into the car and reached for my buckle, which I tugged from his hand. "I've got it." I certainly didn't need the man spoiling me over something that would be over before we returned to work after the holidays.

This was my first fling.

I was a modern-day woman, but I'd always been in a relationship with the person I was having sex with.

But those relationships had hardly turned out, so maybe this would be the answer to all my romantic problems.

Find a guy you like to hang out with and have sex with him a couple of times.

How hard could that be?

No pun intended.

"I'm glad you're here, Tink." He cleared his throat as we drove the short distance to his house, before glancing over at me when he pulled into his garage and turned off the car. It was clear that he was uncomfortable about the whole thing.

"I thought you were a player?" I said, gaping at him.

"What the fuck are you talking about? I am."

"Well, why do you seem so…" I shrugged as a wide grin spread across my face. "Awkward. Isn't this sort of your thing?"

He rolled his eyes. "First of all, nothing about this is *my thing*. I don't talk about having sex with a woman. We just do it. It's just sort of known the moment that we get together.

Everything about this is different. *You're* different. So, I don't want to traumatize you or fuck this up."

I unbuckled my seat belt and slid across the seat and onto his lap. "I hardly think you rocking my world is going to traumatize me. Come on. I thought you didn't have a working heart. Don't go all soft on me now."

He thrust into my bottom. "You don't ever need to worry about anything about me being soft."

I turned and straddled his lap, and his eyes widened. "You aren't used to being friends with a woman, and now we're going to complicate things. I get it. But you needn't worry. I know exactly what this is, and I am so here for it."

"And when we go back to work?"

"I'll get your coffee and read the manuscripts you send and organize your calendar. I probably won't even remember this. I mean, I've had three boyfriends in my life, so I'm not a virgin. But sex has really never been all that noteworthy for me, nor would I have had a hard time being around them once we aren't together. It wasn't very spectacular, you know? Maybe there's something wrong with me, or maybe it's just not my thing. So, I think maybe you're making this a bigger deal than it is. I will act completely professional afterward. Scout's honor." I held up my two fingers.

"I can promise you one thing, Tink," he said, as his lips found their way down my neck.

I started grinding up against him on instinct, and my head fell back. "What do you promise?"

"This will be more than fucking noteworthy. And for the record, my cock finds the word *noteworthy* offensive. And sex is definitely your thing. You've just been dating boys up until now, and you've never been with a man. But I plan on starting things off by dropping to my knees and burying my head between your thighs, licking and tasting you until you cry out my name over and over again."

Holy shitballs.

My head popped up, and I held one hand on each side of his face as I tried to catch my breath.

"Wow, you're really bringing the dirty talk." I bit down on my bottom lip. "But for the record, I've never done that."

"You've never done what?" He placed his hand beneath my chin and forced my eyes to meet his.

"You know… had anyone *bury their face between my thighs,* as you so eloquently put it."

Why was I panting?

"No one has ever tasted you, Tink?" His tongue came out and moved across his plump lips slowly as he studied me.

I cleared my throat and shook my head. "Nope."

"How is that possible?"

I let out a long breath. "So, my high school boyfriend, Scotty, had a nut allergy. The kid wouldn't put anything in his mouth without checking with his mother, so obviously, that was off the table."

He shook his head in disbelief. "Un-fucking-believable. Scotty missed the fuck out. And for the record, I'd risk going into anaphylactic shock just for a taste of your sweet pussy."

"You're insane," I whispered over my laughter.

"And the other two?"

"My first college boyfriend, Bruno, was just more of a wham-bam-thank-you-ma'am type of lover. You know?"

"No. I don't," he said dryly, his eyes searching mine. "Like I said, you've been dating boys."

"And then Dikota had a tongue piercing, so I wasn't about to risk any sort of technical issues down south. So, I put the kibosh on that with him, not that he tried anyway. He was a very selfish lover, if I'm being honest."

"What a surprise. He stole your car, fucked your roommate, and chased his own pleasure. The dickhead was very predictable," he hissed.

"So… you will be entering a territory no man has been before." I chuckled.

"That turns me the fuck on. I want to be the first to taste you. To make you feel so good, you'll never forget who went there first."

Did it just get really hot in here?

I nodded. "I like the sound of that."

"Yeah? And I'd like the sound of you coming on my lips."

"Oh. My. Gosh," I whispered. "I think I'd be open to that."

"That's all I needed to hear." His mouth crashed into mine, and my lips parted, inviting him in.

Our tongues tangled as he pushed the car door open and managed to step out with me in his arms. My legs came around his waist, and our mouths never lost contact.

I couldn't think.

I couldn't breathe.

I tangled my hands in his hair and kissed him harder.

I was not going to overthink this. I was going to enjoy every last second.

Or minutes.

Or maybe even hours.

twenty

. . .

Maddox

I CARRIED her into the house, my mouth on hers, as I walked straight to the bedroom. I dropped her onto my bed, her blonde hair falling all around her like a goddamned angel. And I fucking missed her the minute my lips weren't on hers.

Her brows pinched together as if she were deep in thought.

"Hey, there's no pressure here. Are you having second thoughts?" I asked, waiting for her gaze to meet mine.

"Of course not. But I need to ask you something."

"Ask," I demanded.

"Did you sleep with Heather that night?" she asked.

"Hell, no. I sent her ass home right after dinner. I was pissed at the way she'd treated you." I paused. "But that doesn't mean what you want it to mean."

"What do I want it to mean, Bossman?"

"That I'm the kind of guy who deserves all your goodness."

"Why do you think you don't deserve goodness?" She reached up and ran her fingers along the scruff of my jaw.

"Trust me. I have everything I need. But you… you should

have someone who can give you what you want. What you deserve."

I was just the selfish bastard that wanted her in spite of it. Knowing it couldn't go anywhere. Knowing this would most likely end in disaster. I still wanted it so badly that there was no way to stop it at this point.

Unless she said she wanted to stop.

"You're overthinking it again. This is a fling, so we will keep it casual."

"What does said fling entail?" My lips moved to her neck, and I sucked and licked right beneath her ear, and she moaned. My dick was straining so hard against the zipper on my jeans, desperate to be unleashed.

"Well, I think sex is the foundation of a good fling, right? I don't know. This is more your area of expertise." Her breaths were coming hard and fast.

I continued moving along her neck and down to her collarbone as I spoke against her skin. "Correct, Tink. Lots of sex."

She tugged my head up to look at me.

"There are some rules, Bossman."

Her warm breath tickled my cheek. "Tell me."

"Well, I'm all about that YOLO life." She paused when I looked at her with confusion. "*You only live once.*"

"What the fuck does that even mean? And for the record, I've never talked so much before sex." My tongue trailed down her neck. This was enough talk; it was time to make her feel good.

She tugged my head back up and placed one hand on each side of my face.

"I was saying, I am all about the YOLO life; however… there are still rules."

"Tell me." I raised a brow impatiently.

"If we are going to have sex, then we only have sex with

one another. And when we're done, then we can go back to doing whatever we want."

I thought it over. "I've never played by anyone else's rules, but I haven't had sex with anyone since the day you strolled into my office and became the biggest pain in the ass I've ever met. Plus, I don't want you having sex with anyone else right now. So, this means that your pussy belongs to me for the time being. You're all mine, Georgia Reynolds."

"Oooohhh… I like how possessive you are about our fling. That's a pleasant surprise."

I growled and gripped her hips, grinding my massive cock against her core as I stood between her thighs.

"Look at me," I demanded.

Her eyes found mine as her breaths grew louder, and I continued to rock against her as I spoke. "Lots of sex. Only with each other. We keep it a secret. Act professional at the office. And when we're tired of it, then it ends, and there are no hard feelings. You sure you're okay with that?"

"Don't offend me. I usually get bored fairly quickly. I think I can handle a mutual agreement to sleep together until we don't want to do it anymore. I'm guessing this non-relationship has the lifespan of a yogurt. I give it a week. And then we can go back to being coworkers who annoy one another."

"No one gets sick of my dick in a week, Tink. You'll be begging for it the minute you have a taste."

She sucked in a long breath, and I loved the way she reacted to my filthy mouth. "You talk a big game, Bossman. Why don't you put your money where your mouth is?"

"How about I put my mouth on your pussy?" I leaned down and chuckled against her ear and nipped at the sensitive skin there.

"You are an overachiever at the dirty talk, aren't you?" she asked, her words breathy and laced with need as I pushed to tower over her.

"I aim to be the best at whatever I'm doing, Tink."

"What happens if we do it once and we don't like it?" she asked. Normally, I would be highly annoyed at all this chatter before we got down to business, but I fucking loved the way she shared every thought that entered her head.

"You are doubting the wrong horse. And by horse, I mean that I'm hung like one. I've never left a woman unsatisfied." I smirked as I reached for the hem of her sweater. She had far too many clothes on.

"So cocky," she teased.

"I put the cock in cocky, Tink."

She laughed and sat forward so I could tug the clothing off her.

"Okay, big talker. Let's see you work your magic."

I tossed her sweater and her long-sleeved shirt she wore beneath it onto the floor. She wore a peach-colored lacy bra, and my mouth watered at the sight of her.

"Fuck. These tits haunt my dreams." I reached around her back and unsnapped her bra with one hand, and she fell back onto the bed. I covered her perky tits with my big hands, and they were fucking made for me. A perfect handful.

I grazed my fingers over them, tweaking her hard peaks.

"Really? They aren't that grand," she whispered, and I realized in that moment that she was probably talking because she was nervous. No one had ever made her feel good, and I planned to rectify that tonight. I'd make her feel so good she'd never forget it.

"They're works of fucking art." My mouth moved to cover one breast, and she gasped. My hand worked the other one as I licked and sucked as she arched her back and nearly came off the bed. I moved from one to the next, taking my time, as my hand moved to the band of her bottoms. I slipped beneath the waistband and moved between her thighs, pushing the strap of fabric out of my way and finding her soaked.

Fuck me.

I'd never been so turned on in my life.

"So fucking wet, Tink. This is definitely your thing." I chuckled against her breast as her fingers tangled in my hair.

I pulled away, removing my hand and my mouth from her body, and the loss of contact bordered on painful. Her gaze searched mine, eyes wild, as she placed a hand on her chest to calm her breathing.

"Too many clothes. I need you naked. I can't wait any longer." I gripped the waistband of her bottoms and tugged them down as my fingers moved along her lean, toned thighs before I tossed them onto the floor. Peach panties that matched her bra were waiting beneath, and I was not a patient man. My face came down to rest at the apex of her thighs as I breathed her in. I moved back and slowly pulled her panties down her thighs, fighting the urge to rip them off her body.

She reached up. "I want you naked, too."

I tugged my sweater over my head and let it drop in a heap beside her clothing. She pushed up to rest on her elbows and licked her lips as her gaze moved down my chest and abs. "Impressive. Drop the pants, Bossman."

I studied her, because normally I liked to take control. But it turned me on that she was asking for what she wanted.

I kicked off my shoes before I undid the button and zipper on my jeans and shoved them, along with my briefs, down my legs, kicking them away from me. I stood there looking at her, my cock standing straight up, engorged and eager.

"Wow. You are a chiseled god, Maddox Lancaster." Her words were breathy, and my cock reacted by puffing himself up even more, if that were possible. I moved between her legs, pushing her back as I stroked her cheek.

"You like what you see, Tink?"

"Yes. How about you?"

"If my dick gets any harder, it'll explode. You're so

fucking beautiful," I said, leaning down as my mouth captured hers.

I'd never been one for talk during sex. Or overly telling a woman she was gorgeous. Sure, I'd give an occasional compliment, but I couldn't say enough to this woman. She was perfect in a way I'd never experienced.

And I wanted her more than I'd ever wanted anything or anyone.

My tongue moved in and out of her mouth before I nipped at her bottom lip and traveled down her neck, stopping at each of her breasts.

I gave them equal attention as my hand stroked between her legs, and she moaned.

I kissed my way down her flat stomach, pulling back to see chill bumps covering her golden skin.

I teased her, running my hand back and forth and finding her even more soaked now. My finger teased her entrance, pushing in the slightest bit, and I startled at how tight she was. I pulled back before slipping my finger into my mouth, and I groaned.

"So fucking sweet, Tink."

Her eyes widened, lips parted as she stared at me with surprise. "Thank you."

Jesus. Had she really never been with a man who wanted her the way that I did?

I smirked. "Are you sure you're okay with this?"

She nodded frantically, which made me chuckle. I slowly pulled her to the edge of the bed and pushed her legs farther apart before I dropped to my knees on the floor. I lifted each leg and placed it over my shoulder, looking at her one last time.

"Relax. I've got you, okay? This is going to feel really fucking good."

"Okay." The word was shaky.

I took my time. My tongue swiped along her folds, teasing

and taunting, as she started to writhe. Her fingers yanked at my hair as my mouth found her clit, and I sucked hard, moving my fingers where my tongue had just been.

I stroked her gently at first, waiting for her to find her rhythm.

Her breathing was out of control, and I continued to suck her clit and flick my tongue along the outside as she bucked up against my mouth. I watched her as I slid one finger in, and she tensed at first before relaxing. So fucking tight. I didn't know how my dick would ever fit.

I moved in and out of her before sliding in a second finger. I could feel her clenching around me.

"Maddox," she whisper-hissed.

Her body rocked faster and faster. I followed her rhythm, pumping in and out of her, as my tongue and lips found the same rhythm as I teased her clit relentlessly.

The little noises that escaped her sweet mouth had me so hard I could barely see straight.

Her hips bucked faster and faster.

Desperate and needy.

She panted and gasped.

And I felt it before it happened. The way she tightened around my fingers, the way her hands gripped my hair, the sound of her voice crying out my name as she came apart for me. I stayed right there, waiting for her to ride out every last bit of pleasure.

"Oh my gosh," she said, once her breathing settled. "Wow."

I pushed up to look at her as her chest continued to rise and fall.

"Have you never come before, Tink?" I asked as I moved onto the bed, pulling her up to settle against my chest.

"I know how to please myself, but you're the first man to give me an orgasm," she said, her voice low and sexy.

I wasn't sure why that made me so fucking happy, but it did.

I wanted to be her first.

I wanted to mark her forever.

Make her mine in every way.

Mine.

twenty-one

. . .

Georgia

HE STROKED my hair as his arms wrapped around me. My body was still coming down from the epic orgasm that had just torn through me.

I'd never experienced anything like it.

And now he was holding me in his arms, his hard chest beneath my cheek as he held me.

If this was what a fling was all about, I was so here for it.

Relationships were overrated. Dikota never wanted to cuddle after sex. He said he needed alone time to process, and we would both just lie there, staring at the ceiling.

But this… the after-orgasm cuddle was a close second to what I'd just experienced.

And there was the elephant in the room that would be impossible to ignore.

My hand slid down between us, wrapping around his enormous erection. It was thick, long, and hard as a freaking rock.

Maddox Lancaster really was all man.

His body was a chiseled masterpiece. I'd lost count of his abs, as my eyes had scanned down his chest with admiration, but then he'd dropped his pants to the floor, and I'd gawked in awe at the man and his massive penis.

I'd never seen anything like it.

I sucked in a breath, feeling him grow in my hand as I stroked him. How was that possible?

And how the hell was this enormous thing going to fit inside me?

He chuckled over his rapid breaths, as if he were reading my thoughts.

"You'll be fine, Tink. We'll take our time." He hissed out a breath when my thumb stroked over the tip, feeling the slickness there before sliding back down.

"Okay. Do you have a condom?"

"Yes," he said, his voice gruff. He reached over to the nightstand and pulled open the drawer before tearing at the foil packet with his teeth and dropping the wrapper onto the floor as I continued to stroke him.

I pushed up onto my knees, dropped my hand from where I'd been gripping him, and held it out to him. "Show me how to do it."

He studied me. "Lots of firsts tonight, huh?"

He placed the condom in my hand and guided me to the tip of his ginormous schlong. Was ginormous even a word?

If not, it needed to be. Because there was no other explanation for what I was seeing.

His hand covered mine as I rolled the latex over him.

He startled me when he reached for my hips and shifted me over him. Straddling his hips with my knees as I hovered above Mount Cockasaurus.

Yes… Maddox Lancaster's dick deserved a nickname. That was how spectacular it was.

"You can control the speed and how much you can handle, okay?" he said, his gaze locked with mine. "If it doesn't feel good, we stop. There are other things we can do."

"Okay," I said, positioning myself just above him, his tip

teasing my entrance. And I wanted him so badly that I was determined to make this work. I slid down just a little, flinching at the intrusion. His hands came up and covered my breasts, tweaking my nipples, as a groan slipped from my lips, and I took him in a little bit more.

Inch by glorious inch.

I'd pause and allow myself a minute to adjust to his size as he continued exploring my body before he tugged my head down to his mouth.

He kissed me slowly at first, his tongue slipping in and out, as I took him in a little deeper. He kissed me harder as one hand tangled in my hair and the other traced up and down my back. It was so soothing, the mix of pleasure and pain, I couldn't get enough. I slid down, taking him all the way in, and we both froze for a moment.

It was uncomfortable at first, almost hard to breathe. But I sat up and let out a few breaths as I looked down at him.

His dark eyes were hooded, his lips plump from kissing me, and his fingers were still tracing my breasts.

"So fucking beautiful, Tink."

The way he was looking at me, touching me.

I'd never shared a more intimate moment with a man before.

I was in deep trouble, and I knew it.

But I couldn't stop it if I wanted to.

I slowly lifted up as his fingers intertwined with mine, and I came back down just as slowly at first. I did it again and again.

Somewhere along the way, the pain had turned to pleasure.

I could feel him everywhere.

Our hands connected as I took my time riding him over and over.

He groaned as his hands untangled from mine, and he gripped my hips before sitting forward, and his lips sealed over one breast. He licked and sucked, and we found our rhythm.

He moved to the other breast as he circled my nipple with his tongue, and my head flew back as I arched into him.

Faster.

Harder.

I couldn't get enough.

His fingers moved between us, and he touched me just where I needed him to.

I tightened around him, my body stiffening as the most powerful current ripped through me, and I shook and trembled uncontrollably.

"Fuck," he hissed as he pumped into me once.

Twice.

And then he went right over the edge with me.

A guttural sound left his throat, and he continued moving inside me, tugging at my hair as he pulled my mouth to his.

I'd never felt anything like this.

This made the earlier orgasm seem like a practice round.

My arms, my hands, my fingers… everything tingled. My chest pounded so hard I could hear the thumping in my ears.

Our labored breaths flooded the room as a sliver of moonlight illuminated his handsome face. We stayed this way, with me on top of him and his arms wrapped around me, until we both were able to slow our breathing.

And then he pulled back to look at me.

"What the fuck are you doing to me?" he whispered.

I rested my hand on his cheek. "The same thing you're doing to me."

He nodded before sliding me off him and laying me on the pillow before pushing to stand and walking to the bathroom. I pressed up on my elbows to watch as his muscled butt flexed with each stride from his long, thick thighs. His broad shoulders were cut to perfection, and his back was a work of art.

"I can feel your eyes on me, Tink."

"I'm not trying to hide the fact that I'm staring." I chuckled, but my voice was barely recognizable. It was all husky and sexed up. Had his penis been so big that it had bumped my vocal cords?

The thought had me laughing harder, and Maddox came striding out of the bathroom, more big dick energy than any one man should have.

But he wore it well.

He dove on top of me and tipped me back. His hands found mine again and interlocked our fingers as he pinned them above my head.

"What's so funny, Tink?"

"I just can't believe everything that just happened, you know?" I said.

He rolled onto his back, pulling me with him. "I didn't hurt you, did I?"

There was a softer side to this man that I didn't think he showed many people, and I was honored that he showed it to me often.

"Um, no. I mean, at first, it was a shock to the system," I said, glancing up and smiling at him. "But then it was just… amazing."

"You felt so fucking good. I don't know if I'll ever get enough of you, Tink."

I ran my fingers over his chest, across the light dusting of dark hair, and traced each of his distinct abs. "Careful, Bossman. You don't want to go falling in love with me now."

He didn't laugh. He didn't say a word.

The energy in the room shifted.

I wanted to tell him that I was already hopelessly in love with him.

But I knew it would freak him out.

It was so me to fall for the guy that I couldn't have.

Because this man had made it clear that this was temporary, but that didn't stop me from wanting him.

"Tell me what it was like growing up in a house with all those kids and all that love there," he said, surprising me with the question. His fingers gently traced up and down my back and neck.

"Crazy. Chaotic. Fun. Frustrating," I said. "Being the baby of the family can be difficult sometimes. Everyone thinks they know what's best for me. But at the same time, I never have a day in my life where I don't know how much I'm loved."

"That's the dream, right?" he said, his voice low and serious, as if he was deep in thought.

I pushed up to look at him. "I see the way your grandfather looks at you, Maddox. And I don't know your dad or your brother or your grandmother, but I'm guessing they love you fiercely, too."

He smiled. One of those rare smiles that I got from him. Perfectly white teeth, handsome face, and a smile that reached his dark eyes. "That's because you're all good, Tink. You think everyone is lovable."

"I don't. But I know you are."

Because I'm crazy in love with you.

Maddox wrapped his arms around me a little tighter, and I listened to the sound of his breaths. The way his chest rose and fell with me against him. The rhythmic beating of his heart soothed me. And I dozed off, feeling more relaxed and content than I'd ever been in my life.

When I opened my eyes, the room was pitch dark, so I knew it was still nighttime. I glanced around the room, and Maddox was gone. I reached for my phone and saw that it was just after two o'clock in the morning, and I set it back down on the nightstand.

I pushed to my feet and found his sweater on the floor and pulled it over my head. The warmth of the cashmere draped over me, fitting more like a dress, and I padded through the bedroom and out into the hallway.

Where could he have gone?

It was the middle of the night.

"Maddox?" I whispered.

I heard what sounded like a muffled voice in distress, and I hurried toward the bedroom at the end of the hallway. When I pushed the door open, Maddox had his hands up as he continued to yell, and it sounded like he was saying "help," but it was hard to tell.

I moved to the side of the bed, and I reached for his hands. "Hey, it's me. You're okay."

He pulled his hands away and flailed a little bit, but I moved closer, my hands on each side of his face. "Maddox. Maddox."

I kept my voice calm. I'd heard my mom talk about patients who had night terrors, and I knew I wasn't supposed to wake him, but I couldn't stand seeing him so upset.

I continued saying his name, and he eventually stopped shouting, and his eyes shot open.

He looked terrified at first. Confused. Devastated. I couldn't place all the things I saw in his dark gaze.

"You're okay," I whispered.

"Tink?" He blinked a few times before sitting up and rubbing a hand over his face.

"I came looking for you. I didn't know where you went."

He looked so vulnerable when his gaze met mine. It nearly took my breath away. "I don't normally spend the night with the women that I'm with. I don't do sleepovers."

Yet he'd asked me to stay with him for a few days? It appeared we were both having lots of firsts.

"Why didn't you tell me that?"

"I don't like to advertise the fact that I have nightmares, Georgia. It's not something I'm proud of."

I pushed him down to lie on his back, and I slipped into

the bed beside him, my fingers moving along his jaw in an attempt to comfort him. "Nor should it be something you are ashamed of. Lots of people have nightmares, Maddox."

He let out a long breath. "Fuck. This is complicated. I wanted you to stay here for a few days, but I thought if I slept in another room, I wouldn't wake you up."

"Hey," I said, pushing up on his chest to look at him. The room was dark, but enough light was coming through the blinds to make out his features. "You didn't wake me up. I woke up on my own and came looking for you."

"I'm sorry I wasn't there. I should have told you."

"I forgive you. You're actually pretty cuddly, Bossman."

"You're the only woman I've ever wanted to hold after sex," he said, his voice low and hesitant, as if the admission was something he was uncomfortable sharing.

"Do you think it's my pickleball skills that make me special?" I said, my voice all tease.

"Or the way you just rode me like a fucking jockey at the Kentucky Derby."

I laughed. "Let's go back to sleep, okay?"

"If I do anything—" He paused. "Or if I shout and it scares you, I want you to leave."

"You don't scare me, Maddox." I wrapped my arms around his chest and fell back asleep.

I wasn't scared that Maddox would have a nightmare.

I was only scared that he'd most likely break my heart.

twenty-two

• • •

Maddox

WHEN I WOKE up the following morning, I looked around when I realized Georgia was gone. I surged to my feet, worried that I'd done something to frighten her.

Jesus. I'd fucked up inviting her here. What was I thinking?

I wasn't.

I wanted her with me, and I went for it.

And now she knew about the nightmares.

Outside of Wyle, she was the only one.

I hurried down the hallway, and the smell of bacon flooded my senses. I looked in my bedroom, and she wasn't there, so I pulled on a pair of joggers and my Harvard hoodie and made my way out to the kitchen.

I'd given Hilda the week off for the holidays, not that she ever cooked when she was here.

"My Sharona" played through the speaker on the counter, but the volume was low. Obviously, she didn't want to wake me. She had her back to me, but I could see that she was wearing my black sweater that draped over her petite frame and ended at her mid-thigh. She wore my grandfather's cowboy hat, and she was swaying her hips to the music as she cracked an egg in the pan.

So fucking sexy.

I just took a minute to enjoy the view before I spoke. "What are we doing in here?"

She jumped, dropped the egg on the floor, and let out a little squeal.

I chuckled and walked closer, reaching for some paper towels and wiping up the mess as she watched me.

"Sorry. Didn't mean to scare you."

Once I tossed the raw egg in the garbage, she reached for the cleaner and wiped up the remnants of the egg on the floor to make sure it was gone. She placed her hands on her hips and smiled up at me.

"All that good lovin' made me hungry. I hope it's okay that I made us breakfast."

"Of course it is." I shoved my hands into the pockets of my joggers to keep from reaching for her.

I couldn't get enough of her, and that had never happened to me before.

"I was thinking about this whole fling experience, and I feel like this might be my thing. I misjudged the idea of it." She turned around and cracked another egg in the pan before slipping on a pair of oven mitts from my drawer and pulling the sizzling bacon from the oven. She had two plates out—she'd clearly already found her way around the kitchen—and started plating our food. It smelled damn good.

"What are we talking about?" I asked, pouring us each a glass of orange juice, as she carried the plates to the table.

"We're talking about flings. I mean, this is great. I had two orgasms, I slept like a baby, and now we're eating breakfast together, and it's totally comfortable. This fling is better than any relationship I've ever had." She shrugged and reached for a piece of bacon and bit off the top.

That was because nothing about this was like a typical fling. I never asked a woman to stay with me for days or to sleep at my house. Nor would I have ever slept with a woman in my arms or enjoyed eating breakfast together.

I spent so much time with Georgia daily, and now we'd added fabulous sex to the equation—the best sex I'd ever experienced in my entire fucking life, if I were being honest. And now I was fucked because I only wanted more.

Nothing about this was a fling.

But I'd most likely fuck it up, so I wouldn't admit that to her just yet.

"I see." I forked some hash browns and popped them into my mouth and groaned. Damn, she was a good cook. "This is delicious."

"See what I'm saying? This is a win-win for everyone."

I nodded, fighting back the urge to smile. "Thanks for staying last night. I'm sorry about the nightmare."

"Don't be ridiculous. It takes a lot to scare me, Bossman. Finn used to sleepwalk. One night after I'd watched a super scary movie, he came walking into my bedroom in the middle of the night and just stood over my bed, staring at me. I opened my eyes and screamed. He scared the bejesus out of me." Her head fell back in laughter.

"What did you do?" I studied her as I forked some eggs.

"Well, I didn't know he was sleepwalking, so I lunged from the bed and karate-chopped the poor bastard in the throat. I thought he was messing with me. But my parents came rushing in, and everyone woke up, and then we realized Finn wasn't awake. He wasn't happy the next morning to learn that I'd assaulted him in his sleep. He never came into my room again, but he does occasionally sleepwalk. It's just like having a nightmare, and there's no shame in that." She took a sip of orange juice and then licked her lips after she set her glass down, and my dick immediately responded.

"I've had the same nightmare for years," I admitted. Hell, it was out there now, I may as well explain it.

"What happens in your nightmare? Do you remember?"

I set my fork down. "It's always the same thing. Me finding my mom choking and gasping in her bed. Not knowing what the fuck I'm doing, but I attempt CPR and there's no change. In my nightmare, it goes on and on, but in reality, it all happened very fast. But it's vivid, and it always feels like I'm there. Reliving the worst moment of my life all over again." I cleared my throat. I'd never talked about it with anyone. Yes, Wyle knew I had them, but we didn't discuss the details.

And Georgia had proven herself trustworthy, as nothing I'd shared had ever come back to bite me.

She wasn't looking to sell me out or make a quick buck.

"How often do you have them?"

"I honestly don't know because I live alone and sleep alone."

"So you really never fall asleep with your *lovers*?" she said it so dramatically it was impossible not to laugh.

"You say it like I'm some sort of male escort. There are a lot of women who are down for a good dinner, good sex, and then you part ways. It's not that uncommon."

"I get that," she said, and her lips turned up in the corners before she set my grandfather's hat on the table. "But the after is pretty damn good, right? Or maybe I'm just an affectionate person. But I don't know, Bossman, I liked sleeping with you. Maybe it's because you work me to the bone, so it's just habit to be near you." She smirked.

"The bone, huh? I've got a different bone for you."

"So dirty." She paused for a minute and glanced out the kitchen window before turning back to me. "You know how you didn't like me riding on the scooter, even before you knew me? You knew it was dangerous, right?"

"Yes. Don't even get me started about that motorized piece of shit." I raised a brow.

"Well, sometimes, someone on the outside looking in can see things more clearly." She cleared her throat and took a sip of her juice. "I think you have a lot of trauma from finding your mama the way you did. But I think talking to someone could really help."

I rolled my eyes. "Isn't that what we're doing?"

"We are. And I'll talk to you about it as often as you're willing. But I'm not a trained professional. So I wouldn't know how to help you with the nightmares, you know? And you deserve to sleep peacefully without being haunted by a memory." Her gaze was filled with so much empathy it made my chest squeeze.

"Don't pity me, Tink."

"I would never pity you. You annoy me far too much." She chuckled. "I'm just mentioning it because my mom is a fabulous therapist, and she's helped a lot of people."

"I don't need a shrink."

"Just FYI… if you talk to my mom, never say that word. It's a trigger for her. She finds it offensive. She's a therapist, not a shrink. So she knows things about this that you and I wouldn't."

"Or you could just ride me again, or sit on my face and keep me awake," I said, reaching for the last piece of bacon on my plate.

"I'd be happy to do either," she said, her cheeks flushing pink, and I fucking loved it.

"I'll think about talking to your mom, okay?" I held up my hands when she started clapping like she'd won some big prize. "I'm not making any promises."

"I'll take it."

"So, what do you want to do today?" I asked, because I had her all to myself for a few days. It wasn't like we really had to hide if we went out to eat, because we did it often during our work days together already. We could make it look like we were discussing business. Or was I just trying to find a way to make what we were doing okay? If I were capable of the real deal, I'd just let it be known we were together and talk to my grandfather. She'd have to change job positions, obviously; it would be highly unprofessional to be fucking my assistant.

Which was exactly what I was doing.

But I wasn't about to lose her at work when there was very little chance this would last past the weekend.

I'd just enjoy this time with her. We'd both be over the attraction by next week, and we'd go back to business as usual.

"Let's go cross-country skiing today. I know a great trail."

"Cross-country skiing is so boring, isn't it? Why don't we just go downhill skiing?"

"I told you… I excel at untraditional sports. I suck at downhill. I hate the chairlift. And I don't like going that fast." She shrugged, and she looked so innocent and sweet as she confessed her lack of skills. It made me want to build up her confidence.

"What if we do one day of each? And when we go downhill skiing, I'll tuck you in front of me and control the speed."

"Wow. This is like finding out that the Tin Man has a heart. Look at you, softy."

"What did I tell you about calling me soft?" I said, rushing to my feet and pulling her from the chair. I flipped her over my shoulder, and my hand found her ass as I jogged down the hallway with her. She was laughing hysterically when I dropped her onto the bed.

Her eyes scanned my joggers to see my eager dick pointing at her. He had a mind of his own, and he had it bad for Georgia Reynolds.

"Well, clearly, soft is not the right word for you. How about we take care of that in the shower together?"

"You want to shower with me, Tink?" I asked, as I moved closer and lifted her arms before tugging my sweater over her head and finding her completely bare beneath.

She sucked in a breath and nodded before reaching

forward and pulling my joggers down my legs and then pushing to her feet and sliding her hands beneath my hoodie.

This woman's touch did something to me. It made me feel things I'd never allowed myself to feel.

I reached for her hand and led her into the bathroom before turning on the shower. I'd never showered with a woman before.

It always felt too intimate.

But I was all about firsts with this girl.

She stepped into the oversized walk-in shower first, her head fell back, and she laughed as the water sprayed down on her gorgeous face.

"What's so funny?" I held her against my body, my throbbing cock poking at her lower belly.

"I just can't believe I'm showering with my boss. I guess I've taken inappropriate to a whole new level."

I didn't like her joking about being unprofessional. I was her fucking boss. I was the one who'd crossed the line. The truth was Georgia was overqualified for the job she'd been given. I should have moved her to a different department a few weeks ago when I'd started giving her manuscripts to read.

"There's nothing inappropriate about you," I hissed, tipping her chin up so her gaze would meet mine.

"Buckle up, Bossman. I'll show you inappropriate."

And before I could process what was happening, she'd dropped to her knees and gripped my dick before guiding it between her lips.

And just when I thought things couldn't get better, Georgia Reynolds gave me the best blow job of my life.

twenty-three

. . .

Georgia

I'D NEVER BEEN a fan of the blow job before. I'd avoided it at all costs… but not today. I'd enjoyed it, which was hard to wrap my head around.

I'd come to learn over the last twenty-four hours, that pleasing Maddox Lancaster was a complete turn-on for me. The way he'd groaned and thrust and completely come undone—it was a sight to see.

It made me feel empowered and sexy and wanted.

And here I stood, with this beautiful man who had just returned the favor by dropping to his knees and burying his head between my thighs until I cried out his name and could barely stand. He'd then followed it up by washing my hair.

No man had ever washed my hair before.

He massaged my scalp, and I groaned as he carefully rinsed my hair, making sure the soap didn't go into my eyes.

I lathered up my hands with soap and proceeded to wash his body as he stood there with his arms crossed over his muscular chest, watching me.

Fling or no fling, this surpassed all expectations.

If it ended tomorrow and no man ever touched me again, I would not complain.

"You keep covering my cock in suds, and I'll have you drop to your knees so I can fuck that sweet mouth of yours again." His voice was gruff, eyes hooded as he watched me.

I chuckled and rinsed off my hands and turned off the water.

He wrapped a towel around me before doing the same to himself, and we spent the next forty-five minutes getting dressed and ready for the day.

Together.

We talked, and we laughed, and he stayed in the bathroom after he was done, watching me apply my makeup and blow-dry my hair.

And we were out the door shortly after.

Cross-country skiing, here we come.

"We're going too fast!" I shouted as he guided me down the mountain. His legs were on each side of mine, his arms wrapped around me, and if I wasn't wearing my white ski bibs and matching jacket, I would feel the erection driving into my lower back even more.

I'd insisted we cover every inch of our faces, just in case someone from the office spotted us out here. Cross-country skiing had been much easier, as we were completely alone all day on the trail.

But the resorts here were busy, so this was the plan. And considering it was freezing outside, being bundled up wasn't a problem.

"Stop whining. We're barely moving," he grumped against my ear, which was covered in my favorite white snow hat with an oversized pom-pom.

We'd spent the last five nights together at his house. I'd only left once to go look at a rental house that had come on the market while Maddox had some work to catch up on, and I'd stopped by my place to grab my ski clothes.

The crazy thing was I wasn't bored or irritated or ready to leave.

I kept waiting for him to call it done, but he hadn't yet. And we hadn't discussed it. We'd had endless sex, eaten every meal together, watched a ton of movies, and had our two outings trying out our skis on both a flat surface and a large mountain.

We would be heading back to the office soon, and I didn't know what that meant. We'd just go back to being boss and employee?

That was the plan, and I wasn't going to fight it because this fling had done worlds of good for my confidence. I now knew what I wanted out of a relationship, and I would no longer settle for selfish assholes who chased their own pleasure or stole my car. So, I wouldn't regret this, even if it was short-lived.

Even if it hurt, which I knew it would.

But I'd keep that all to myself. I'd made this deal, and I was going to enjoy it while it lasted and deal with repercussions later.

Maddox hadn't had another nightmare since our first night together, and it was the first thing he asked me every morning.

We came to a stop at the bottom of the mountain, and he moved in front of me, pulling off his goggles.

"You did better that time, aside from endlessly complaining about the speed." His dark eyes searched my goggle-covered gaze.

I popped them up slightly so he could see me. "Good. We need to get going."

I let my goggles fall back against my face, and he chuckled. He'd laughed more over the last few days than he had in all the weeks I'd known him. And that made me happy.

At the very least, we were friends.

I was just the one who'd fallen in love with my friend.

My unattainable, broody, grumpy, gorgeous friend.

"Remember, if my brother hits on you, you have to be firm with him." We unsnapped our skis and dropped them off in the lodge, trading out our ski boots for our shoes before we made our way to the parking lot. He pulled the passenger door open for me and helped me inside before reaching for my seat belt and pulling it across my body and snapping it into place. I didn't try to stop him. I'd learned that these were the ways that Maddox showed me he cared. By worrying about my car or buckling my seat belt, giving me more orgasms than any one woman deserved, or encouraging me to try things like downhill skiing, even though I didn't enjoy it. My hands were freezing, and he got into the driver's seat and cranked up the heat. I used my teeth to tug off my gloves when I felt my phone vibrate in my pocket.

"Isn't your brother bringing a date?"

"I don't know. The dude is very secretive."

"Hmmm… it must run in the family." I found my phone and then squealed when I read the email from the property manager. "I got the house. I can move in over the weekend. I'll be in my own place before we go back to work."

Maddox stared straight ahead as he turned down the final street and then into his long driveway. Once he pulled into the garage, he turned off the car but didn't say anything.

"Hello? Did you hear me?"

He turned to face me. He looked… agitated.

Upset.

Disappointed, maybe?

Was I reading into things?

"Congratulations. I'm happy for you."

"You can't muster up a little more enthusiasm?"

"I thought you were staying with me until we went back

to work. What if I have someone move you in so you don't have to leave?"

My jaw fell open. For a guy who only had flings, he'd surprised me more times than I could count. He'd been attentive and thoughtful, and we talked about things I'd never talked about with any man before.

He wanted to know what I liked in the bedroom—which was all things Maddox Lancaster. What my dreams were. What my favorite subject in school was. Favorite movie.

I mean, I wasn't a pro at this whole thing, but I'd been in yearlong relationships that didn't go this deep.

"I don't even really have any furniture, if I'm being honest. So there won't be a lot to move in. I've got my dishes and my kitchen stuff, some cute decorations, and things to hang on the wall. It won't take long."

"What will you sleep on?"

"I'll probably get my bed from my parents' house."

"That's madness," he hissed.

I tugged the goggles completely off my head now that we were in the garage. "It's not madness. This is how normal people live. They save up and then furnish their new place. The first step was getting the house. The next step will be furnishing it."

He studied me for a long moment, a habit I was growing used to. "I have some things in storage. Why don't I send them over?"

"What kind of things?" I raised a brow because this had come out of left field.

"A bed. A couch. A table and chairs. I wasn't able to use them."

"You weren't able to use them in your mansion?" I pressed. The whole thing seemed suspicious.

"Correct. Us *abnormal people* sometimes purchase too many things, and they don't fit." He pushed out of the car and came around to open my door, but I was already out.

"It just seems odd that you have all the things that I need." I followed him inside.

He whipped around, and my chest slammed into his. "I have extra furniture that I'm not using, Georgia. And you need furniture. Stop making this more difficult than it needs to be."

"Fine. I'll pay you for it," I said, our eyes locked on one another.

He groaned. "Are you really going to make me say it?"

"Say what?"

"I have more money than I know what to do with. I don't need you to pay me for furniture that I'm not using anyway. Isn't this what friends do?" He smirked.

My shoulders relaxed. "I suppose. So, we really are friends, aren't we?"

"Well, if you were a really good friend, you'd let me take you to the bedroom and have my way with you before my brother gets here."

"I could live with that," I said over my laughter.

"Good." He kicked off his shoes and tossed his coat onto the couch. "Don't ask your parents for the bed. I've got one, and I'll get it all moved over there."

"You're so sexy when you talk about furniture and moving," I said over a fit of giggles. He rushed me and tossed me over his shoulder.

"I'll show you sexy, Georgia Reynolds."

He carried me to his bedroom and dropped me onto the bed. He bent down and tugged off my boots one at a time and tossed them onto the floor. He peeled off each item of clothing that I wore, one at a time.

"How many pieces of clothing can one woman possibly wear?" he grouched, and I laughed and shook my head.

"It was cold out there."

Once he had me completely bare, he stared down at me. "Yeah? How about I warm you up, baby?"

My chest squeezed. I didn't know if it was the way that he was looking at me, or that he'd just called me baby.

I sucked in a breath and nodded. He tugged his sweater over his head and pushed his jeans down, along with his briefs. I'd never tire of seeing this man naked.

He crawled over me, his mouth crashing into mine.

And then he kissed his way down my neck and my chest. His hands were everywhere.

"I love your fucking body so much, Tink. I want to mark you as mine in every way."

Fling. Fling. Fling.

It's not real.

"I want you," I whispered.

He settled between my thighs and looked at me with the most mischievous look on his face before he buried himself there. He took his time. Teasing and licking and bringing me just to the edge and then pulling back.

"Please, Maddox."

He paused and his gaze locked with mine. His lips were shiny with my desire, and I squirmed beneath him. He slipped a finger inside me, and then another, before his mouth sealed over my clit.

And that was all it took. I went right over the edge, just like I always did with him.

I tried not to think about the fact that it would all be ending soon.

Because right now… this felt like forever.

Before I even caught my breath, he glanced at the clock and reminded me that his brother would be here shortly. So, we both hurried into the bathroom to take a quick shower, where I dropped to my knees and returned the favor. The water fell down his muscled chest when he found his release and a feral sound escaped his lips. It was the sexiest thing I'd ever seen.

After, we dried off quickly, both of us still floating from the high we'd just experienced.

"Are you sure you want me here with Wyle?" I asked as we hurried out to the kitchen once we were dressed.

"Yes. We're friends. Why wouldn't I want you to meet my brother? I've met your family."

I shrugged. "That's true. And I'm looking forward to meeting him."

The doorbell rang, and Maddox poured me a glass of wine and then made his way to the door.

"I thought you were bringing someone." I heard Maddox ask, and a voice that was very similar to his chuckled.

"Yeah. That didn't work out. She was a stage-five clinger." When they came around the corner, Wyle Lancaster's gaze moved to me.

He resembled Maddox with his dark eyes and intense stare, but his hair was lighter. He was maybe an inch or two shorter and not as lean as his older brother. But he was fit and gorgeous and definitely had the Lancaster good looks.

"Who do we have here?"

"I told you I was inviting a friend. This is Georgia Reynolds. She works for Lancaster Press." Maddox cleared his throat and moved around the bar to pour his brother a glass of wine.

"Ahh… and what do you do for the company, Georgia?" he purred. He didn't have his brother's broody demeanor. The man was definitely a flirt, and he reached for my hand and kissed the back of it.

Before I could respond, Maddox slapped his hand away from me, which made us both laugh. "She's my administrative assistant. Don't be inappropriate."

Wyle had a big grin on his face, and he nodded. "I see. You're his admin, and you eat together when you aren't working? Is that allowed?"

Well, he'd just had his head buried between my legs thirty minutes ago, so I'm guessing we've broken multiple rules.

"We were working." Maddox handed him the glass of wine and then looked at me. "He's just fucking with me. This guy has never followed a rule in his life."

"This is true. But my brother tends to stick to certain rules. So, this is a nice surprise." He clinked his glass with mine just as the doorbell rang.

"I hate surprises," Maddox said as he moved toward the door to get what I assumed was the dinner that he'd ordered for the three of us.

"So, what rules is it that your brother sticks to?" I asked.

"Well, Georgia, this may surprise you, but my brother would normally not be dining with a woman he worked with when the office was closed." He winked and leaned close to me. "Nor would he ever bring a woman to a casual dinner with his brother. He takes dates to events, not to dinner at his home. But this isn't an event, is it?"

I took a sip of wine to think about how I would respond. "This isn't a date. We're just friends."

"Maddox doesn't have any female friends, unless you count our new stepmother." He turned when his brother walked in before glancing back at me quickly, keeping his voice low. "I have a hunch you're special."

Was I special?

Would I be special next week when we returned to our normal lives?

I sure hoped so.

twenty-four

. . .

Maddox

WHEN THE DELIVERY arrived at her new place, her brothers eyed the furniture and then smirked at me. All three of them were there. Her parents had been there. Her sister was there. Hugh's fiancée was there.

They all came out to see her put her clothes in her closet.

The only one missing was little Gracie, who was on some sort of play date, whatever the hell that meant.

Georgia had a few things that would go on the desk that I'd also lied and said that I had.

I'd ordered everything from a furniture store in the city after she'd taken me over to see her new place, and I'd then had to hire movers to bring it all here and pretend that it was coming from a storage locker and not directly from a store.

Because the girl was proud and wanted to prove she could do things on her own.

But the truth was, she already had.

She'd been far more than an assistant to me at this point, and not because I was fucking her, but because she'd worked her ass off.

I was counting this as a bonus that she'd more than earned from her diligent work ethic.

Hugh, Cage, and Finn stood outside with me, waiting for the furniture to arrive, because they thought they'd have to help move it in.

I'd been surrounded by the Reynolds family all day, and I'd repeated my bullshit excuse that I'd just been in the neighborhood and wanted to offer help to my assistant on her move.

Her brothers knew there was something going on between us. She'd been staying at my place for a week. I didn't think that her parents knew what was going on, so they'd been overly grateful that I was such a hands-on boss.

Their words, not mine.

But I was a hands-on boss, wasn't I?

Hell, I'd had my hands all over her just a few hours ago. Tomorrow, we were heading back to work, so this was our last night doing our so-called fling. And the whole thing seemed crazy now. I'd made up all these damn rules, and now I had no intention of following them.

"Hmmm... are we supposed to believe that this stuff is used?" Hugh smirked as he clapped me on the shoulder.

The two guys that had just arrived started unloading, and I leaned close to them. "You made sure all the tags and wrapping was off of everything already, right?"

"Yep. And we threw away all the evidence like you asked," one of the smart-asses said, and all three of Georgia's brothers laughed.

"It's not *evidence*. It's trash." I shook my head. More laughter, as I was obviously completely caught at this point. We watched as they started pulling everything out of the truck. There was a couch, coffee table, desk, bed, dresser, and dining table and chairs.

Georgia was inside the house with Lila and Brinkley unloading some dishes and décor that she'd brought from her apartment in the city, which had apparently come furnished.

Her parents had gone to the market to load her up with groceries.

"Pretty slick, dude. Is this part of the employee benefits package?" Cage said, and he barked out a laugh.

"She has gone above and beyond at work. She's far more than an assistant, so it's more of a bonus."

"Ignore him. He's still pissed because he got woken up in the middle of the night because Mrs. Lamprose thought her turtle was dying," Finn said before covering his mouth to hide his laughter.

"The damn thing had the hiccups. These people are insane," Cage hissed. "Who fucking calls their vet in the middle of the night about the hiccups?"

I shrugged. "I didn't even know turtles went to the doctor."

"It's called small-town madness," Hugh said. "This is really nice of you, brother."

I nodded. "It's not a big deal."

The two dudes finished unloading just as Georgia walked out with Lila and Brinkley behind her.

"Wow. This was all in your storage shed?" Georgia asked, as she ran her fingers over the white dresser and gaped at all the furniture. "It looks brand-new."

"My decorator over-ordered, so I'm glad we can use it somewhere," I said.

Brinkley narrowed her gaze at me as Georgia and Lila ran over and plopped down on the couch, which was sitting in the middle of the driveway.

"How you doing?" one of the movers asked as he moved closer to Georgia.

Was he fucking kidding me?

He was hitting on my fucking—friend.

"She's doing fine," I growled, which only earned me more laughs. The fucking Reynolds family apparently found humor in everything. "And you can go ahead and start carrying it in."

And the next few hours were absolute madness.

Her parents were there. Everyone was helping put things away, her brothers were making endless smart-ass comments every time they were alone with me in a room, and it wasn't a horrible day like I'd expected it to be.

They were all saying their goodbyes, and I was ready to be alone with her. I needed to talk to her about extending our... situation.

We'd lost today, so adding a few more days wasn't going to hurt anything.

We were grown-ups, after all. We could be professional at work.

"I just can't get over what a great boss you are, Maddox," Bradford said as he shook my hand.

"I'm his only friend in town, Dad. Leave him alone," Georgia said, and she winced at me as if she were nervous I was bothered by the comment.

I wasn't.

I actually wanted to tell him I was a hell of a lot more than her boss. But when I fucked it all up in a few days, I wouldn't want her family hating me.

"Of course. She's doing a great job at work. And she's right, she's been really helpful to me since I moved to town."

"I'll bet she has," Brinkley said under her breath as she stood right behind me.

Next was Georgia's mom, who hugged me, hugged her daughter, and then made her rounds to everyone there.

It wasn't even normal how loving these people were. My father was normally blackmailing us to make us show up to something.

Everyone was making their way out the door, and I was fascinated by how long this whole departure took. She wasn't leaving the country. She was only moving a few blocks away.

The last person out the door was Brinkley, and she smiled

at me but raised a brow before she spoke. "That was really nice that you had all that furniture sitting in storage. Thanks for helping out Georgie."

"Of course. Happy to help."

She then reached up to hug me and leaned close to my ear. "But if you hurt her, I will hunt you down and torture you slowly."

I didn't hide my surprise at her words, but then her head fell back in laughter. "You are too easy, Bossman. I'm kidding."

"What's going on over here?" Georgia asked as she came back inside from walking her parents out.

Brinkley pointed two fingers at her eyes and then back at me. "He knows what's going on."

More laughter.

I couldn't keep up with all the warnings and jokes.

"Love you. I'll see you tomorrow," Georgia said. "Thanks for helping."

Brinkley waved at both of us and walked out the door.

And we were alone.

"So, you survived a full day with the Reynoldses." She shrugged. "I didn't think you were going to stay the whole time."

"Well, I needed to be here for the furniture. Make sure it all got delivered correctly." And I wanted to be with her, as crazy as that sounded.

"Thanks for everything. I feel bad that I ruined our last night. That took a lot longer than I thought it would."

I moved to the couch and sat down. Her brothers had hung photos and art on the walls, and the place looked like she'd lived there for months. The Reynolds family was as impressive as an expensive decorator with a team of professionals working for them.

"About that… I wanted to discuss some options," I said as she walked over and sat beside me.

"What kind of options?"

"Well, seeing as we lost our last day, I wouldn't mind lengthening the agreement if you were open to it. It might be awkward being at work with me bossing you around, though."

She threw her head back in a full-bodied laugh. "You could try *not* bossing me around, seeing as I am pretty damn good at my job. But I would be open to the extension option."

"Yeah?" I asked, and I'd be a fucking turtle with the hiccups if my chest didn't squeeze with excitement.

She moved so quickly she caught me off guard. She was on my lap and straddling me, one hand on each side of my face. "I'm not bored with you just yet, Bossman."

"Are you really going to make me sleep here tonight?"

"Did you see that free-standing clawfoot tub in my bathroom?"

"I don't take baths."

"You also don't sleep in bed with the women you have sex with, and we changed that, didn't we? Take a bath with me." She put her hands together like she was praying.

I studied her pretty face. Her hair was tied back in two braids that fell over her shoulders, and she wore a pair of denim overalls with a hooded sweater beneath it. And all fucking day I thought about unhooking those buckles and dragging her into the bathroom.

"I'll make a deal with you," she said.

"Let me hear it."

"I know you don't have clothes here. And the bed isn't made yet. So how about we soak in that cute tub together, because that's something I've never done with a man and I don't think you have either, so it would be another first for both of us. And then we'll dry off, and I'll pack up some work clothes and sleep at your house. But after tonight, we take turns at each other's house until this *arrangement* is over. Fair is fair."

This was her argument with cross-country skiing, which was a fairly miserable sport, if I were being honest. It was slow, and there was no excitement, but the fact that she'd packed lunch for us and let me follow behind her and watch her cute ass maneuver through the trail made it tolerable.

"Fine. Deal." I pushed to my feet, and her legs wrapped around my waist as we moved through her tiny, little one-bedroom house. It was cute, and it felt like Georgia, and I didn't actually mind being here at all.

Because apparently, I liked being wherever she was.

And that was something I couldn't wrap my head around. I set her on her feet, and her phone buzzed, and she pulled it from her back pocket.

"It's a text from your brother. He said you aren't answering your phone."

"Is that bastard still texting you? He's so fucking needy lately," I hissed. She and Wyle had hit it off, which was no surprise because he liked everyone, and she was one of the most likable people I'd ever known.

He'd pulled me to the side after our dinner and told me not to fuck it up. I'd reminded him we were just friends, but he saw right through it.

And Georgia had taken us all around town the following day, showing him around. She didn't make us wear disguises or stay incognito because she said having my brother along with us changed the dynamic, and no one would be talking about it.

Wyle had gone back to New York, but we'd had a good visit.

I checked my phone and saw all the screenshots of the story breaking about our father marrying his best friend's daughter. And the fact that they were expecting a baby was apparently the big story of the day.

I texted him back and told him it would eventually blow over.

But after seeing how normal Georgia's family was and then reading this shit about my father, it irritated me.

"Hey. What happened? Where'd you go?" She turned off the water in the tub once it was full and reached for the hem of my sweater before tugging it up until I helped her pull it over my head.

"That story broke about my dad and Claire. It will probably be the talk of the office for a while." I reached for her overalls and unbuckled them. The denim fell to the floor in a heap before I tugged her hoodie over her head.

She looked up at me as I reached around her and unhooked her bra. "He is who he is, Maddox. That has nothing to do with you and who you are. Tune out all the noise."

"And how do you recommend I do that, Tink?" I nipped at her mouth.

"You make peace with it. You have no control over him or his choices, so you can't be held accountable for them. You're a good man, Maddox Lancaster. That's all that matters."

Goddamn, she was sweet.

"You sound like a therapist."

"Meh. The apple never falls far from the tree. Now, drop your pants and get in the tub, Bossman."

I laughed. Hell, I'd never laughed more than I had since I'd met her.

So, I did what she said, and I climbed into the tub that looked like it was older than dirt.

And then she slipped in after me and settled between my legs.

And for the first time in my life, I didn't mind taking a bath at all.

Because I didn't mind anything as long as she was with me.

twenty-five

. . .

Georgia

WE'D BEEN BACK at the office for two weeks, and I'd just been bumped from the top of the ping-pong championship by Craig in marketing, and I groaned when I set my paddle down in defeat. The guy had apparently been practicing while we'd been off work for that week after Christmas, and I'd been too busy boning Bossman to think about ping-pong.

Everyone was clapping me on the back and telling me I'd get back up there again, and I almost felt bad for Craig that no one seemed thrilled by his win.

"Good game. You smoked me," I said, smiling up at him when he set his paddle down and came to my side of the table.

"So, I won the game, but can I win the girl?" He waggled his brows.

What? Where did that come from?

I laughed nervously. Sure, Craig had flirted with me a few times, but nothing extreme. "I think moving your name to the top of the whiteboard is a big enough win for the day, right?"

He moved closer. "I'm serious, Georgia. I've been sneaking out on my breaks and making Freddy play with me every day just to impress you."

Damn. I'd been much happier when I was sitting in the top spot. Beating me did not make me want to date him; it made me want to get better and beat him.

"Well, I am impressed with your ping-pong skills, Craig," I said, taking a step back until my butt hit the edge of the table.

"Is that the only thing you're impressed with?" he purred and crowded me once again. I wasn't loving this side of Craig. Nor was I impressed with his lack of ability to read the room.

"I think you're a great guy, but I'm seeing someone." Was I seeing someone? I mean, I was in the midst of the world's longest fling that had been extended multiple times. But what were we? We weren't anything official.

But it felt like… everything.

How sad was it that the best relationship I'd ever had wasn't even an actual relationship? It was a secret.

A deliciously dirty little secret.

"Really? It seems like you're always at work. I didn't think you would have time for a boyfriend."

Wow. Way to analyze my life with absolutely no knowledge or facts. We literally spent twenty minutes a day together in a group while playing ping-pong.

Note to self… Craig was a bit judgy. I think his ping-pong success was already going to his head.

"It's not serious, but we aren't seeing other people."

"Well, what if I told you I was a serious guy?"

"I would thank you for that information." I shrugged. What the hell was going on?

"When your *not-serious* relationship implodes, I'll be here, Georgia."

He was so intense. He appeared to be a guy who was maybe three minutes away from grabbing a boom box and resting it on his shoulder and serenading me.

This had come out of left field.

"Georgia," a deep voice barked from behind me. I whipped around to see Maddox standing there, looking broody as always, and I didn't miss the way the veins in his neck were bulging and his hands were fisted at his sides. "Lunch is over. My office. Now."

Hello, Bossman.

I liked seeing him all worked up.

Craig just stood there, and I had no choice but to put my hands on his chest and push him back gently at first, and then harder when I realized he wasn't budging.

"Excuse me." I slipped between him and the ping-pong table and made my way toward the stairs, where my ever-angry boss-slash-lover glared past me at the man who'd just asked me out.

I hurried up the stairs and into his office, and he was hot on my heels before slamming the door and facing me.

"What the fuck was that?"

"What do you mean?"

"With Anus-hole," he growled, moving closer to me as his hands wrapped around my wrists.

"Anus-hole?"

"That asshole, Craig. That's his last name."

Laughter bellowed from my belly, and my entire body shook. "His name is Craig Anistilo."

"Same thing. What the fuck was that about?"

"He asked me out. It was not a big deal."

"And what did you say?" He tightened his grip on me, pulling me against his body.

"I said no. I told him that I was seeing someone, but it wasn't serious."

His gaze softened, and he released my wrists. "He's fucking fired."

"What?" I gaped and shook my head. "You can't fire him."

"I sure as fuck can. I own the company. He shouldn't be asking out coworkers. It's unprofessional."

"That's rich, seeing as you're fucking your assistant," I huffed and marched toward the door.

He was fast. He moved around me and stood against the door. "Is that what I'm doing? Fucking my assistant? Spending every day with her, every night? Talking, laughing, taking fucking bubble baths? I think it's a bit more than that, yeah?"

"Don't play the victim card. The ball has been in your court the entire time. You're the one who wants to keep it casual, not me." My vision blurred as my eyes watered, and a lump formed in my throat.

His hand moved to my neck, his fingers resting on my cheek. "I don't want to keep it casual. I want you, Georgia Reynolds. I don't want some dumb fuck asking you out at the office. I want everyone to know that you're mine. Because you are, and we both know it."

"I can live with that," I said as a tear rolled down my cheek, and his thumb swiped it away. "So, what are you going to do about it?"

"Well, you're fired, for starters." He let me go and moved toward his desk, back in business mode.

"What? You're firing me?"

"I can't be fucking my assistant, Tink."

I shook my head in disbelief. "But you own the company."

"It's still inappropriate." He picked up his phone and dialed. "Hi, Virginia. Put out an ad for a new front-desk receptionist." I could hear her talking frantically in the background, and he held the phone away from his face and rolled his eyes. "No. You aren't fired. You're my new admin." More shouting as he pulled the receiver away again and winked at me, like he hadn't just fired me and left me hanging. "She's not fired, either. She's been promoted to creative director. Send out an office email, please, and let everyone know about the changes. And also, make it known that the new creative director and I are dating, as well. Your first task as my admin is to spread the word. And make sure Craig is aware."

I heard her squealing before he slammed the receiver down and looked up at me.

"I'm the creative director? Do we need to run this by anyone first?"

"I'd already gotten it approved this morning by the board. That's what I was coming to tell you when I found that dick-fucker hitting on you."

"What does this new position entail?"

"You're going to do exactly what you've been doing, minus the monotonous stuff. You'll give input with cover designs, continue reading manuscripts, give feedback on blurbs, and help me find new talent."

"Will I still be picking up your dry cleaning and bringing you coffee?" I raised a brow and moved closer to him, coming around his desk.

"I'm not letting Virginia touch my clothing. She spilled coffee all over the front desk twice this week already. So, yes. If you're willing to handle my dry cleaning, I'd appreciate it. And the coffee…"

I rested my hands on his shoulders as one leg came around each side of him so I was straddling him. "What about the coffee?"

"I mean, no one makes it as good as you."

"You just want to find a reason to keep me coming in here for you."

"I want to find a reason to keep you *coming*, Georgia Reynolds." His lips moved to my neck, and I felt him harden beneath me.

"I thought you didn't do relationships, Bossman," I whispered, and my voice was hoarse and filled with desire.

"That's before I started *doing* you. And now I can't get enough." He kissed along my throat and down to my collarbone. "I want to take you to dinner and ski down a mountain without wearing enough gear to suffocate myself. I want everyone to know that we're together."

"Mrs. Runither will be so disappointed," I groaned as he nibbled my earlobe. "She keeps asking me about you."

His head shot up with concern as his gaze locked with mine. "She punched me in the dick yesterday when I went to pick up that to-go order for us."

A wide grin spread across my face. "Did she?"

"I think she was trying to slyly graze my goods, but she stumbled and literally junk-punched me. I mean, the woman is old enough to be my grandmother. Who the fuck does that?"

"She's a dirty old bird." I laughed. "You didn't mention it when you got home last night."

He sighed, a softness filling his dark gaze. "Because I missed you, and when I got home, all I wanted to do was feed you, get you naked, and then sit with you under the stars."

"We barely ate."

"Exactly." He smirked before his face turned serious. "This is not something I've ever done before, Tink. I'm most likely going to fuck it up."

"Well, you sucked at the fling. I mean, obviously, it was my first, but every day, you were asking for an extension," I teased, grinding up against his erection. His hands gripped my hips as I continued talking. "Maybe you'll be better at this."

He groaned. "Stand up."

I pouted but did what he commanded.

"Bend over my desk, Tink. I want to celebrate your promotion." He tugged up my skirt and then reached into his wallet and pulled out a condom, tearing the top off with his teeth as he quickly covered himself. His hands landed on my ass, and he squeezed. "Do you want me to fuck you in this office one last time as my assistant?"

I nodded, desire pooling between my legs. He pulled my

lace thong to the side and swiped between my folds before moaning against my ear. "Always so wet for me."

"Always," I whispered.

He teased my entrance before turning my head so he could kiss me. I wiggled against him, eager for him to give me what I needed. And with one quick thrust, he pushed inside me. I used my hand to cover my mouth to muffle the noises that were escaping.

It wasn't our first time having sex in this office. But it was the first time that it had happened in the middle of the day with people here.

But it was also the first time that it had happened with the man who was now officially my boyfriend.

I gripped the edge of the desk as desire built.

His hand came around my waist, dropping lower and touching me exactly where I needed him to.

He always knew what I needed.

"Fuck," he hissed in my ear. "So fucking good."

"Yes," I whispered, but I couldn't hold on any longer. "Maddox."

"Come for me, baby," he said, his voice low and demanding.

And that was exactly what I did.

And nothing had ever felt better.

Because I was undeniably in love with this man.

twenty-six

• • •

Maddox

RELATIONSHIPS WERE UNDERRATED. I'd been missing out. It wouldn't have mattered because there wasn't anyone in the world that I would have wanted to do this with before now. Life had a way of working out. Of giving you what you needed.

And I needed Georgia Reynolds.

We'd been officially dating for two weeks now, and I had no complaints. I'd always felt suffocated by the women I'd spent time with in the past. A few dates had always been enough.

But my appetite for this woman was insatiable.

And today was proof of how crazy I was about her because I'd agreed to come to Hugh Reynolds' house tonight for a poker game that he was hosting.

This was not typically my thing.

I wasn't big on guys' nights or small talk.

But hanging out with Georgia's brothers and their friends was not as bad as I'd expected it to be. Georgia and I had gone to dinner with her parents twice, and I'd even been to two family dinners since we'd made it official. But her siblings had just laughed because, apparently, they'd known we were together before we'd ever admitted it.

I was seated around an oval-shaped poker table covered in green felt. I sat between Hugh's best friends, Brax and Travis. Finn was across from me, sitting between Hugh and Cage. We'd finished playing and were just drinking and shooting the shit now, and Travis was bitching about Finn taking everyone's money.

"You take our money and have the nerve to stare at your phone the whole night?" Travis grumped.

The dude made me seem like a ray of sunshine. Travis was also Lila's brother, and he was a self-proclaimed moody bastard. But he blamed it on the fact that his new baby boy did not sleep much.

"It's Reese," Finn said as he typed into his phone. "We haven't talked much because she's in a different time zone."

I had no idea what we were talking about, and Hugh picked up on it. "Reese is Finn's best friend. She's also my mom's best friend's daughter, and we all grew up together. She's been in London the past six months, and they can't go very long without talking."

"They're like two fucking schoolgirls. Why don't you just date her already?" Cage said over his laughter, and Finn's head shot up with a death glare. I may not have known them long, but I could recognize when someone had crossed the line, and Cage definitely had.

"It's fucking Reese, asshole. She's my best friend. And if you recall, she was engaged to someone."

"*Was* being the point of my question. She isn't engaged *now*," Cage said as he reached for his beer and took a pull.

Finn flipped him the bird and ignored him as he continued texting.

"He'd never risk fucking that up," Hugh finally said, reaching for some pizza rolls in the middle of the table and popping them into his mouth.

"So, how about you?" Brax asked, turning his attention to me. "You and Georgie are a thing, right? How does that work at the office?"

It works fucking great. We spent every waking minute together. We had sex at work and at home. But I obviously wouldn't be sharing that.

"She's not my assistant anymore. She's the creative director, and she's kicking ass at work. So, it works just fine."

"He knows he'll be hunted down and tortured slowly if he hurts her," Cage said as he winked at me.

"I'm not afraid of you assholes. But Brinkley terrifies the shit out of me. Every time I see her, she whispers some kind of threat in my ear, but then follows it with a friendly goodbye."

Hugh had just taken a long pull from his bottle, and he coughed so hard, Cage pounded on his back.

"I'm fine." He barked out a laugh. "Fucking Brinks. She's the most terrifying Reynolds out there. Georgia is all sunshine and unicorns. But Brinkley, man, she doesn't play around. Just don't fuck it up." Hugh smirked.

"Trust me, there's a very good chance I'll fuck it up. This is new for me," I admitted, because they were all good dudes.

"Listen, if these two can pull it off, you'll be fine." Travis flicked his thumb at Hugh and Brax.

"When you know, you know," Hugh said. "Man, did I get hit hard when Lila came home last summer."

"He was so pussy whipped over Lila. I saw it long before any of these fuckers did," Brax said.

"Do not use the word pussy and my sister in the same sentence when I'm sitting here. I do not want to hear that. And speaking of pussy-whipped motherfuckers, take a look in the mirror, dickhead."

They went on to tell me how he'd fallen hard for his girlfriend Frannie, and now, they were inseparable. They were living together, and he was thinking of proposing soon.

My stomach wrenched. I didn't have a fucking clue what I was doing, but I knew I was crazy about her.

I hadn't told her that I loved her, which was cowardly. Because I did. But I knew once I said the words, there would be no going back.

"Hey, don't overthink it. Everyone goes at their own pace. I fought it every step of the way," Hugh said as he studied me.

"Things are going well."

"You doing something special for her birthday?" Cage asked. "The girl loves her birthday. She celebrates it all month, so get ready for all the birthday talk."

My chest squeezed. I didn't know when her birthday was. We'd talked about so much, but that had never come up. I should have checked her fucking paperwork from her employment file. This is the shit I should know.

I cleared my throat. "When's her birthday? She hasn't talked about it."

Finn barked out a laugh when he set his phone down. "Her middle name ought to give you a good hint. Georgana Valentine Reynolds."

"Her birthday is on fucking Valentine's Day?" I asked. Of course, it was. It was so her to have a holiday for a birthday.

Everyone laughed.

"It sure is," Cage said, shaking his head.

"You look stressed. Don't worry about it; it's not for two weeks. You've got time to plan something."

I nodded. "But it should be good, right? It's not only her birthday, but it's Valentine's Day. This is something people in relationships celebrate the shit out of. Fuck. I could take her on a trip?" I thought it over. She'd mentioned wanting to go to Paris someday. But then I remembered what the fifteenth was. "Shit. That won't work. Georgia has a client flying in the next day. It's an author she loves, and she thinks we should sign her. But the woman has a tight schedule, and that was the only time she could make it to Cottonwood Cove. Tink's real excited about it, so I can't ask her to move it."

"Tink?" Travis raised a brow and chuckled.

Fuck. Had I said it aloud?

"Says the dude who calls his wife, shmoopie." Hugh gave him shit and then glanced back at me.

"You don't need to take her anywhere. She's all about sentiment. Hell, Lila's favorite place is the cove. It's our spot. You find a special place and bring some food. Some wine. Some flowers." Hugh shrugged.

"Who would have ever guessed you'd be such a sappy bastard?" Cage said. "But I agree with him. Women love that romantic shit. And Georgie is pretty tender-hearted. She'll eat it up."

We'd go somewhere outside so we could sit under the stars. That much I knew. But we didn't really have a place outside of my backyard.

"What about that big pond where she used to skate all the time?" Finn asked. "You'd have to drive up the mountain a bit, but no one's ever out there. It's pretty dead over there, so that could work. Georgie used to make me go with her all the time so she could show me how good she was on skates."

"She's mentioned that place. She likes it there, huh? I guess it's better than cross-country skiing." I shrugged.

"I'm glad she has you now because the last time she took me cross-country skiing, we were out there for seven hours. I froze my ass off," Hugh said.

I laughed. "I hear you. It was a long day. And boring as hell. But seeing her skate sounds a hell of a lot better. And the pond will still be frozen in February?"

They all laughed now.

"Welcome to Cottonwood Cove, brother. It won't start to warm up until the end of March," Brax said over a mouthful of pizza rolls.

Okay, so I had a plan. I'd take her at night. Under the

stars. A picnic. I'd buy her some new skates. Maybe drive up earlier in the day and set things up. I could do this.

Maybe I wasn't so bad at this boyfriend shit.

I wasn't dreading it. I was looking forward to surprising her.

"You've got this," Finn said, holding his bottle up in cheers. "And she's going to the city with you this weekend for the reception for your dad and his new wife, right?"

My chest squeezed. I was dreading an evening with my dad and my childhood friend who was now knocked up with his child and tied to him for life. They were throwing a reception at the hotel—a party after the vows sort of thing. It was for the public since they'd been rampant in the press. My grandfather thought it would be best to show a united front of support for the newlyweds.

"Yep. We'll go for the weekend." I cleared my throat.

"Relax, brother. Georgia loves everyone," Hugh said.

I didn't doubt that for a minute. She'd see the good in him. I was looking forward to her meeting my grandmother, and I knew she loved my grandfather and Wyle. But I didn't like the idea of my father being around Georgia.

Nor did I like the idea of the press finding out we were together and what that would mean for her.

I'd always kept my private life private, but that was easy because I didn't have anything I cared about before now.

She'd be photographed as we'd already agreed to a red carpet and giving the media a bit of a show. I'd been photographed with women before. But I wasn't dating them. And once they realized we worked together and she was spending the weekend with me, it would be news for a hot minute.

And I worried that might freak her out.

"Yeah. It'll be good," I said.

Hopefully, she wouldn't run for the hills after a weekend with the Lancasters.

We'd taken the helicopter to the city after work, and we'd been at the hotel for an hour. We were getting changed for the reception now, and I poured myself a generous glass of whiskey as I sat on the bed. Georgia had gone with her sister to find a dress a few days earlier, back in Cottonwood Cove, and she hadn't shown it to me yet. She'd shooed me out of the bathroom so she could change, and she wanted to surprise me.

The event was black tie, and I was wearing a tailored black tux.

My phone vibrated, and I glanced down to see a message from my brother.

WYLE

My date is already annoying me.

Shocker. Who is she?

WYLE

Remember Brandy, that girl I went to prep school with? She still lives in the city, and she reached out and offered to be my plus one.

The girl who stalked you right before you left for college?

WYLE

Stalked is a bit strong.

I thought you filed a restraining order.

WYLE

I was in high school. I was being dramatic. I've come to learn that she's just passionate.

Why is she annoying you now if she's so spectacular?

WYLE

Because she won't stop taking selfies of us and posting them. And you know how I feel about being photographed. She's some sort of influencer.

Good luck with that, brother. See you downstairs in twenty minutes.

The bathroom door swung open and out walked the most beautiful woman I'd ever laid eyes on. That had already been established, but this—this was next level.

She wore a black velvet strapless gown that hugged her curves in all the right places. There was a slit running up her leg, exposing her thigh and making it so she could still walk in the gown. Nude, sexy-as-hell heels were strapped around her delicate ankles, and she stopped in front of me. Her hair was slicked back in an elegant twist at the nape of her neck, and it took everything I had not to press her up against the wall and push into her right here, right now.

I moved to stand, my hands finding hers as our fingers intertwined. "You're so fucking beautiful."

"You look pretty good yourself, Bossman," she whispered.

"You sure you're okay with all of this tonight? You know the press is getting a photo, and your face is going to be all over the internet tomorrow."

She smiled and lifted one shoulder as she tipped her head to the side. "I want to be with you. So, if this is part of your life, then it will be part of mine."

So loyal.

So honest.

So willing to give herself to me.

Say it, dickhead. Stop being a fucking pussy.

My hand came around the side of her neck, fingers splayed across her gorgeous cheek. "I need to tell you something."

A thick ball lodged in my throat, making it difficult to speak. Not because I wasn't feeling it—it was the exact opposite.

I felt it all.

It was too much in a million ways, yet I only wanted more, which made no sense.

Loving someone was not in my plans.

But I was in too deep. There was no turning back.

"Tell me," she said. She didn't hide her concern as she searched my gaze. "Are you okay? You can tell me anything."

This was what I was talking about.

There was no turning back.

"I—" I paused to clear my throat. "I love you, Georgia."

I'd never said those words to any woman aside from my mother and grandmother. And now I'd said them, and I didn't have the urge to run. But my heart raced as if I'd crossed some imaginary line that had made me vulnerable in a way.

I didn't mind it, though.

I wanted her to know how I felt.

Needed her to know how I felt.

She sucked in a breath, her mouth falling into a perfect O. As if she never thought I'd say those words.

Neither did I. But here we are.

"I've loved you for a long time now." She blinked a few times as two tears slipped down her cheek. I ran the pad of my thumb over her tears and swiped them away.

"Me, too. It just took me a while to get here."

"It doesn't matter how we got here. We're here now, and that's all that matters," she whispered.

She was right.

Now we just needed to find our new normal together.

I just hoped after a night with the Lancasters, she wouldn't be running for the door.

twenty-seven

. . .

Georgia

MADDOX LANCASTER LOVED ME.

I'd known it for a while now, but I never thought he'd actually admit it.

I felt it every time he looked at me. Every time he kissed me.

He wasn't a man who tossed those words around casually.

And he'd taken that risk for me.

I'd had a few guys I'd dated before tell me they loved me, but it never felt like this.

It was the look in Maddox's eyes when he'd pledged his love to me that felt like my world had shifted in a way.

Like nothing would ever be the same again.

Hell, when Dikota had told me he loved me, it was over a bowl of ramen noodles, and his eyes hadn't left the TV screen. It was sort of like an *I love you, can you pass the salt* moment.

I'd known it wasn't forever.

Nothing had ever felt like forever before this moment.

So, I was going to enjoy it because I knew what we shared was rare. I knew that Maddox didn't take these words lightly, and he was a man who meant what he said.

He loved me.

There was no question, and I'd never experienced that before now outside of my family.

But then his phone rang a couple dozen times, and he cursed when he realized they were waiting for us downstairs, and we had to hurry out the door.

I knew that Maddox was concerned this would overwhelm me, but it didn't. I just found the whole thing odd, but I was channeling my inner royal tonight and going with the flow.

"One more," the guy in the flannel shirt who'd been shouting endless questions at us said, as he jogged along the red carpet, following us to the end before we'd stepped inside the hotel.

Was it weird as hell that we were staying at this hotel, and we had to make our way outside to walk the red carpet and reenter the hotel?

Yes. Not the best use of time, but I guess this was more about appearances tonight, and everyone in the family needed to be seen supporting Davis and Claire's nuptials.

I hadn't even met them yet, as we'd been ushered out the back door of the hotel where we'd slipped into a fancy black car, and I'd requested beer in my champagne flute because I didn't want to get too tipsy on the bubbly stuff before I met his family. We'd sipped our cocktails and pulled back in front of the hotel, where Maddox proceeded to get out of the car and assisted me and my gorgeous black dress out, as well.

We walked. We smiled. There were a couple of photographers out there taking pictures and shouting questions. Light flashes made it difficult to see, but I just blinked in between stops when we'd walk and try to refocus.

Maddox leaned in multiple times and reminded me not to respond to their incessant questions.

He'd also distracted me by whispering naughty things in my ear the entire walk from the car to the hotel.

"I can't wait to get you back to the room so I can slip my hands beneath your dress, slide your panties over, and fuck you senseless."

"I have to keep my jacket buttoned so they won't see how hard and swollen my cock is right now at just the sight of you in this dress."

I'd chuckled and tried to play it off, squeezing his hand in warning, as desire pooled between my thighs.

After the last photo was taken, my handsome date held up his hand. "That's the last one."

"Mr. Lancaster, is this lovely lady just a friend, or is she someone special?" the eager photographer shouted.

Maddox paused and glanced over at me. I could see his wheels turning, trying to decide how he wanted to handle things. "This lovely lady is my girlfriend, and she's most definitely someone special."

"How long have you two been together?" someone shouted.

"Who is she?" another man called out.

Maddox intertwined our fingers and looked over one last time. "You got your story. That's all I have to say about it. Goodnight."

And then he led me inside.

Once we entered the lobby, there was security everywhere. At least, I assumed that was who they were because they were wearing black suits and appeared to be speaking into some sort of earpiece as their eyes scanned the area around us.

One of the men approached. "Maddox, you're looking well."

"Thank you, Jared. This is my girlfriend, Georgia Reynolds."

The suit guy nodded. "Nice to meet you. I'll escort you both to the banquet room."

They were obviously monitoring who came in and out of

the lobby. As we followed him down the hallway, I glanced over to see another man in a suit following behind us.

Sheesh. This was serious business.

"This only happens when there is a big event. You've been to this hotel before with me, and security wasn't necessary." Maddox kept his voice low, as if he were concerned that this was too much for me.

"I'm not freaked out by this. Jared seems very nice." I shrugged, and the large man leading us to the party chuckled.

"It's her first family event," Maddox said, his hand tightening around mine.

"Welcome to the family." Jared paused in front of a door and held out his hand for us to step inside.

Maddox leaned down close to my ear. "You ready for this?"

"Of course. Stop worrying. So far, so good, Bossman."

He kissed my forehead and pulled the door open. My jaw dropped, and the extravagance of the room nearly stole my breath. There were multiple crystal chandeliers overhead, a live band playing jazz music, and there were tables with white linens and chairs around each one. This wasn't a large party. It was intimate, yet there was definitely something very formal about it. Starting with the way we entered the event to the fact that there were several security guards standing in the corners of the room here, as well.

"About damn time," Wyle said as he glared at his brother before smiling at me. "You look beautiful, Georgia."

"Thank you. You look very handsome in your tails."

The woman beside him cleared her throat, waiting for an introduction. She wore a body-hugging long, red dress with cutouts that left very little to the imagination. But she pulled it off, and gravity was definitely on her side. She had some giant knockers, and they looked like they were standing tall and proud without any support from the gown.

"Sorry. This is Brandy. Brandy, you remember my brother, Maddox. And this is his girlfriend, Georgia Reynolds."

"Oh, my. You're a lucky woman to land one of the Lancaster boys, huh?" Before I could respond, she whipped around, her back knocking me in the chest, and she held her phone above her head and took a photo of us. "Should I tag you?"

"Um. Sure?" I shook my head, startled by her greeting.

"What's your username?" she asked as she quickly typed into her phone.

"It's just Georgia Reynolds." I glanced up to see Maddox shooting his brother a look, and he didn't hide his annoyance.

"We're going to go get a drink," Maddox said, tugging me away from Brandy, and Wyle frowned, clearly not wanting us to leave him alone with her.

"There he is. You sure look sharp tonight, son." A man who was the same height as Maddox, but built more like Wyle, stood in front of us and shook my boyfriend's hand. He had dark, familiar eyes, the same as his son's. His hair was dark, with gray mixed in, and it worked for him. But I couldn't imagine my father shaking our hands. The whole exchange was very formal and cold. It wasn't hard to see that they weren't close. They behaved more like acquaintances. There was a beautiful woman beside him who looked to be about my age, maybe a few years older, and I assumed she must be his new wife.

"Congratulations, Dad. This is Georgia Reynolds. Georgia, this is my father, Davis Lancaster, and his wife, Claire." I'd heard all the details about her being his best friend's daughter and a childhood friend of Maddox and Wyle's. I knew that this was uncomfortable for them to wrap their heads around. Especially with all the anger around the way he'd treated their mother toward the end of her life.

"Georgia, it's a pleasure to meet you. My father sang your praises. He tells me you've got quite an eye in the publishing world and have brought on a few new authors at Lancaster Press." He shook my hand, as well. "You've obviously been busy, seeing as you started as his personal assistant, and now, you're here as his date. The apple doesn't fall far from the tree, does it, Maddox?"

His words startled me because he was smiling and laughing, yet he'd just insulted me. Maddox's entire body stiffened beside me, and I could feel the anger radiating from his shoulders.

"Davis, that's not funny." His wife gave me an apologetic look. "Hey there, I'm Claire. His better half, obviously." She had a genuine smile and gave me and Maddox each a hug.

"I'm sorry if that came off harsh. I meant no offense. It's the Lancaster sense of humor." Davis patted me on the shoulder, and Maddox's gaze moved from me to his father.

"It's not. It's just *your* sense of humor, which is interesting, seeing as you're celebrating your nuptials to your best friend's daughter, who is half your age."

I squeezed his hand and smiled. "You don't need to apologize. I'm a lucky girl, no question. You have an amazing son, and I'm glad I'm not the only one who sees it. Congratulations to you both. I'm so happy to be here to celebrate your special day."

"Thank you, Georgia. It means a lot to us that you're both here. I know it's a bit strange for you, Maddox, and I am sorry about that." She looked from me to the brooding man beside me, and his shoulders relaxed a bit.

"It's fine. Have a good night. I'm going to go introduce Georgia to Grandmother."

With a curt nod, Maddox led me away. I gave a quick wave and hurried to keep up.

"Let's get a drink first," he said. "I could use one."

"Hey." I tugged on his hand to force him to face me. "I'm not upset. This is actually fun for me. I've never been to a party like this, and I'm having a good time because I'm with you. Your father did not offend me. It's not my first rodeo with the backhanded compliment. I can handle myself, so please stop worrying."

"He's such a fucking hypocrite," he hissed. "I don't even like him being around you."

"He's your father. Your entire family is here, and I'm looking forward to meeting everyone. Let's get that drink and then go find your grandparents."

His face relaxed, his eyes softened, and he nodded. "Always the little fairy, spreading all that goodness, Tink."

I pushed up on my tiptoes and gave him a chaste kiss on the lips just as a server approached. "What can I get you both from the bar?"

"A whiskey straight up for me, and the lady will have whatever the best beer you have is. Pour it into a wine glass, please."

The woman smiled and nodded. "I'll find you with your drinks."

"Bossman, the fact that you just ordered me a beer in a wine glass at this fancy party means you're not nearly as stuffy as I give you credit for."

He rolled his eyes. "Keep up that smart mouth, and I'll show you how stuffy I am when I bury my face between your thighs and make you come so many—"

"Maddox. It's been way too long. Introduce us to your special friend."

He didn't miss a beat. The man could go from dirty talk to small talk faster than most people could change a TV channel.

"John, it's good to see you here. This is my girlfriend, Georgia Reynolds. Georgia, these are Claire's parents, John and Bev Strauss. They were also very close friends of my mother's."

"It's so lovely to meet you, Georgia. We've known this handsome guy since he was in diapers," Bev said.

"It's a pleasure to meet you. I'm sure you've got some

good stories." I chuckled. "Congratulations on your daughter's marriage and the new baby."

"Well, obviously, her marrying one of our best friends was a bit of a surprise at first, but at the end of the day, she's happy. And that's all that matters," she said.

"You were all right with this?" Maddox kept his voice low as he studied John.

"What have I been telling you these last few years, Maddox?" He paused to sip his champagne just as the server found us and handed Maddox and me each our drinks. She winked at me when she glanced at the beer in the wine glass, and I smiled.

"Yeah, yeah. Life is all about forgiveness," Maddox groaned. "Not everything is forgivable, John."

"Agreed. And trust me when I tell you that we didn't speak to your father for some time all those years ago when he was acting like a fool while your mother was sick. You know that. And we didn't speak to him for weeks after Claire told us about their relationship. But cutting them off hurts us, not him. He's always been a selfish man, Maddox. There's no argument there. But he's not the devil that you think he is. He does love you and Wyle, and I do believe that he loves our daughter. She certainly seems to love him. We raised her to be a strong woman, and we need to trust that she knows what she's doing."

Maddox sipped his whiskey and contemplated the older man's words. "I hope you're right about that. And I certainly hope he does better by her than he did by my mother."

"The thing that you didn't see was the years that your father grieved for your mother, both while she was sick and after her passing. You and Wyle were so angry that I don't think you were able to see it. You blamed him, and I do understand your anger about what happened. But, Maddox, ALS is a horrible illness, and that's what took her life. And carrying all this anger around is not good for you." He placed a hand on Maddox's shoulder.

"Well, thank you for the insight. I do appreciate it, and I will keep it in mind. But tonight is a celebration, so let's focus on that, shall we?" Maddox tipped his glass and then pulled it to his lips.

"I could not agree more," Bev said, blinking her eyes a few times as they were wet with emotion, and she looked over and smiled at me.

"All right. Nice to see you both. We're going to go say hello to my grandparents. If you'll excuse us."

We said our goodbyes and walked a few feet away to where his grandparents were standing and chatting with another couple.

When they turned to look at us, they excused themselves, and all their attention was suddenly on me.

twenty-eight

• • •

Maddox

WE'D BEEN STANDING HERE for almost half an hour, with my grandparents gushing over Georgia. They loved her. I wasn't surprised. She was a breath of fresh air, especially amongst this stuffy group.

She laughed and talked with her hands flailing, and everyone in her vicinity was drawn to her.

She was sunshine and goodness.

Something I never thought I deserved.

But being the greedy bastard I was, I'd taken the leap with her.

And everything was changing.

Being at my father's reception would normally be torture for me, but I was having a good time. I'd replayed John's words over a few times in my head as I watched my girlfriend and grandmother talk about everything from holiday gift wrap to their favorite flower.

"ALS is an illness, and that's what took her life. And carrying all this anger around is not good for you."

There was a lot of truth to both. What I couldn't get past was that she suffered through this brutal illness without the man that she loved by her side. That was almost as painful as the physical pain that she suffered. I resented my father for that. And I didn't know how to get past it.

After my last nightmare a few days ago, I'd agreed to go talk to Georgia's mother. It went against everything I believed in.

1. *I didn't like asking for help. I had figured my own shit out for most of my life, and going against that felt unnatural.*
2. *I was dating Georgia. Having her mom as my therapist seemed… wrong? But, apparently, there is no wrong way to ask for help, according to the ball of sunshine I was dating.*
3. *I'd talked about my mother with Georgia, which was not something I normally did. But now I'd be inviting another person into my tragic memory, and I wasn't sure how I felt about it.*

"It's time to take your seats. Dinner is about to be served," the woman who had been bringing us our cocktails said, as she and a few other servers ushered us to our assigned seats.

We were at the head table with my grandparents, Wyle, and Brandy, who had tried to take a selfie with me a few minutes ago, and I'd shut that shit down by covering her phone with my huge hand. This wasn't a media show. We'd agreed to the photo out front, and that was where the buck stopped, as far as I was concerned. Wyle had finally reached for her phone in frustration and dropped it into his coat pocket, and she nodded and apologized.

My father and Claire were at our table, as well, and so were her parents.

We took our seats, Wyle and I each sitting on either side of my father. Georgia was the star of the party, and I sat back and chuckled as she talked nonstop to everyone at the table like she'd known them her whole life.

It hit me in that moment that my mother was very similar. She never fit in at these events. She was down-to-earth and fun, and people were drawn to her in the same way.

Georgia had everything under control, and I'd been worried for no reason at all.

Even my father's asshole joke didn't cause her to miss a beat. She knew who she was, and no one else's opinion played a part in that.

Because the world was Georgia Reynolds' fucking oyster. She didn't care about money or expensive things; she was just comfortable in her own skin.

Maybe that was what had drawn me to her.

There was a lightness, a peace, and an ease that surrounded me when I was with her.

Like I'd finally found where I belonged after feeling misplaced for so long since my mother's passing.

Georgia Reynolds felt like home.

And I fucking loved it.

We ate.

We drank.

We laughed.

And when Georgia got the band to play some of her crazy-ass seventies songs, she dragged me out to the dance floor.

I thought my brother was going to lose his shit because he laughed so hard at the sight.

I was the broody bastard at family events—not the guy having a good time and dancing at his father's wedding reception.

Looks like Georgia Reynolds just got herself another first.

We'd been back from our weekend in the city for a couple days, and the internet had been flooded with photos the day after my father's wedding reception. Me admitting that I had a girlfriend publicly for the first time had been a bigger story than my father's celebration with his new, much younger wife.

And Georgia hadn't been the slightest bit fazed by it. She didn't read what was being posted, and she laughed it off when people in town were calling her a celebrity.

She was one of the rare women who could handle this without being affected in any way, shape, or form.

Her brothers had said they were having a guys' night the day after we returned, but instead, they'd taken me out to the pond where I'd be surprising her on her birthday. A hotel in the city would have been my pick, but this was Georgia, and sitting outside in the freezing cold, eating ribs and cake with her putting an ice-skating show on for me was much more her speed. So, I'd been ordering all sorts of stuff to make it special for her. I had two guys that would go out there early and get things set up for us, and when we showed up, the place would light up like the fucking Fourth of July.

"I'm heading out to my meeting," I said, pausing in the doorway as she stared at her computer monitor. Georgia was still working from her desk while I interviewed a few people for Virginia's position. We were transitioning everyone to their new job titles, but Georgia was covering the tasks as my assistant as well as that of the new creative director.

There had been zero comments about her promotion and the fact that she was dating the boss. Because everyone here knew how hard she worked, and they also probably knew I'd fire their ass if they said one unkind word about her.

She chuckled. "Tell my mom I said hi."

I held my finger to my lips. The last thing I needed was for everyone in the office to find out I was going to therapy. But I'd made this promise to her that I'd go once, and I was a man of my word, even if I'd moped all morning about it.

"I'll be back." I leaned over her desk. "Tell fucking Craig

to stop volunteering to challenge you at ping-pong. He lost. It's over," I hissed. Yeah, my girl had returned from our trip and smoked his ass, and I loved watching every minute of it. The dude had spent his vacation time playing ping-pong so that he could beat her, just so he could ask her out. Now she was back at the top, and he needed to sit his ass down.

"Maybe you should mention this hostility you have about someone challenging me at ping-pong to my mother." She raised a brow.

I wrapped a hand around the back of her neck and kissed her hard before leaving.

Alana's office wasn't far from mine, but it was cold as hell outside, so I drove there. I hurried inside just as the snow started coming down again. That was one thing I hadn't fully gotten used to yet. The bone-chilling cold showed no sign of going away anytime soon.

I jogged inside and up the stairs and knocked on her door. She pulled it open and gave me a hug.

Alana Reynolds was that storybook kind of mother. She made Sunday dinners and got excited about buying her children thoughtful presents and genuinely loved each one of them. It was impossible to miss when you were at their house. Both she and Bradford were as good as it gets.

That was why I was surprised they'd warmed up to me.

I wasn't the easiest to love. It took me a while to warm up to people.

It usually took me a lifetime to trust.

Alana guided me to the couch across from her chair, and it was exactly how I'd seen this play out in movies. My brother had gone to therapy after Mom was gone, per my grandmother's insistence. But he never talked about it, just like I never talked about the nightmares. We both always shrugged it off and said we were fine.

"Is this normal that I'm coming to you when I'm dating

your daughter?" I asked, sitting forward on the couch and folding my hands together where they rested on my knees.

"Well, let me ask you this. If your girlfriend's mother wasn't a therapist, would you be going at all?"

I thought over the question. "No."

"I guess we have our answer, then. This is something that can help, and if this is the only way to get you here, I'd call it a win." She smiled, her blonde hair, the same color as Georgia's, rested on her shoulders. "It's certainly not abnormal to me. And everything we talk about will stay right here in this office, okay?"

I nodded. And we spent the next forty minutes dissecting my childhood, my relationship with my parents, and the horrible night that I found my mother. I never expected to go this deep so quickly, but here we were.

Diving into a big pile of traumatic horse shit.

"So, you were angry with your father before your mother's passing?" she asked, black-rimmed glasses resting on her nose and eyes filled with empathy.

"Fu—sorry. Yes."

"Maddox, I have five children. You are free to speak however you want to speak in here. There's no judgment. These are sensitive topics, so don't censor yourself on my account."

"Okay." I shrugged. "Fuck, yes. He'd been caught having affairs numerous times while she was sick. He wasn't sly. He was sloppy. And thoughtless. He hurt her terribly, and I fucking hate him for that."

"I can imagine. It was a betrayal to you and Wyle, too. And seeing your mother hurt is not easy on a child, especially while watching her battle a horrible disease." She paused and tapped her pen against her lips. "Was there ever talk of her entering a facility toward the end? It seems like a very traumatic thing for two teenage boys to be dealing with when your father wasn't present to support you."

I scrubbed a hand down my face. This was not my favorite topic. "She wasn't particularly keen on leaving our house, and with the resources we had, she was able to have the best care money could buy. But I also think my father played a role in that decision, from what I overheard once."

"What did you hear?" she asked.

"I heard them arguing a few months before she died when he'd graced us all with his presence and then visibly winced when he saw how much she'd deteriorated since he'd last seen her. They were arguing, and she said she didn't want us to see her like this any longer. I think she knew she was at the end, but she also wanted us with her at the same time, if that makes sense?"

"It does. She wanted every last minute with you. I can understand that. Yet her need to protect you had her discussing other options?"

"Yes. She mentioned going to a hospital, but my father didn't like that option because it would make things more public. She was very hidden away at our home, as was her illness. I think if people knew how bad it had gotten, they wouldn't have been too keen on seeing my father out there flaunting his affairs and attending events several days a week while his wife was at home fighting for her life."

"So, he hired the best nurses and had you and Wyle there with her until the end. It sounds like it was his way of giving her what she wanted, as long as it didn't involve himself being there."

"Correct." I cleared my throat. The lump forming there was making it difficult to talk. I'd never thought about it that way.

"Have you ever asked your father why he wasn't around?"

"We've argued about it many times. The bottom line is, he's selfish. He didn't want to be there to see her deteriorate.

Her illness was a massive inconvenience in his life. And once she got sick, he had no use for her."

She nodded. "Do you hold him responsible for her death?"

"In a way, yes. I believe he contributed to her suffering, at the very least,"

I said, moving to my feet because I was antsy. I walked toward the window and stared outside at the falling snow. Cars were driving slowly, and the grassy area next to her office was covered in fresh white snow.

"He also left you and Wyle to deal with it all. Do you resent him for that?"

I let out a long breath. "No. I'm grateful I was with her till the end."

"But a lot of that responsibility fell on your shoulders, right? You tried to shield Wyle the best you could, and you carried all of that weight. Not typical for a high school kid."

"We had good nurses. I still had my fair share of fun in high school. The illness took her fairly quickly, and things didn't get really bad until the very end. So, I was fine."

"But you were a child. And seeing your mother take her last breath was traumatic, am I right? You were the only one there at that moment."

"Sure." I turned around to face her, my hands shoved in my pockets.

"I think all of that trauma and all this anger toward your father is festering inside you, and that's the reason for the nightmares. But as you talk about it more and let go, you will be able to move forward. But you have to let go of some of this, Maddox."

"So, I should just forgive my father for what he did to her? And then we can all live a happy life?" My tone had more bite than I meant it to. But why did he just get a pass from everyone? After what he'd done, he didn't deserve that.

"That's not what I'm suggesting, Maddox." She raised a

brow, and I made my way back to the couch, sitting back down to face her.

"Okay, let's hear it."

Her lips turned up the slightest bit in the corners, and her eyes were full of empathy as she watched me. "I think we need to talk about your anger, and then put it in the right place. Does that make sense?"

I scrubbed a hand down my face. I was fucking exhausted from this conversation. I didn't like digging all this shit up. "Not really."

"Fair enough." She chuckled. "So, your mom's disease took her life, correct?"

"Yes." I was trying not to bark at her, but the questions were frustrating me.

"So, we can hate ALS for taking a beautiful woman's life far too early. It's fair to be angry about."

"Agreed."

"And we can be disappointed in your father for being a crappy husband and a crappy father when all three of you needed him most."

I narrowed my gaze. "It's what he did to my mother that angers me. I don't care about that man."

"Is that true, Maddox? Would you still be attending his reception and going to family events if you didn't care about him at all?"

"I don't have a choice. He's family."

"You always have a choice." She held her hand up when I opened my mouth to spew something angry. "What I'm saying is, your father let you down. He let your mother down. He let your brother down. But he isn't responsible for your mother's death. He wasn't there for her, or for you, but he isn't the reason that she's not here. And I think you're mixing up those feelings and holding him responsible for her death. But the truth is that even if he had been a decent husband and a good man, she still wouldn't be here today. Isn't that right?"

I leaned back against the couch, letting my head tip so I was looking up at the ceiling. "That's true. But it didn't help her when she was suffering."

"Agreed. But you said that your mother never said a bad word about him, right? She loved him even despite his betrayal."

"Because she was a good fucking human," I hissed. "And he's not."

"And that stinks, because you had a parent who always put you first, and she's not here. And I think you're angry at him for not only the way he treated your mother, but for the way he's treated you and Wyle. I mean, you stayed. You were there with her. Who took care of you?"

"It's fine. I survived, didn't I?" My voice was barely recognizable as it was laced with pain and anger and grief.

"You did. But you were young, and you shouldn't have had all that responsibility on your shoulders. So, you have every right to be angry with your father for not showing up for you and your brother. For betraying your mother. For not being the father that you needed. Those are all fair emotions, and you can decide what to do with them. But I think a little part of you doesn't want to completely write him off."

"I can't. I'm forced to see him at family events."

"Really? What would happen if you didn't attend?" she asked, and I pinched the bridge of my nose.

"It would disappoint my grandparents. They've been good to me, to my brother, to my mother. So I go for them."

"Is there any part of you that wants a relationship with him?"

"No," I growled, looking away before finishing the statement. "I mean, now I'm even more tied to him because he's going to have a baby. I can't turn my back on my sister or brother."

"You are allowed to do whatever makes you happy, Maddox. And what I've seen of you and Georgia, I think you're both very happy together."

"Absolutely," I said. "Without question, she's the best thing that's happened to me."

"You said she's your first serious relationship. The first woman you've loved since your mother's passing, right?"

"She is."

"I think that's a sign that you're ready to move on. To let go of some of this sadness. You deserve that. And whether or not you continue a relationship with your father is up to you. But you need to know that you're also allowed to stop hating him. That would not be a sign of you being disloyal to your mother. So I want you to think about what you really want moving forward. Don't worry about your grandparents. They are going to love your father and love you regardless of what either of you do. I think they've proven that by being so forgiving of his actions." She pushed to her feet and reached for my hand, waiting for me to look up at her. "You're allowed to be happy, Maddox. Your mother would want that for you."

Fuck me.

This shit was hitting every fucking nerve in my body.

I nodded, the lump so thick in my throat it was difficult to swallow, let alone speak.

So, I didn't.

I pushed to my feet, and I just wrapped my arms around her and hugged her.

And for today, this was enough.

I wanted to stop thinking about it and get home to my girl.

She was all I needed.

And that was what made me happy.

twenty-nine

. . .

Georgia

MY LEGS WERE GENTLY PUSHED APART, and I squirmed against the sweetest sensation between my thighs. My eyes blinked a couple times, and I startled when I realized I wasn't dreaming. I glanced down to see a bare-chested Maddox, his eyes hooded as he looked up at me, and he licked his lips as I was sprawled in the middle of his bed.

"Happy Birthday, and Happy Valentine's Day, Tink."

Well, this was definitely one for the books, because no one had ever woken me up on my birthday quite like this. And I was here for it.

"Thank you," I said, my voice sleepy and laced with need as my fingers tangled in his hair.

"I want to start your day off right." He dropped back down, his tongue flicking and teasing my most sensitive area before his mouth covered my clit. My head fell back, and I moaned, the sensation so overpowering. I squirmed and writhed, and he took me right to the edge over and over before pulling back. His finger slipped inside, moving slowly at first before sliding a second finger in as his tongue continued working its magic. And this time… he didn't pull back.

My entire body started to shake, and I tugged harder on his hair as stars exploded behind my eyes. I nearly arched off the bed, but he held me there, his hand resting over my lower stomach, as I exploded.

"Maddox!" I shouted, tremors rocking through me.

So powerful.

So strong.

So epically delicious.

Look at me, being all poetic. That was what this man did to me. And he stayed right there, letting me ride out every last bit of pleasure.

Once my body stopped quaking and my breathing settled, he slid up the bed beside me, one hand on my cheek and the other on my waist.

"Happy Valentine's Day, birthday girl." He kissed my forehead and then my nose and my cheeks before stopping on my lips. I never would have guessed this man was such a romantic, but he was. He'd been acting awfully cocky since my brothers had told him when my birthday was. I hadn't intentionally kept it a secret. It just hadn't come up yet. Our relationship was a whirlwind in some ways. And in other ways, it felt like I'd known this man forever.

"Happy Valentine's Day. I have a present for you."

"Today is all about you."

"No. It's also about us." He wouldn't tell me where we were going tonight, but he'd been very distracted the last few days, so I knew he was up to something.

He pressed up against me, and his erection poked me in the lower belly, which made me laugh.

"How about I start out by returning the favor?" I slipped my hand inside the waistband of his joggers and was pleased that there were no briefs to work through, as my fingers wrapped around his thick, hard erection.

"I'd rather be inside you, baby," he said as I stroked him a few times.

"I told you it's been thirty days since I got on the pill, and I've never been with anyone without protection. You said that you haven't either, so what if we don't use a condom?" I whispered because I was dying to feel him with nothing between us.

His hand found my cheek, and he pushed my hair away from my face. "You want my bare cock inside you, don't you?"

I could feel my cheeks heat. The man had a filthy mouth, and I was embarrassed to admit that I loved it. I bit down on my bottom lip. "I do."

"I do, too. There is no better gift that you could give me."

I was already naked, as I'd grown accustomed to sleeping this way now. He pushed to his feet and peeled off his joggers within seconds, which made me laugh, before he dove onto the bed, shoving my legs apart as he settled between my thighs.

"Someone's eager this morning," I said.

He smiled this wide grin, with perfect white teeth and sexy scruff peppered around his jaw. "That's because I have so many surprises for you today."

My chest squeezed at his words.

"I didn't know you were so into surprises."

His eyes softened. "I never have been. Never cared about Valentine's Day. Never thought birthdays were that big of a deal. But celebrating the day that you came into the world—" He paused and looked away for a moment before his eyes returned to mine. "It's my new favorite day of the year, Tink."

My breath lodged in my throat.

The love that I felt for this man was something I never knew was possible. It was everything. I never knew my heart could completely belong to another person, but it did.

He teased my entrance with the tip of his erection before he moved forward, slowly, his dark eyes locked with mine as he filled me. Inch by glorious inch.

The feel of him bare was indescribable.

His hands found mine and intertwined our fingers, holding them just above my head.

My eyes squeezed shut, and I gasped once he was all the way in.

"Eyes on me, baby." His voice was strained yet commanding.

My gaze snapped open and locked with his.

It was more intense as we watched one another and found our rhythm. His large hands still covered mine, and something shifted between us. A love so strong that I didn't think either one of us saw this coming.

"I fucking love you," he said. "You know that, right?"

"Yes, of course. I love you so much," I whispered.

Sensation built, and our pace quickened. He released one of my hands so he could slide his fingers between our bodies, knowing exactly where to touch me.

Exactly what I needed.

My back arched, and I groaned.

And I exploded again. My body was exhausted and exhilarated all at the same time.

He pumped into me once more.

Twice.

And then he growled my name as he followed me into oblivion.

Our breaths were labored, and once we both calmed down, he pulled out of me and went to the bathroom. He returned with a towel and pressed it between my legs. It was warm and soothing, and he took his time cleaning me up.

The doorbell rang, and I startled. "Who's here?"

"It's your first present. Get dressed and meet me out there." He tugged his joggers on before pulling his Harvard hoodie over his head, glancing over to wink at me as he slipped out of the room.

I hurried to my feet and got dressed as quickly as I could.

As I pulled my hair into a bun, I glanced down at my phone to see multiple texts in the sibling group chat.

BRINKLEY

Happy Birthday to my favorite sister! I hope you and Bossman are doing all sorts of naughty things to kick off your special day. And Happy Valentine's Day to everyone else.

CAGE

Why in the motherfucking hell would you put that in a group text? May you never do naughty things with anyone, Georgie. But Happy Birthday. I'm endlessly proud of you and love you. Happy Valentine's Day to the rest of you romantic saps.

FINN

I agree with Cage on this one. I'm going to ignore that part of the message, Brinks. Maybe you two can share that kind of shit on a separate thread. Happy Birthday, Georgie.

HUGH

Do whatever makes you happy today, Georgie girl. I love you, and I'm wishing you a kickass year. You deserve all the good in life.

CAGE

Wow. That was deep.

BRINKLEY

Can we please talk about how sappy Hugh is now that he's in love? Cage, you're an endless grump. Finn, stop being Cage's bitch.

Hey, guys! Thank you for the birthday wishes. I can't believe I'm another year older. I'll be thirty before I know it.

FINN

You're twenty-three...

But someday, right? LOL. I'm having a great day so far, but I won't even tell you all the naughty things I've done already.

CAGE

Please don't. <puking emoji>

FINN

Some things are better left unsaid. <covering eyes emoji>

HUGH

You do you, Georgie girl. <shrugging emoji> <heart eyes emoji>

BRINKLEY

Go girl, go. <thumbs-up emoji>

Happy Valentine's Day. I love you. <blowing kisses emoji>

I tucked my phone into my back pocket and hurried out of the bathroom.

When I padded down the long hallway and out to the great room, I found Maddox in the kitchen with Sal Roberts, a friend of my father's.

"Hi, Sal," I said, and it came out as more of a question.

He laughed. "Hey, Georgia. Happy Birthday."

I moved next to Maddox, who was standing on one side of the kitchen island, while the older man stood on the other side. Sal had a large white roll of paper that he'd just pulled from the kitchen counter.

"Thank you. What's going on here?"

"I'll be out back taking some measurements. I'll let

Maddox fill you in." He smirked and made his way out the door.

A large black box sat on the island with a white bow on it. I reached for my collarbone and rubbed my fingers over my star necklace. This gift would be really hard to top.

"Happy Birthday, baby," he said, pushing the box toward me.

I untied the ribbon and pulled off the lid, and found four pickleball racquets and several sets of balls inside. My head tipped back as laughter escaped. Damn. He really did pay attention.

"You got me pickleball gear!" I squealed. "You really do love me."

He tugged me into his arms. "I mean, you're the county champ, right?"

"Damn straight, Bossman. Thank you. So, what's Sal doing here?"

"Hugh gave me his number, and we've already met a few times before today, but he needed to get a few more measurements before they break ground next week."

"Measurements for what?"

"I'm having a pickleball court put in the backyard for you. So, you can play whenever you want now." What in the absolute hell had I done to deserve this man?

He never tried to change me. He loved me just the way I was.

I lunged into his arms as he lifted me off the floor, and my legs wrapped around his waist.

"I don't know what I did to deserve you, but I feel like the luckiest girl in the world."

"I'm the lucky one, Tink." He kissed me. "And you'll get your Valentine's gift tonight."

"I already have everything I want right here."

And that was the truth.

Maddox and I had picked up takeout from Reynolds', and he refused to tell me where he was taking me.

We talked and drove up the mountain a bit, and I quickly figured out what he was up to.

"Are you taking me to the pond?" I asked with a chuckle.

It was as if someone had literally climbed inside my head and shared every single thing that I would want and put it all into one day.

He pulled down the dirt road, which made it clear that he'd been here before. I saw two trucks coming from the opposite direction, which was surprising because there was never traffic up here.

"I don't know how all these people know about the pond. It's pretty private. Only the locals know about this place, and no one comes up here at night," I said, watching as they both passed us on the narrow road.

He just smiled and kept driving. When we came around the corner, my mouth fell open. There were twinkle lights in the trees that surrounded the pond. It had always been my favorite place to sneak away to.

The place I'd first learned to skate.

Sometimes I'd drive here when I was in high school, park my car, and just bundle up and listen to music out here and daydream.

It was always so clear at night, and the stars danced in the distance when I looked out the window.

There was a large blanket and candles placed in a line down the dirt path toward the frozen pond.

"It's so beautiful," I whispered.

"That's what those guys were setting up for us." He winked.

"Is it a fire hazard?"

He barked out a laugh. "The candles are on batteries, Tink.

Hugh gave me some good ideas for how to light the place up at night."

"I still need to give you your gift, but now I feel like a crappy girlfriend because I didn't transform your favorite spot and turn it into a winter wonderland." I reached over the seat to grab the package when we came to a stop a few feet from where our blanket was.

"Don't be ridiculous. You gave me my gift this morning." He waggled his brows when he turned to face me.

I pressed the button on the light above us and handed him his gift. My stomach fluttered with nerves because I'd wanted it to be special.

He pulled off the first package and unwrapped it before flipping through the pages of the small rectangular book. "A coupon book, huh?"

I climbed over the seat, moving onto his lap, as he held up the last two gifts so I could settle on his lap. I could never get close enough to this man. He wrapped his arms around me as he read each one to himself, laughing as he turned each page.

"Good for one life-changing blow job, huh?" He nipped at my ear.

"Of course, that's the one you focus on. Not the day of teaching you how to play pickleball or reading a romance book to you aloud."

"I love it," he said, and he turned my face so he could kiss me. "Best gift I've ever received."

"You're too easy." I chuckled and pushed the other package in front of him. He opened the white box with the red bow wrapped around it and pulled out the T-shirt that read: *My girlfriend won the county pickleball championship, and all I got was this stupid T-shirt.*

His head fell back in hysterical laughter.

Maddox Lancaster's laugh was music to my ears.

"I love it, baby." He kissed my cheek, and I took the T-shirt and the coupon book and placed them in the back seat, pushing the final package toward him.

He tore off the red-and-white polka-dot paper and then opened the lid to the box. I heard the inhale of his breath as he studied the photos in the large frame with two cutouts.

There was one picture of him and Wyle and their mom sitting on the back porch beneath the stars. The other picture was of me and Maddox, curled up on the outdoor couch in his backyard, with the stars twinkling above us.

"Georgia," he whispered. "Where did you get this?"

"I asked Wyle if he had a good photo of the three of you, and he asked your grandmother. She said she had boxes of photos from your mom. So, that night, when you thought I was doing a girls' night with Brinkley and Lila, I had actually gone out to the city and had dinner with your grandparents, and we went through a bunch of boxes of photos. When I saw this one, I knew it was what I was looking for."

His eyes were wet with emotion, and I turned to face him so I was straddling him as his hands ran through my hair, tucking it behind my ear.

"That's exactly how I felt when I found you." He pulled me close and kissed me. "Thank you."

"I mean, it's not a pickleball court or a transformed ice-skating pond." I smiled. "But I'm glad you like it. And I want you to know that I love everything you did, but if you did nothing, I'd be okay with that, too. Because the best gift I've ever received is you."

"Right back at you, baby. Now, let's get you out there so you can show me all your moves. I've got one more gift for you in the trunk. Let's go."

"There's nothing left to give me," I said, climbing off his lap when he pushed the door open. I started jogging down toward the ice.

"I've got skates for you!" he shouted after me, but I didn't stop running.

I paused at the blanket that had flowers and a bakery box there. And when I turned around, I saw him walking my way, wearing his black ski coat and carrying our dinner and another box with a bow on it.

"I'll give you a little preview without skates. And then I'll put them on for the big finale. I can twirl barefoot if I want to," I said over my laughter, as I moved onto the pond that looked like glass with the moon shining down on it. I held my hands out to the sides and spun around.

He set the food down on the blanket and shook his head. "All right, then. Let me see it."

I moved to the middle of the ice and spun around as he watched me and held up his phone to take a picture.

"Okay, one more twirl, then we'll eat." I moved farther onto the ice and heard a crunching noise beneath my feet. My stomach twisted, knowing something was wrong, just as the ice beneath me opened up—and swallowed me whole.

thirty

. . .

Maddox

THERE ARE moments in your life that you know are going to be life-changing the minute they happen.

I'd experienced it before.

I dropped the bag of food, dropped my phone, and started sprinting before I could truly process what was happening.

"Georgia!" A voice I didn't recognize left my throat as I moved quickly toward the pond.

She'd been twirling.

Laughing.

Smiling.

My angel. My love.

And then she literally disappeared beneath the ice.

There was no warning.

Like she'd stepped into a hole and fallen right inside it. I'd heard her gasp. And then she was gone.

Terror moved through every bone in my body, but I knew I had a short time to get to her, so I reacted.

I made it to the edge and tugged off my coat, knowing I would need it to be dry when I pulled her out. I dropped down on my stomach and slid as fast as I could toward the center of the pond. I knew stepping on the ice would be too risky.

I needed to get to the hole and get her out.

"Georgia!" I screamed as I got closer. Something beneath me pounded on the ice and I realized it was her trying to get out.

I screamed her name again as the hole was only inches from my reach.

I kept my lower body on the ice and shoved my head down inside the freezing cold water.

And that was when I saw the tint of red flowing around her as she floated in front of me in her white coat.

I silently begged her to give me her hand, but she was lifeless, and her body swayed just out of my reach. I pushed further into the abyss and grasped her coat as the red water darkened, and I realized it was blood. I tugged as hard as I could, sliding my body back as I pulled her head through the hole, and blood moved from the top of her head and down her face.

I pushed to my knees and pulled her out as a guttural sound left my lips. My hands shook as I touched her everywhere, covering her cheeks and shaking her.

"Baby, please," I begged. I pulled her as far as I could from the center of the ice so we wouldn't risk falling through.

Fuck.

The word repeated over and over in my head.

Once we were close to the edge, I pressed my ear to her mouth, and she wasn't breathing. Her lips were blue. I turned her on her side and hit her on the back as water spewed from her mouth, and then I leaned down to listen for a breath.

Nothing.

Fucking nothing.

I unzipped her jacket, placing one hand over the other, and pumped my hands into her chest as I shouted and wailed words that weren't coherent.

"Twenty-nine, thirty," I said. "Breathe, baby."

I tipped her head back, plugged her nose, and breathed. I saw her chest rise, and I leaned back down and gave her another breath.

She coughed and made a wheezing sound, and I placed my ear against her mouth again, and thanked God that she was breathing, but she still lay there completely lifeless.

A sob escaped, and I swiped at my face, unsure if they were tears or water.

Everything moved in slow motion, and I knew I needed to act fast.

I picked her up and tossed her over my shoulder, grabbing my coat as I sprinted up toward the blanket. I reached for my phone and the edge of the flannel blanket, yanking it hard as everything flew into the air around it, and I raced toward the car. I opened the door and started stripping her clothes off of her as I dialed 911 on speakerphone. I wrapped her in the blanket and then put my coat around her.

"I need help. My girlfriend fell through the ice. She's unconscious." My voice didn't sound like my own. It was shrill and panicked, and I was on the verge of losing it.

The operator shouted all sorts of orders at me, and when I realized there was no way for anyone to get to us quicker than I could get her to the hospital, I moved behind the wheel, with Georgia in my arms, and raced down the mountain.

"I'm on my way to the hospital." I ended the call and demanded Siri dial Hugh Reynolds.

"My man. How did it go?"

A strained sob left my throat again as I raced down the road.

"Maddox." Hugh's voice was laced with panic.

"She fell through the fucking ice!" I shouted, finding my voice now. "I don't have time to get her to the city. I'm going to the closest hospital."

"The hospital is a few blocks from Reynolds'. You're close. Is she breathing?"

I couldn't speak again as I looked down at her as she lay lifeless on my lap. "Breathe, baby!"

I ended the call and swiped at my eyes. My vision blurred as I approached a red light. I laid on the horn and flew right through it, knowing the hospital was not far. I pushed the gas pedal down and sped into the hospital parking lot, driving over a curb to get there faster. When I pulled in front of the emergency room, I put the car in park just as a group of people came flying out the door, and I lifted Georgia in my arms, hurrying out of the car. I didn't know how they knew we were coming, but I figured Hugh must have made a call. Blood poured from her head down her face, and three men reached to take her from me.

I didn't let go at first, and I choked on a sob.

"Sir, we need to see what's going on. Please, let us take her."

I held on to her hand when they took her from me, and I followed them over to the gurney where they laid her down.

Her hand slipped from mine as they hurried inside, and I followed them, quickly answering their questions as fast as I could, but everything was happening so fast.

"How long do you think she was under the water?" one of the men asked me, as another group of people hurried in our direction to help when we moved through the waiting room.

"Maybe two minutes?" I shook my head. "I don't fucking know. She wasn't breathing at first. But she coughed up a lot of water. I did CPR, and she started breathing."

They moved her toward the double doors, and the guy talking stopped me. "You need to wait here. We will do everything we can and be out as quickly as possible. Where did the head injury come from?"

"I don't fucking know. I think she hit her head when she

fell in or maybe she hit it beneath the ice when she was trying to get out," I said, shaking my head with disbelief.

"Okay. Thank you. We'll be out as quickly as we can."

I stood there, staring at the double doors where they'd taken her, and rage suddenly took over. No fucking way was I standing out here.

She needed me.

I pushed through the doors, and two guys moved toward me and asked me to leave, and I swung.

"I'm fucking staying with her!" I wailed, just as two arms came around me from behind and squeezed tight.

"I've got him. He's just upset." It was Hugh's voice.

"We need you both out of here. We can't help her if we're fighting you."

I threw my hands in the air in surrender, and Hugh walked backward through the doors as he kept hold of me. Once we were out in the hallway, he turned me around to face him and wrapped his arms around me.

"You're okay. Breathe. Tell me what happened." His voice was eerily calm.

I stepped back, looking down to see my hands covered in blood. My clothes were covered in blood and soaked. "I don't know. She ran down to the ice while I was setting the food down. And we were talking. We were fucking talking. And then she just fell through the ice. There was no warning. She was just gone."

I leaned against the wall. I couldn't catch my breath.

I couldn't fucking live in a world that Georgia Reynolds wasn't in.

Not now that I'd experienced life with her in it.

"Jesus. You've got blood all over you." He reached for my hands and took his coat off and put it around my shoulders. "Where is the blood coming from?"

"It was coming from her head," I said, staring down at my bloody hands. "She was unconscious. She never spoke."

"Was she breathing?" Hugh's voice cracked, and my eyes snapped up, and I saw the panic.

"Not at first. I did CPR, and she started breathing. But she wasn't conscious. I don't know what the fuck happened. I'm so fucking sorry. I let her go out on that ice. I fucking let her go out on the ice!" I shouted and turned and punched the wall.

Hugh grabbed me again, just as Cage and Finn came running around the corner. The next hour was filled with all of Georgia's family members showing up. There were tears and questions, and they hugged me, repeating over and over that it wasn't my fault. Lila brought me dry clothes, and Cage and Finn dragged me over to the bathroom and forced me to go in the stall and change. When I came out, I washed the blood from my hands and then fell against the wall beside the sink, sliding down to the floor and letting myself break down. They moved on each side of me, sitting on the floor as they cried right along with me.

When Brinkley arrived, she paced for the longest time and then went and got a hot tea and insisted I drink it while she paced some more.

The next few hours were brutal. We were told that Georgia had suffered a traumatic brain injury when she'd fallen through the ice and most likely hit her head hard enough to split it open. She was in a coma, and they had no idea how long it would be until she woke up.

I called my grandfather, who had a friend that was a prominent neurosurgeon in San Francisco, and he flew on our helicopter to give a second opinion. No one thought she was in a state to be moved, so we'd bring doctors here and do whatever it took to make sure she got the best care.

We were able to sit in her room in the ICU, and the Reynoldses had all agreed to take shifts, as the hospital didn't want more than two people in her room at a time.

I wasn't big on taking shifts.

I was here, and I wasn't leaving.

When the sun came up in the morning, I blinked a few times, my hand covering hers and my head resting beside her waist on the bed. I'd slept in the chair on one side of her bed, with Alana on the other.

"Good morning, Tink," I whispered. "Can you hear me, baby?"

Nothing.

She looked peaceful, not a sign of distress other than the gash that they'd stitched up at the top of her forehead.

Her hair was wild and wavy from being submerged in freezing cold water.

I squeezed my eyes closed as I remembered how she looked when I'd pulled her out. Her lips were blue, her body lifeless.

Just like my mother had been.

Was I fucking cursed?

The two most important women in my life had put their lives in my hands.

I'd failed the first time.

We had no idea if Tink had suffered a loss of oxygen to the brain. Dr. Lexington, my grandfather's doctor friend, had agreed with Dr. Pruitt here in Cottonwood Cove.

Time would tell.

Fucking endless years of schooling, and that was the diagnosis?

Time would fucking tell?

Time had never been much of a friend to me.

It had taken my mom too soon.

I rubbed my thumb over the back of her limp hand and glanced over to see her mother sleeping in the other chair.

"I didn't get to give you your other gift. It wasn't just the skates in that box, Georgia. There was a key to the house," I said, my voice cracking on the last word. "*Our* house, Tink. The one with the pickleball court. I promise I'll play as much as you want me to if you wake up. If you let me know that you're in there."

I gave her hand a slight squeeze. Nothing.

My head fell forward and rested on our joined hands.

"Please, baby. I need you."

"Hey," Alana said, and I raised my head to look at her. "How is she?"

"The same."

We both knew that the longer she stayed in this state, the worse it would be.

"Maddox." She stood and stroked her daughter's hair away from her face. "You saved her life."

My eyes widened. "After I nearly killed her?"

"The ice breaking was not your fault. The boys told you to take her there. I would have told you to take her there. It's her favorite place. And you responded quickly. I don't even know how you pulled her out of there so fast and performed CPR and got her to the hospital, all within minutes. That is why she's here and still breathing."

"I should have gone out on the ice and checked it first."

"Why would anyone think to do that? And honestly, if you had gone out there first and fallen in, she would have gone after you just like you did for her. But she wouldn't have had the strength to pull you out, and then you'd both be gone." Her words broke on a sob. "My daughter is very strong, Maddox. She's a fighter. Always has been."

Dr. Pruitt walked in and talked to us a little more about the fact that he knew nothing about her condition or her future.

I hated him for it.

I hated everyone right now.

A nurse came in to change her IV, and I saw a bruise on Georgia's arm, and I lost my shit.

"Does anyone know what the fuck they're doing? You can't just keep poking her!" I raged, just as Bradford and

Hugh arrived. Alana kissed my cheek and went home to shower as her father and brother said that they would take turns coming in so that I didn't have to leave.

Because I wasn't fucking leaving.

Hugh pulled me out into the hallway, handed me a coffee, and told me to settle the fuck down.

"Punching walls and screaming at everyone is not going to make her wake up faster, brother." He raised a brow as I sipped the black coffee.

"How do you know? Maybe she'll wake up and tell me to shut the fuck up," I said dryly.

Hugh barked out a laugh, but it wasn't nearly as loud as it usually was, and I didn't miss the dark circles beneath his eyes.

The Reynoldses were all suffering, just like me. I was just the one being a total dickhead because that was how I usually dealt with things.

"You might be right. There's nothing Georgie loves more than calling people out if they aren't behaving." He scrubbed a hand down his face.

"Is it bad that I don't want to give up my spot in the room? I know you're all taking shifts, but I don't want to leave, Hugh."

"Nah, Maddox. This is where you need to be, and we all respect that. Everyone's out in the waiting room. Lila went to get bagels and muffins. The family will be taking over this hospital until she wakes up. And we can take turns coming in and out of the room. You stay right there with your girl. She'll want to see you first when she wakes up."

I nodded. "Thank you. And I'll try not to scream at anyone for the next hour or so."

He nodded and forced a smile. But it wasn't genuine, because none of us could smile right now. I turned to walk back into the room, and he clapped his hand on my shoulder. "I'm sorry I told you to take her there. I'm so fucking sorry."

Jesus. He was blaming himself, too?

I turned around and wrapped my arms around him. "Don't do that."

"It was my idea."

I pulled back. "If you would have seen her face when we pulled up. Hell, I probably could have gotten her to agree to marry me in that moment, because she was so fucking happy we were there."

"Yeah. She loves that fucking place. Dad made some calls, and we're trying to figure out how the fucking ice cracked in these temperatures. We've been skating on that ice for years."

I shrugged just as Bradford called me to come back in.

I hurried inside, hoping something had happened, but it was just more updates about her heart rate being slow now.

I took back residence in my chair, reached for her hand, and promised her I would be there when she woke up.

But the sunlight that filled the room during the day would darken in the evening. Another night without my girl.

Another night where we couldn't sit beneath the stars.

Brinkley and Finn had taken shifts coming in with me during the late hours.

Cage had come for several hours and sat with me.

Lila and Hugh were there the following morning, taking turns in the chair on the other side of her bed.

The days and the nights blurred.

Alana had urged me to go home and sleep and take a shower. But I wasn't leaving until I knew she was okay.

Period. End of story.

The room had filled with flowers from everyone in town.

The largest arrangement that arrived was from my father, who'd called me multiple times a day to check on her.

Who the fuck would have guessed that Georgia Reynolds would be the reason I would take calls from my father?

But he was genuinely concerned about her because she'd been nothing but kind to him.

Wyle called constantly, as did my grandparents.

Everyone loved her.

I'd put them in touch with Alana, who was much better at updating people, because I didn't want to talk to anyone but the one person I couldn't talk to.

"I'm going to go down to the cafeteria and get you a sandwich. You haven't eaten anything today," Alana said when the room darkened and we were getting ready for our third night of sleeping in a chair. She'd left during the day and brought food for everyone at the hospital, but I had no appetite.

I nodded, not because I wanted food, but because I could use a minute alone. I didn't want to break down in front of Georgia's mother. Hell, she'd given birth to my girl, and I knew she was hurting. But holding it in was killing me.

I wrapped both hands around my girl's dainty hand, and I let the tears fall.

"Baby, I need you to wake up. I never thought I would love anyone the way that I love you. And now that you've awakened that, I don't know what to do with it." I sniffed and tried to stop the tears from falling. "I can't be in a world that you aren't in. So please, please, Tink. Don't leave me."

The lump lodged in my throat made it difficult to breathe. I fell forward, my head resting on her hip. Her hand wrapped in mine.

And that was when I felt it.

Her finger moved along the back of my hand. Soothing and healing and bringing me back to life.

My head sprung up to look at her. Her eyes were blinking. Her hand squeezing mine back.

I glanced at the outdated clock hanging on the wall.

Forty-eight hours and twenty-nine minutes of pure hell.

Georgia's dark gaze locked with mine.

She was awake.

thirty-one

. . .

Georgia

EVERYONE BUSTLED around me as I tried to process all that was happening.

Dr. Pruitt, my parents, my siblings—everyone explaining the events of the last two days.

The only one not speaking was my boyfriend, who'd sat silently in the chair as people came in and out of the room.

I'd heard him when I was sleeping, or as they liked to call it, when I was in a coma.

I'd heard them all talking around me.

But Maddox was the one I'd heard endlessly. I had flashes of the car ride to the hospital with him, sobbing as he held me in his lap. I couldn't recall the specific words, but I felt the impact. The pain. The desperation in his voice.

And here in the hospital, I heard the words.

How badly he needed me.

But I wasn't leaving Maddox. It would take a lot more than an ice bath and a concussion to pull me away from this man. I was just resting. Just tired.

But I knew it was time to wake up because his sadness rocked me.

I hated that he was hurting.

He'd cried when my eyes had opened. Kissed every inch of my face and ran out to get the doctor, and then my mother came running in shortly after.

And from that moment on, there'd been too many people in the room. We hadn't been alone. But every time I looked over at him, he was watching me.

Silently observing.

He looked exhausted.

Dark circles that were a mix of black and purple settled beneath his eyes. His scruff was overgrown, and he was wearing Hugh's hoodie, along with a pair of joggers.

My mother told me that Maddox had never left the hospital. Not to get something to eat. Not to go home and sleep or change clothes or take a shower.

He'd refused to leave me.

But he'd barely spoken to me, as all my siblings, my niece, and my parents crowded the room the morning after I'd woken up.

"Hey, I'm going to let you be with your family, okay? I'm going to head out." Maddox kissed my forehead, and when he pulled back and my gaze locked with his, I knew something was off.

He looked… sad and distant and lost.

Maybe it was exhaustion, I wasn't sure.

"Yeah. Of course. I'm fine. Thanks for—" My eyes welled, and I looked away. They'd all told me what happened numerous times, and I had flashes of memories, but I knew that Maddox had saved my life. "Pulling me out, and breathing for me, and staying with me."

There wasn't enough that I could say to thank him. My words were jumbled, and even though I'd slept for two days, I was exhausted.

He put his finger to my lips. "You are the one who saved yourself, Tink. You nearly burst through that ice. You're stronger than you think. Get some rest."

His hand slipped from mine, and I missed him the minute he backed away from me.

For whatever reason, it felt like goodbye.

I'd fought to come back to him, and now he seemed to be the one pulling away.

CAGE

How does it feel to be home? Do you need anything? Are you okay to be by yourself?

BRINKLEY

She's been home for five minutes. Perhaps you could wait a little bit before you start firing off the questions.

FINN

Mom said that you didn't want her to stay with you tonight. You sure you're okay to be by yourself?

HUGH

Lila and I could bring you dinner tonight?

I'm good, guys. I haven't been alone in days. I just want to have a little quiet time, take a bath, and get in bed early.

The elephant in the room was the fact that my boyfriend had left the hospital three days ago, and I hadn't heard from him since. I'd called and texted, but he hadn't responded. And they were all afraid to ask about it because no one wanted to upset me. But everyone had clearly noticed his absence.

No one more than me.

And it hurt like hell.

BRINKLEY

You sure you don't want to sleep at Mom and Dad's house tonight?

HUGH

You also have a room at my house. You don't need to be alone.

I know you're all worried because Maddox has disappeared on me. But I'm a grown-up. I don't need to sleep at Mom and Dad's or at Hugh's house. I do know how to be alone. I'm fine here.

HUGH

He's processing, Georgie. It was a lot. He blames himself for the accident. The dude was an absolute mess.

CAGE

No question that he loves you. Just give him time. He'll come around.

FINN

It was scary. We thought we'd lost you, Georgie. Everyone deals with things differently.

BRINKLEY

Yeah. I don't give fucking grace to anyone that hurts my sister. So, if he doesn't get his act together quickly, he can suck it. There, I said it.

FINN

There are times I feel like Brinks would be better suited to be a mob boss than a sports reporter.

HUGH

Yes. She's totally giving off gangster vibes at the moment. You terrify me sometimes, Brinks.

CAGE

Normally, I'd agree with you, Brinks. But I saw the man. I saw the torment and the hurt. He gave her fucking CPR and brought her back to life. I think he gets a pass while he figures his shit out.

BRINKLEY

Touché. I suppose he does deserve credit for pulling you out of the freezing cold water, breathing life back into you, and hauling ass down to the hospital. Even mafia bosses can give passes sometimes.

You do realize I'm on this thread, right? I know what he did, and I'm grateful. I'm not mad at Maddox for running. He's scared, and I get it. I just hope he finds his way back to me.

FINN

Should you go find him?

Nope. He knows how I feel. I'm not a mystery in any way, shape, or form. I've been honest with him. So, he'll have to come back on his own, otherwise this will keep happening every time he gets scared.

HUGH

Fuck. That was deep, girl.

CAGE

You amaze me, Georgie. I don't give you enough credit for how much you've grown up. I'm proud of you.

FINN

Did someone steal Cage's phone?

CAGE

<middle finger emoji>

BRINKLEY

Fine. We let the bastard live. For now. But he best figure out his shit quickly.

HUGH

Or what? Horse head in the bed?

CAGE

Can we not talk about dead animals, please? I took a few days off work to be at the hospital, and Mrs. Remington has been blowing up my phone with texts letting me know that Mr. Wigglestein was still single. Guess the fuck what? I'm still single. The pug is no different from any other dude out there trying to survive.

FINN

The fact that you put yourself in the same league as the pug says a lot. You choose to be single, brother. There is a slew of women who wouldn't mind being Mrs. Doctor Reynolds.

BRINKLEY

Wait. If you marry a doctor, you don't get to use the title of doctor in your salutation, do you?

HUGH

No fucking way. If you marry a football player, you don't get to call yourself a quarterback.

CAGE

What the fuck are you people talking about? Are you drunk?

FINN

I'm three sheets to drunkville. It was a joke. Duh. You people have no sense of humor.

HUGH

Did you just say, duh? That word is so over. Hell, it hasn't been used in your lifetime.

BRINKLEY

Let's reel it back in. You still there, Georgie?

Yes. I'm enjoying the riveting conversation. Getting in the tub. Love you, guys.

CAGE

Text when you get out, please. You did have a serious concussion, and I know that you would like to have us all call the coma a "long nap", but the truth is, you were in a coma.

FINN

Wow. You really are a doctor. Impressive advice, Dr. Reynolds.

HUGH

Well, even if it was a long nap, you should still let us know when you're out of the tub. You did hit your head hard. I don't need to be a doctor to know that's dangerous.

BRINKLEY

I'm at your front door, Georgie. Open up. I'm sleeping over.

FINN

Well, that's another way to go about it. She said she wanted to be alone, so why not go right over there and insist she let you in? <laughing face emoji>

BRINKLEY

<middle finger emoji>

I padded to the door and pulled it open to see my sister holding a bag from Cottonwood Café.

"I got you the mac and cheese. I know it's your favorite." She walked in and dropped the bag onto the counter before wrapping her arms around me.

The tears started to fall. And for the first time since my accident, I let myself fall apart. I cried for what happened and the trauma that it put everyone through. I cried for the fact that my favorite place was now tainted by this horrible accident. But mostly, I cried because the man that I loved was hurting, and I couldn't help him.

"You're okay, Georgie," Brinkley said, and there was a crack in her voice when she said my name.

I pulled back and swiped at my face. "Wow. You were willing to deal with Mrs. Runither just to get me my favorite pasta?"

"It's the duty of being a big sister. But she didn't ask about me tonight. She only talked about you." She moved toward the bag and pulled out the two containers, setting them up at the little island counter where the two barstools sat.

"Really? That's so unlike her."

"Well, she started out by asking if you were okay. But then her questions were all about you and the hot billionaire, and if you were boinking him. She commented on his height. His hands. That he appeared to have large feet. And that his broody demeanor probably made him a lion in the bedroom."

My jaw hung open, and my tears turned to laughter. "She is unbelievable."

Brinkley handed me a fork, and she sat beside me and took a bite. "It is damn good. Totally worth the awkward conversation."

I groaned as the warm cheese hit my system. "I get the fascination with the man. Hell, I've been fascinated by him since the moment we met."

"You love him, huh?"

"I do."

"Have you told him?"

"Yes. We've said it to one another and I heard him say it when I was," I paused to hold my pointer and middle fingers on each hand to make air quotes, "*taking a long nap*. I know he loves me. I've known for a while."

"Damn. That's kind of hot."

"What?" I smiled and searched her gaze.

"That he stayed by your side during your hospitalized nap time and declared his love. And then he ran away when you woke up because the pain of almost losing you was too much. Sounds like a great romance book."

I chuckled. "Yeah, but that's why romance books are fiction. Living that is not as charming. You don't want to have to go through hell to be together, you know? But I'll mention it to Ashlan. She could probably use that plot in one of her books."

There was a knock on the door, and I startled.

"Do you think Bossman sent you more flowers?" Brinkley chuckled as she glanced around my apartment at the endless arrangements that he'd sent since he'd left the hospital and hadn't said where he was going.

I moved to my feet, and when I opened the door, my

mouth fell open. Dylan, Everly, Ashlan, Charlotte, and Vivian stood there. Vivian had a large pink bakery box in her hands.

"What is happening?" I shouted, and they rushed toward me one at a time.

Once they'd hugged me and Brinkley and pulled off their coats, Vivian handed me the box of pastries.

"We thought you might want some cupcakes when you got out of the hospital." She kissed my cheek.

Everly flicked her finger at Dylan. "We needed to see that you were okay. And money bags over here had her husband send the helicopter for us, and then we grabbed her in the city, and here we are."

"We know you're exhausted. We're just here for a few hours. We can eat cupcakes and laugh like old times." Ashlan wrapped an arm over my shoulder and rested her head there.

"You knew, didn't you?" I chuckled and glanced at my sister.

"I'm a reporter, Georgie, I know all things. Of course, I knew. Plus, someone had to tell them where your new place was. So, we figured I'd feed you real food first, and then we'd binge on Vivi's cupcakes." She carried the bakery box down to the coffee table, and we all found spots on the couch and huddled together.

"I can't believe you guys are here," I said, and my bottom lip started to tremble. Tears broke free, and once they started, I couldn't stop them.

But I felt all the love right here in this room, and it was exactly what I needed.

"I know you went through some serious trauma," Charlotte said, "but Brinks gave us the short version about what's happening with Maddox. Boys are so freaking stupid sometimes. I swear, they put us through hell before they sweep us off our feet."

Everly reached for a tissue on the coffee table and wiped at the tears falling down my face. "It's all going to be okay,

Georgie. Everyone handles trauma differently. Trust me, I can vouch for that. I was a runner myself. Sometimes, the fear of losing someone is so overpowering you can't think straight."

"But no one runs forever. He'll figure it out," Vivi said, handing me a chocolate cupcake with pink icing formed into the prettiest flower. "I know these are your favorite."

"Cupcakes make everything better, don't they?" Ashlan said as she reached for a vanilla pastry from the box.

"They really do." Brinkley took a big bite of the pink, sugary icing and groaned. "This is a good temporary fix."

"So, tell us about Maddox Lancaster. Wolf knows him and says he's a brilliant guy, and he really likes him," Dylan said before wincing. "Or do we hate him now? Because I can blow up a photo of him and get us some darts, and we can beat the shit out of him on paper if you want."

I laughed and I cried all at the same time.

Though my body was still recovering, and my heart was aching… family always made everything better.

Even if my heart was beyond repair, I wasn't alone.

But the thought had my chest aching again.

Because I wondered if Maddox was alone.

Suffering all by himself.

And the thought of him hurting made my entire body ache.

thirty-two

. . .

Maddox

THERE WAS a knock on my hotel room door, and I groaned. I'd already ordered dinner, and I didn't want to be bothered by anyone.

I'd come straight here after I'd left the hospital.

After I knew Georgia was okay.

Everything had come crashing down on me when she opened her eyes.

It hadn't happened when she'd fallen through the ice, or when I'd given her CPR. Almost like my body had been in fight-or-flight mode, and I'd fought like hell to get her to the hospital. To make sure she was okay.

But from the minute those sapphire blues had locked with mine… The minute I'd heard her hoarse voice speak…

My body had had a visceral reaction.

Flashbacks of my mother not responding when I'd breathed into her mouth and desperately pumped my hands down on her chest. Memories of her lifeless body being taken from our home.

I felt like I was reliving it all over again.

And I couldn't get the thought of Georgia lying on the ice with blue lips, her body completely still, out of my head.

Allowing myself to love someone the way that I loved her had been a reckless decision.

I'd fucked up.

Because I would not survive losing this woman.

I looked through the peephole and groaned. Why the fuck was Wyle here?

I pulled the door open. "Did you not get my text that said I was fine and that I didn't want company?"

He strolled past me. "Of course, I got it. I just don't give a fuck what you said."

I moved to the minibar of my suite and poured myself another whiskey straight up and tipped my head back, allowing the cool liquid to warm my throat.

"So, what's the plan, Maddox? You're just going to hide out here because your girlfriend almost died? I thought you were the mature brother."

"Fuck you. You have no idea what went down. You have no fucking idea what I've gone through. The shit in my head." I pointed my finger in his face, and he slapped it away.

"Don't be a dick. I've asked you hundreds of times to talk to me after that night with Mom, and you shut me down over and over. So don't play that card with me, brother. Tell me what happened with Georgia. I know she fell through the ice, and you got her to the hospital. But I want to know what's going on in that head of yours. What's got you so fucked up?"

I shoved past him and dropped to sit on the chair next to the desk that I'd been working at. "It's just too much, you know? She almost died, Wyle. I took her out there. And she was dancing out on the fucking ice like a little fairy, and then —" I looked away and glanced out the window at the tall buildings outside as the last bit of sunlight disappeared behind the clouds. "She was gone. Without warning. And when I pulled her out…"

He poured himself a drink and pulled up a chair beside

the table and moved it right in front of me, our knees almost touching. "That had to be fucking terrifying. Was she breathing when you pulled her out?"

I sucked in a deep breath before letting all the air exit my lungs. "Her lips were blue. She wasn't breathing. I turned her to the side and slapped her back hard, trying to expel the water from her airways. And then I did CPR until she started breathing. And there was all this blood and I didn't know what the fuck to do. I called 911, but they couldn't get there quick enough. So, I wrapped her up, and she was completely lifeless. Unconscious. But I knew she was breathing."

He covered my hand with his, and I startled. Lancasters weren't touchy-feely people. "That had to bring up some memories about the night you found Mom."

"It didn't at first. Not until after she woke up. And then it hit me like a ton of fucking bricks." I scrubbed a hand over my face. "Fuck, Wyle. If I lost her, I'd be done. So fucking done. How did I let myself get here?"

"You love her, and loving someone is scary as hell. But you're hiding here in the city, talking about how she could have died, and you would have lost her—yet you aren't with her now, when she needs you most?"

My head snapped up. "I was there when she needed me. I never left her."

"Yeah. You stayed when she was in a coma, brother. And then you took off the minute she woke up. That's a little fucked up."

"I'm in too fucking deep, Wyle. I needed to know she was okay, but this is too much for me. I've got to be careful moving forward. It hurts too much. And I took her out there, you know? What kind of shit boyfriend am I? I nearly killed her on Valentine's Day. The first girl I've ever loved. I'm not cut out for this shit."

He tipped his head back and finished the amber liquid in his rocks glass and set it down on the desk. "Listen to yourself. You're making no fucking sense. First of all, her falling through the ice had nothing to do with you. It was shitty luck. Shit happens, Maddox—we both know that. It was out of your control. You could have taken her to a fancy restaurant and gotten into a car accident on the way there. That would not be any more your fault than this was. A shit boyfriend does not plunge half his body into the freezing water, which, by the way, you could have fallen through that ice yourself. Going out there was risky. But you did it because you love her. You fucking risked your life for her, man." He slapped me on the arm when I stared out the window and waited for me to look at him. "Seeing her like that, I'm sure it fucked you up. Especially after what happened with Mom. But Georgia didn't die, Maddox. She's alive and well. And there's always a risk when you love someone, but we're all going to die eventually. There's no risk-free way around it. It doesn't mean that you stop loving just because you might lose that person someday. Guess what, *Harvard*, you will. We all will. You just have to love the best you can while you can, right?"

His eyes searched mine, and I shook my head. "What the fuck is happening here? Who are you, and what have you done with my unemotional brother?"

"Hey, I guess this was a wake-up call for all of us. I think we all shut down after we lost Mom, and, man, she would be so pissed about that. She was all about feelings, you know? About loving one another."

"Yeah." I nodded. I was so tired, and I didn't know what the fuck I was doing anymore.

"She would be so pissed at you right now." He barked out a laugh.

"Fuck you. She would not. She never got mad at me."

A wide grin spread across his face. "True. But… you went through all those heroic measures to save the girl. Hell, you breathed life into her and wouldn't leave her side. And then she wakes up, and you tap out? That's fucked up, brother."

I scrubbed a hand down my face. "I get it. I'm a dumbass. The truth is, I didn't know I was capable of loving someone the way that I love her, and that scares the shit out of me."

"You've never been a coward. Man the fuck up."

"Okay, can we give the offensive pep talk a rest and let me process this? How did you know I was even here?" I hissed.

"Hugh Reynolds must have gotten my number out of his sister's phone. He called me. Said he was worried about you. He'd gone by your house, and no one at the office had seen you since you left the hospital. So, I called the hotel, found out you were here, and came right over. I was actually in the city, meeting with Grandfather. I think I'm going to join the world again. You've inspired me. I agreed to take a position working with Dad. I'm interested in real estate. What can I say?"

"Well, aren't you just full of surprises?"

There was another knock on the door, and I rolled my eyes. "When I told the front desk I did not want to be disturbed, that seems to have been an invitation to knock on my door every five fucking minutes."

"Listen, I'm meeting a woman down at the bar. But I sent this surprise to you myself. You're welcome." He marched to the door and pulled it open, and I stood there, stunned to see Alana Reynolds on the other side of the door.

"What are you doing here?"

"She's your therapist. Hugh and I both thought you were due for a session. You've got an hour, and the helicopter is waiting to take her home." Wyle shrugged and winked at me.

The little fucker.

"I'm sorry you came all this way," I said, holding my hand out for her to walk in.

"Good luck, Alana. He's a tough nut to crack," Wyle said as he made his way out the door before letting it shut behind him.

I pulled a chair out beside the table, and she took her seat.

"Can I get you something to drink?" I asked.

"I'm good for now, but thank you."

I settled in the chair across from her. "Should you be away from Georgia right now?"

She smiled. "Georgia is okay, Maddox. She was released from the hospital, and her cousins all flew to Cottonwood Cove to surprise her, and she's doing really well. I stopped by this afternoon and saw all the arrangements that you sent."

I cleared my throat. "I wanted her to know that I was thinking of her."

"I think she knows."

"You don't seem like you're pissed at me…" I leaned back in my chair.

"I'm not. I'm your therapist right now, and I'm here to talk about you. You are clearly going through something, and I want to help you."

"I left your daughter when she needed me most," I said, raising a brow, almost begging her to get angry with me. That would make things easier.

Her eyes widened. "My daughter needed you most when you pulled her out of the ice and rushed her to the hospital. How could I be anything other than grateful? I know how much you love Georgia."

"I don't know why I ran. And now, I don't really know how to fix it. This feeling that I could lose her—it's overpowering me. I'm drowning in fear," I admitted.

She leaned forward and took my hand. "I know why you ran."

"Why?"

"Those first few days in the hospital, when she was in a coma and we didn't know if she was going to wake up, you were in shock. You'd experienced something traumatizing, just like she did. But yours wasn't visible to the outside world. But that fear, the flashbacks of that terrorizing moment, seeing her the way you did…" She swiped at the tear running down her face. "Doing what you did that day was not easy. You stayed calm and in control. You did what needed to be done. And now… it's not easy either. To process all that happened. To realize that you love someone so deeply, and the fear of losing them hits you smack dab in the face. Especially when you combine all of this with the fact that you've been through a similar trauma with your mother, and you didn't get this outcome. It's human nature to think of all that could have gone wrong. So… you're processing it all, Maddox."

"But she needs me."

"Georgia is a strong girl. But I do think you talking to her about this would be helpful for both of you. She knows you love her. That's not what's hurting her."

"What do you mean? Is she not recovering well?" I pushed to my feet as my heart started racing.

She stood, a kind smile spreading across her face. "No. She's physically on the road to recovery and doing well. She's hurting because she knows that you're hurting. She doesn't like knowing that you're alone and dealing with this on your own."

"My sweet fucking fairy," I whispered under my breath, but Alana chuckled, which made me think she heard me.

"I have one-hundred-percent faith in you, Maddox Lancaster." She squeezed my hand.

"I guess I've been bashing my father for leaving my mother when she was sick, and now, look at the way that I ran." I shrugged. I hated the thought that I could be anything like him. "I guess that makes me a hypocrite."

"You and your father are very different people, Maddox. I know that. You know that. You didn't leave Georgia when she needed you. No one is questioning your loyalty. Taking a step away when you're terrified is okay. What he did was completely different. But maybe there's a part of you that can forgive some of his actions, because they stemmed from fear.

Yes, he made some really bad choices after that, and that's on him. And what you do moving forward is on you."

She leaned up and kissed my cheek. "You're a good man, Maddox. I have all the faith in you. I'll see you back in Cottonwood Cove next week for our usual appointment?"

"Thanks for coming. I'm going to figure this out."

"I don't doubt that for a minute." She held her hand up. "I've got a helicopter to catch."

"Thanks again," I said as she made her way down the hallway.

I closed the door and squeezed my eyes closed.

What the fuck was I doing? Was I really going to let fear stop me from being with the woman I loved?

Fuck no.

Time to sober up and get my shit together.

And by *get my shit together,* I meant get my girl back.

Because nothing worked without her.

thirty-three

. . .

Georgia

I WALKED into the office and was greeted by a face that I didn't recognize. She looked to be a little older than me, with a kind smile.

"Hey, I'm Georgia. You must be the new receptionist?"

"Georgia, hey. Yes. I've only been here for a week. My name is Halle, and I started when you were in the hospital. Everyone was so worried. I've been so excited to meet you as you were in a meeting the day that I interviewed with your boyfriend," she said, before covering her mouth and shaking her head. "Am I supposed to know that? Anyway, I haven't seen the boss since I started here. Will he be in today, too?"

"That's okay. It's not a secret that we're together." I'd leave out the fact that I hadn't heard from said boyfriend in several days. "He hasn't been in?"

"No. Not since I started here last week."

So much had happened in the last week and a half. It felt like years had passed.

Maddox and I had declared our love to one another, I'd fallen through the ice, died, come back, slipped into a coma, recovered as quickly as I'd been wounded, and the man whom I normally spoke to a hundred times a day, who hadn't left my side the entire time I was in a coma, had left without saying where he was going.

But he owned the company. He couldn't hide forever.

"Well, he'll be in soon. It's great to meet you. Welcome to the team. You're going to love working here."

I made my way toward the stairs, and everyone came out of their offices to greet me. They'd all sent flowers and cookies and all sorts of treats while I'd been in the hospital. I took turns hugging everyone, and even Nadia Wright looked emotional when she squeezed my hand.

"We've missed you. Both of you. Is Maddox coming back today?"

A lump formed in my throat, but I forced a smile. "He'll be back soon. He's just taking care of a few things."

Freddy and Craig told me they'd be waiting for me at lunch to defend my ping-pong title.

Sydney told me she had lots of good office scoop to fill me in on, and she followed me up the stairs. "I was crying at the office one day because I'd been so worried about you, and Freddy consoled me. He's since taken me to dinner, and we're sort of secretly dating."

"I love that." I shook my head and smiled. "Two of my favorite people are dating. That's amazing."

"Ahhh… we missed all that sunshine at the office, Georgia. So happy you're back. Where's the boss?"

I cleared my throat. "He is taking care of a few things for his family. He'll be back soon. I'll see you at lunch."

"Thank you. I'm guessing he's the one who sent all the flowers this morning?" she said as she turned to jog down the stairs.

I hadn't received any flowers this morning. I'd gotten a few more arrangements yesterday, and I always sent a text letting him know that I received them, and I missed him. I wasn't going to beg him to come back to me. Not after all we'd been through. I knew he was going through something, and he needed to do it on his own.

He never responded to the texts. He just sent more flowers.

Bossman never did anything the easy way.

Like picking up a phone and telling me what he was going through.

Nope. He just filled my house with peonies and hydrangeas and every single card said the same thing.

I love you. M.

"Georgia!" Virginia squealed from behind my old desk. My chest squeezed at the sight of her sitting in my spot. The place where it all started.

That felt like it was so long ago.

"Hi! Thanks so much for all the sweet treats you dropped off for me at the hospital."

"Of course. Boy, did we miss you. The boss called to make sure your office was all set up for you this morning."

"Oh, really? Did he say when he was coming in?" I asked, trying not to sound desperate.

She looked at me, a little puzzled. Obviously, everyone knew we were together, but they didn't know that he'd left after I'd woken up or that we hadn't spoken in days.

"He didn't say. But I'm guessing he's the one who sent you all the gorgeous arrangements. I had them brought into your office."

I moved around the corner, and she was right behind me. There was a nameplate on the wall outside my office that read: *Georgia Reynolds, Creative Director*.

My breath lodged in my throat when I stepped inside to see the white desk, floor-to-ceiling bookshelves that ran along one wall, and every open surface was covered with a floral arrangement.

I needed a minute.

I was confused and tired and suddenly feeling angry that

the man just kept sending flowers that I didn't care about instead of showing up and talking to me.

"I'm just going to get settled in here. Thanks for everything."

She smiled. "Should I bring you a cup of coffee?"

"I'm okay for now, but thank you." I closed the door, desperate for a minute alone.

It hurt that everyone was asking about him, and they all expected me to know where he was.

Because he was my boyfriend, after all.

And the man that I loved.

He didn't get to just run away from me every time he was scared.

I picked up my phone and let out a long breath.

> Hey. Stop sending the arrangements. Enough flowers have been sacrificed for the fact that you're too cowardly to tell me what's going on.

> And, of course, you aren't going to answer. That's your thing, right? Well, I'm done with this ridiculous situation.

> Yes, it was scary. I hate that our first Valentine's Day together is tainted by all the trauma that went on. But you don't see me running away, do you?

> I died. You brought me back. We're all good. Get over it.

> I'm throwing all the flowers in the garbage. I'm not accepting another delivery until you speak to me.

I spent the next few hours going through emails and reading a few submissions.

"Hey," Sydney said as she stood in the doorway. "We ordered takeout in honor of your first day back. Can you sneak away for lunch now?"

She glanced around the room at the floral arrangements and gasped. I hadn't lived up to the threat of throwing them in the garbage. That was just me having a meltdown. "I would never have guessed Maddox Lancaster was such a romantic guy. He always seems so intimidating and grumpy to everyone else. But with you…" She moved to one of the arrangements and leaned down to smell the peonies. "He's just so different with you."

"In what way?" I asked because I needed a reminder at the moment.

"It's something that's hard to explain. But you know how we both love our romance books?"

"Yes."

"Well, the hero is always so consumed by the heroine, right? That's what we love so much. And that's how Maddox is with you. It's like no one else exists." She shrugged as she walked toward the door. "We were all imagining that he was glued to your side when you were in the hospital, and no one knew if you were going to wake up or not. That must have been terrifying for him. You know, when you realize you've found your person and then you think you might have lost them… Ahhh… I can't imagine."

I thought about her words as I followed her down the stairs. My chest was heavy, and I stopped in the lounge where they had pizza and salads set up. There was a cake that read: *Welcome Back!* It had an ice skate on it with a big red X, which actually made me chuckle for the first time since I thought about the accident.

My father had done some digging and found out that a kid had taken his snowmobile on the ice earlier that day, and someone had reported him to the park district, and he'd been cited. But they hadn't made it out to check the ice for safety yet.

Not many people went out there, so unfortunately, I'd most likely been the first person to step out on the ice after.

I hadn't had much of an appetite since I'd returned home from the hospital, but I picked at my pizza and tried hard to focus on the conversation.

But my mind kept wandering to Maddox.

And what Sydney had said.

I pulled out my phone and sent another text.

> Ignore those earlier texts. The flowers are fine. You can keep sending them for as long as you need to. I love you, Bossman.

Freddy convinced me to play a game of ping-pong, and the only reason I was beating him was because he kept getting distracted by Sydney, who was cheering and giggling as we rallied back and forth. My head wasn't in it.

And my heart… it wasn't even mine anymore.

"Lunch break is over," a deep voice said from behind me. "Get back to work."

I whipped around to see Maddox standing there in a pair of dark jeans, a crisp white button-up, and a navy blue sports coat. He held a large white box with a pretty red ribbon tied around it.

Everyone hustled, saying their hellos and welcome backs to him, and, of course, he completely ignored them.

But his dark eyes were on me.

"Such leading man energy," Sydney whispered as she squeezed my arm and moved toward her office.

"Hey."

"Hey," I said, not moving, the ping-pong paddle still in my hand.

"I got your texts, and I know you're tired of the flowers, so I thought I'd come see you instead."

"I don't need flowers, Maddox," I whispered as a tear streamed down my cheek.

"What do you need, Tink?"

I set the paddle down when he moved closer, and I looked up at him. "I need you."

"I'm yours. I have been since the first day you fluttered into my office." He set the package down on the ping-pong table, and his hand landed on my neck, fingers grazing my cheek.

"Why'd you leave?"

He sucked in a deep breath and then let it out. "Because nearly losing you made me realize how much I love you, and that scared the shit out of me. I don't want to live in a world that you aren't in, Georgia."

"I don't either. But I'm not running away from you because of it." I raised a brow in challenge.

"Well, if you ran, I would catch you. Every single fucking time."

"You can't run from this," I whispered.

"I know. I'm sorry, Tink. That's why I'm here. It was cowardly, and I don't have an excuse other than I was terrified I was going to lose you. I give you my word it won't happen again." He leaned forward and swiped at the tears running down my face as his forehead rested against mine.

"I accept your apology. Please don't tell me that those are the skates you were giving to me on Valentine's Day," I said, glancing at the white box.

"Hell no. You're never putting on another pair of skates, if I have a say in it. We're keeping you on solid ground, moving forward." He pulled back and handed me the box. "But there was something else in that box with the skates that I never got to give you. So, I went with something different."

I took the bow off as his hand settled on my hip, and he smiled. I pulled out a pink helmet that had my name painted in white on the side. "What is this for?"

"Pickleball, baby. I'm not letting you play any sports without the proper equipment ever again. In fact, you should wear it when you play ping-pong. Who knows what could happen with that little ball?"

My head tipped back in a fit of laughter. It felt so good to laugh again. "I am not wearing this helmet at the office to play ping-pong, you overbearing brute of a man."

"Look inside the helmet. There's a surprise tucked in there at the top."

I flipped it over and saw something gold and sparkly. Tugging the key out of the interior strap, I held it up. "What's this?"

"A house key. I wanted to ask you to move in with me before you fucking plunged into the ice, and I thought my world had come to an end." He tugged me against his body.

"You want me to live with you, huh?" I bit down on my bottom lip.

"I really do."

"I'm on a lease at my rental house, though." I shrugged, knowing that he wouldn't care about that.

"I bought your rental house weeks ago. I'm your landlord, baby. And I insist that you move in with your boyfriend. I've hated every second that I've been away from you."

"Me, too."

"So, is that a yes?" He bent his knees so that he was at eye level with me.

"It's always a yes for you."

His mouth crashed into mine, his tongue slipping inside, with not a care in the world that we were in the middle of the office. I heard clapping and cheering, and we both pulled away.

Maddox glanced over at everyone watching and rolled his eyes. "Does no one know how to work anymore?"

His voice was all tease, and he gently kissed the stitches that still remained on my forehead before scooping me up and cradling me in his arms as everyone laughed. He took the stairs two at a time as he hurried me to my office, passing Virginia and holding his hand up like he didn't have time for questions. I chuckled as I held the key in my grip like it was a lifeline.

Our lifeline.

The start of our future.

And I couldn't wait to get started.

thirty-four

• • •

Maddox

"AND THAT'S how you do it. Winners gonna win, and losers gonna lose!" Georgia shouted, doing some sort of crazy dance as she twirled around in her little skirt with tights beneath it because it was still chilly in Cottonwood Cove.

She refused to wear the helmet I'd bought her, even though the freaking ball pegged her in the cheek when she was playing with her brother, Cage, last week. He'd looked over at me sheepishly when I'd growled at him, and the rest of her siblings thought it was hilarious.

Normally, I despised losing. But losing to this girl felt like a win.

I loved her excitement and enthusiasm for the smallest things in life. She'd already taught me so much about living. Here I'd been the one born into this wealthy family, where I'd never wanted for anything. I'd traveled the world and experienced things most people would never experience. Yet Georgia Reynolds was teaching me about life.

About living.

Really living.

Playing pickleball, picnics at the park, walking along the cove, and Sunday dinners with family.

We'd been living together for two weeks, and to say that things were good would be a massive understatement.

I wanted things that I'd never thought I'd want.

And they all revolved around her.

I followed her inside as the sun was just starting to go down, and she said that she had a surprise for me.

"What are you up to?" I asked as we walked through the opening at the back of the house that was all glass, and the entire wall opened to the outdoors. We left it open when we were home because we were backed up to mountains and a gorgeous view of the ocean.

"I know it's hard to lose, so I'm going to do something nice for you. You just sit down on that couch, Bossman. I'll be right back."

I rolled my eyes because she loved to rub it in when she beat me. I acted annoyed, even though I fucking loved every second of it.

I sat back on the large sectional couch and glanced around the room. There were photos hanging on the walls now.

Pictures of my brother and me and even the photo we'd taken at my father's reception hung in a gorgeous frame on the wall. The photo of my brother and me with my mother was blown up and hanging amongst the others, as well. Photos of Georgia's family donned the walls, too. But my favorite photo was the one of me and my girl sitting under the stars. It was what we did every night now before we went to bed.

And as corny as it sounded, I thanked my lucky fucking stars every single day for this girl.

For the way she'd breathed life back into me.

The irony was not lost on me. Even though I'd been the one who'd literally resuscitated her, she'd actually been the one to bring me back to life.

"You ready?" she shouted from around the corner.

"Born ready, baby," I said, using the words she'd said to me so many times.

"Alexa, play 'Slow Ride' by Foghat," she ordered our little speaker in the kitchen.

The next thing I knew, her odd choice of music started playing loudly. It was the song she always played now, since I'd told her that was the day that I'd fallen in love with her without even knowing it. The day she'd danced around my closet like a fucking rock star.

She came around the corner wearing her pickleball skirt, minus the tights, a little white tank top, and my grandfather's cowboy hat. She wore her infamous wide grin as she strode toward me, and her feet were bare.

She started singing the lyrics to me, and I leaned back, enjoying the show.

She moved closer, climbing onto my lap, one leg moving to each side so she was straddling me.

My hands moved up her toned, lean thighs, and she just continued singing as she smiled down at me.

My fingers moved to the apex of her thighs, and I stroked over her thin lace panties as her head fell back, and she gasped.

We couldn't get enough of each other.

And it wasn't for lack of effort.

Her hands found my shoulders as I slipped my fingers beneath her panties.

"You want a slow ride, baby?" I purred, and she bit down on that juicy bottom lip of hers as I stroked along all her wetness as she groaned.

I reached down and shoved my joggers down my thighs, freeing my ever-eager cock, who couldn't get enough of this gorgeous woman. Her gaze locked with mine, two dimples on full display as she smiled before sliding down my thick erection, inch by glorious fucking inch.

I held her still once I was all the way in, because I just

wanted to savor the moment. Because when I was with this woman, I was exactly where I wanted to be.

I'd found my home and my joy and my happiness in this little bundle of a beautiful woman with sapphire eyes, a heart of gold, and the sweetest pussy known to man.

I gripped her hips and helped her slide up and down my erection, slowly at first. I tugged at her tank top and pulled down the straps, needing to see her beautiful body, nudging her bra down as my mouth came over her perfect tits, one at a time. I flicked my tongue at her hard peaks as she sucked in a breath and her head fell back.

She rode me into fucking oblivion.

And I never wanted it to end.

Her hands gripped my shoulders, and I knew exactly what she needed.

Because I knew every inch of this woman's body.

I moved my hand between us, rubbing little circles over her clit, just the way she liked it.

"Yesss," she hissed, as she moved faster.

I wrapped my hand around her neck and pulled her mouth down to mine, and I kissed her hard. My tongue slid in and out at the same rhythm as my dick.

She moaned into my mouth just as she exploded.

Her body shook as little gasps left her sexy mouth, and I pumped into her once more.

And that was all it took.

I went right over the edge with her.

Just like I always did.

WYLE

I think I'm going to buy a place in Cottonwood Cove. Now that I'm living in the city, I want to have a place I can go to on the weekends.

I'd been telling him how we took the boat out the last few weekends, and he knew how much I liked living here now.

Dad said he wants to get a place here now, too. You're all so fucking clingy.

WYLE

It's all your fault.

How is this my fault?

WYLE

When the grumpiest dude on the planet is living his best life, people take notice, dickhead.

Because I'm happy, you're all going to punish me by moving here?

He knew I was kidding, because having Wyle nearby had been really nice. My family was slowly healing from all the anger and loss that we'd experienced. My father wasn't my favorite person, nor did I ever think we'd be close, but I wasn't going to ice him out anymore. Claire was a good woman, and they were having a baby, and for whatever reason, I didn't want to miss out on that. We still had work to do, but we were moving in the right direction.

WYLE

Damn straight. Can Georgia set me up with some of her friends?

Well, the fact that you want her to set you up with multiple women is a bad sign. She's not going to go for that.

WYLE

I don't know. Your girl is pretty soft on me. She baked me my favorite cookies when I was in town last week. You better watch your back, brother.

Not a fucking chance. She likes the broody, brilliant type.

WYLE

Even though you're an arrogant fucker, I'm happy for you, Maddox. You deserve this.

Now you're going soft on me?

WYLE

Nothing soft over here, brother. And if you tell anyone what I said, I'll deny it and tell them that you used to sleep with that penguin stuffed animal Mom got you until you were thirteen.

That was you, asshole. Love you, too.

WYLE

Yeah, yeah, yeah. Love you, dickhead. See you in a few days. You're coming to look at spec homes with me on Saturday.

I laughed when I set my phone down and looked back at my computer monitor. Our numbers were up this year, and we'd signed several new authors to our client list, thanks to my girlfriend's keen eye for discovering talent.

I didn't even like calling her that.

Girlfriend didn't do her justice.

Because she wasn't just my girlfriend, or a coworker or even a friend.

She was *everything.*

There was a knock on the door, and before I responded, she was pushing it open.

She strode toward me wearing a white button-up, a sexy-as-fuck black pencil skirt, and a pair of pink stilettos. She came around my desk and rested her ass on the edge as her legs settled between mine.

"How'd it go?" I asked.

"We signed her to a two-book deal. Easy breezy," she said, clapping her hands together twice and smiling. "Ashlan Thomas is officially a client of Lancaster Press."

Georgia wanted to run the meeting on her own with her cousin, as she was building her portfolio of clients, and the fact that she was working directly with Mara Skye and Ashlan Thomas was impressive for someone in their first year of publishing.

But she knew books.

She knew the market.

She had a brilliant eye for design and worked closely with the cover designers to create the perfect packaging.

"You're amazing. How does it feel to have two of the most sought-after authors out there requesting to work with you?" My hands rubbed along the outside of her thighs.

"Pretty damn good. It's crazy, you know?"

"What?"

"Well, when I came to work here, I didn't know what I wanted to do with my life. I'd just gotten out of a miserable relationship. I'd studied art and really loved being creative, but I'd felt all this pressure to have a job that could support me." She shrugged as her hand found mine, and she interlaced our fingers. "And then I found you, and everything literally fell into place. I know what I want in both my personal life and my professional life, and that's all because I fell in love with you, Bossman. You helped me figure out who I was."

I tugged her down to sit on my lap and wrapped my arms

around her. "And you helped me figure out that there was more to life than just working and making money."

Her head tipped back, resting against my shoulder, and she looked up at me. "What more did you find?"

"That I could actually enjoy the fucking life I'd been born into instead of resenting it. That I did still know how to laugh, even though it had been a long time since I'd done it. And you're fucking funny, baby." I nipped at her bottom lip, and she chuckled.

"What else?"

My thumb traced along her cheekbone. "That I could love again, Tink. That's the gift you gave me. Because after losing my mom, I really didn't think I'd ever allow myself to go there again. To let myself love someone so much that it would hurt to lose them. And I felt it that day you fell through the ice. That terror that I knew I would never recover from. But here we are, living and loving, and that doesn't even scare me anymore."

"So basically, what you're telling me is that you can't live without me?" Her glossy pink lips turned up in the corners, two dimples on full display, and sapphire eyes that could see into a soul that I didn't even know I had.

"That's exactly what I'm saying. Which is why we're going to wrap you in bubble wrap for that family pickleball tournament you planned for this weekend."

"Not a chance. I can't smoke everyone if I'm being constrained." She laughed. "Wyle texted that he's going to be here for the tournament."

"He told me. He's looking for a house here now, too. Look at you, healing all the broken Lancasters and putting us back together."

"I told you, I have a knack for odd sports."

"You have a knack for making everything better, Georgia Reynolds."

"And you have a knack for making me feel like I'm the only girl in the room," she whispered.

"You are the only girl in the room." My voice was all tease as I raised a brow at her.

But she was right. It didn't matter if we were alone or in a room full of people.

She was the only one I saw.

The only one I needed.

"Such a smart-ass," she said, rubbing her nose against mine.

"You know how we sit under the stars every night because it's our favorite thing to do?"

"Yeah?" She pulled back to look at me.

"Well, when you're looking up at the stars and talking about all the things that you see, and I tease you because I can't see any of it?" I paused, and my gaze locked with hers.

"Yes. Which is why I want you to go get your eyes checked."

"I don't need my eyes checked, baby. The reason I don't see what you see when you look up at the sky is because I'm always looking at you. Even with all the stars out at night, I don't want to look anywhere else. Because I have everything I need. Everything I want. It's right in front of me."

"You just beat out every book boyfriend I've ever put on a pedestal with that confession," she whispered. "You're the perfect leading man."

"Oh, yeah?" My fingers tangled in her hair as I pulled her closer, her lips just a breath away.

"Yeah." The word came out all breathy. "You're ridiculously handsome and protective and broody. Bossy as hell. But you're sweet and romantic when we're alone. And don't even get me started on your filthy mouth when it comes to sex. You're the whole package, Bossman. I'm the luckiest girl on the planet."

"We both are. I love you, Tink."

"I love you. And we get to write our own happily ever after, don't we?"

"Damn straight. We've been writing it since the day you strode into my office."

And that was the truth.

I didn't even believe in that happily ever after bullshit before I met Georgia Reynolds.

But now I was a sappy bastard who wanted it all.

And now that I'd found her, I was never letting go.

epilogue

. . .

Georgia

WE'D JUST CLEANED up after having everyone over for dinner and a heated game of pickleball, where Finn gave me a real run for my money. The bastard had never even played, but he'd clearly gotten the same pickleball gene as me.

My parents had come by to watch, and my dad barbecued so Maddox could ref the games. Everyone but Brinkley had been here, as she'd had a big press conference to attend for some famous football quarterback that she couldn't stand. But my sister never let anything or anyone keep her from getting her story.

Cage had tried to teach Gracie how to play, but teaching wasn't his thing, as he had the patience of a Labrador puppy. So, she and I had had a lot of fun just tossing the ball back and forth to one another, trying to get it over the net.

Baby steps.

Wyle had stopped by, and everyone in my family loved him. He was working with Brax to find a home. Brax owned the real estate company in town, and he'd taken him out to see a spec home that Travis and his company had built a few months back. He showed us photos, and we all loved the property, which was walking distance from our house.

He and Hugh both challenged me to another round of pickleball, and I loved every moment of it. Having everyone here. The sun was shining, and it was a perfect day for a barbecue.

But then, Cupid shot an arrow straight into my heart when I glanced over to see Maddox bent down, Gracie's back to his chest, with his hands covering hers as she held the racquet, and he gently swung her arms back and forth, letting her feel the motion.

That was when Hugh had scored a point against me. Which was a small miracle in itself because he and Lila weren't remotely focused on the game as they had agreed to have an outdoor wedding at our house this summer, seeing as we had the big yard with views of the ocean, and they could look right down at the cove, which was their favorite spot in the world.

It was Maddox's idea. They'd been tossing out venues they were considering, and none had felt quite right for them. He suggested they do a tented area out in the backyard, and I'd gasped when he also suggested the pickleball court would make a perfect dance floor.

I'd agreed, of course.

Weddings before pickleball.

I was reasonable, especially when it came to love.

And it would only be covered for a few days, so I could live with that.

So, they'd walked the property, taking photos and talking about potential ideas for where to set things up. And we'd all given suggestions, as well.

Everyone had just left, and Maddox and I were settling on the couch to watch a movie.

"You were really sweet with Gracie today," I said as I leaned against him. "I think you'd be a great dad someday."

We'd talked about it—marriage and kids—often, and it was something we both wanted, but we weren't in a hurry to grow our family just yet. I was just finding my way in my new career and enjoying my life with this man beside me.

"I never thought that would be something I'd want, but you've changed my outlook on a lot of things." He kissed my forehead. "My fear is that they won't all be like her, you know? I mean, Gracie is the best. I'd have a dozen kids if I knew they were going to turn out like her. But if we get a little shit like Wyle? Then we're completely fucked."

I laughed hysterically, and he smiled as he watched me. He loved his brother, but they also loved to give one another a hard time. "I think we'll be fine with whatever we get."

"Yeah. I hope we have lots of little girls that look just like you and have all your goodness. It'll make the world a better place to have more Georgia—" He paused. "You will be taking my last name. You know that, right?"

"You don't want to be a Reynolds?" I teased.

"I already feel like one. Your family has a way of seeping in. Answer the question, Tink."

"When you ask *the question,* I will be happy to take your name… I mean, pending I say yes," I said over more laughter.

He rolled his eyes. "Well, I can assure you I won't be asking at any fucking ice-skating rink. But I'll come up with something special when that day comes."

"Maybe we could take a drive on Scooty, and you could ask me as our hair is blowing in the breeze and we're cruising down Main Street. We could get some mac and cheese after and get sexually harassed by Mrs. Runither."

"Not a fucking chance. I'm going to dazzle the fuck out of you."

"You already do every day," I said, because it was the truth.

I'd never known life could be this good. I'd always been a happy person with a positive outlook. But I couldn't have dreamed up all that had happened over the last few months.

Where I'd started.

Where I was now.

Who I was with, and how happy he made me.

And I was a girl who believed in fairy tales wholeheartedly.

But this one—this one was my favorite.

My phone vibrated on the coffee table, and I leaned forward and saw that it was Brinkley. I answered and put her on speakerphone.

"Hey, how did the press conference go?"

"Not freaking good," she said, and her voice cracked on the last word, causing me to shoot forward, my back ramrod straight. Brinkley rarely got upset, and when she did, it was usually for a good reason.

"What happened?"

"Lincoln freaking Hendrix happened." She sniffed.

"What did he do?"

"Everyone wants to know what that arrogant bastard is going to do next year. His contract is up, and he hasn't announced where he's going to play. And he always lets that asshole, Tex McGuire, break the big news. He never calls on me or acknowledges me when we're all gathered after games, no matter how persistent I am. He's a misogynist pig."

"Yes, you've mentioned that before," I said, glancing over at Maddox, who was listening attentively, as well.

"So, I found out where he was before the press conference. And maybe I snuck into the men's bathroom when I saw him go in there. I mean, so what!" she shouted. "We all pee, right? It's not fair that all the male reporters get the benefit of catching him off guard while I'm in the women's bathroom with who? There are no quarterbacks in that bathroom."

A small laugh escaped Maddox's lips, and I covered my smile. "That's true."

"So, I caught him off guard. I mean, it's not like I saw his package. He hadn't unzipped. But obviously, he's got issues there because he freaked out on me for being in there."

"Did he lay a fucking hand on you?" Maddox hissed.

"No, no, nothing like that. But he shouted about no one giving him a fucking second to himself. *Guess what, genius?* You're the GOAT of the NFL. You don't get a second to yourself. That's the deal."

"Did you say that?" I asked, because Brinkley was like a dog with a bone when she wanted something.

"I did. And then I just asked him to tell me if he had decided who he was going to play for. He's the hottest free agent on the market. It's the story everyone wants to break. And my asshole boss wants this story. *At all costs.* Those were his exact words."

"And did he answer you?"

"He did not. He pointed his finger in my face and said something like, *shame on you.* I shouted the same thing back at him as he stormed out of the bathroom. And then he goes and has me banned from the conference. Security literally escorted me out of the building."

"No!" I gasped. "That's horrible."

"It's not even the worst part."

"What happened?" Maddox asked, his tone hard, but I could hear the concern.

And that was when it happened. Brinkley started crying. I could only think of three times in my life that I'd seen my sister cry. One was when my mother washed her favorite white cashmere sweater with Hugh's red football socks. The next was when we found out that our aunt Beth had passed away from cancer. And the last time was when we'd found out that our father also had cancer, which was now in remission.

"Brinks," I said, my heart aching for her.

"He called me out publicly in the press conference and said I crossed a line. He actually said my name on national television. And my boss just called to tell me I needed to take an unpaid leave. It's the same thing as being fired, but he's keeping the door open *in case* I recover from this because he knows I'm good at my job."

"Hey. You've said for so long that you're tired of working for him and you'd rather be a freelance reporter. You're an amazing journalist, Brinks. This is your time to take that leap."

It was quiet on the other end, aside from a few sniffs, and then she cleared her throat. "That's true. I do have a lot of money saved up, and I wouldn't need to pay this high rent and stay in the city. I can come rent a place back home for a few months until I figure it out."

"Yes. That sounds like a great plan. You can build your freelance business."

"I like the sound of that. But I am not living in Hugh and Lila's casita, and I'm sure as hell not tucking tail and living with Mom and Dad. I need my own place. I'll find a cute house, and I can work from home, too," she said, her voice sounding upbeat now, like she had a plan and was going to be okay.

"Hey, we just had the floors redone on that rental house that Georgia was living in, and I was going to have a few more renovations done to it, but it's yours for as long as you need if you want it," Maddox said, stroking my hair. "And it's already furnished."

I smirked at him because I'd recently learned that none of that furniture had belonged to him. He had purchased it all for me so I wouldn't have to wait.

"Really? You haven't rented it out?"

"I wasn't planning on it. I figured we'd just offer it to family that came into town," he said.

"Well, I insist on paying rent. That's the only way I'll agree to move in. I don't need a handout, even if I was just publicly humiliated."

"You fucking Reynoldses and your pride about handouts

is exhausting. Fine. Rent is one dollar a month. Don't be late. We'll kick your ass to the curb."

My boyfriend tried to keep his voice even, but I heard the humor.

"Deal. And I'll make you guys dinner whenever you want."

"You don't cook," I reminded her.

"Well, now that I'm an unemployed sports journalist, I'll have more time on my hands. Maybe I'll start making jam in jars. Or growing my own vegetables. Yes, that's what I'll do. And then I'll go to Lincoln Hendrix's next game and chuck big melons at him from the stands," she seethed.

"This kind of anger isn't healthy," I reminded her. "Put him in your rearview mirror and move forward. When one door closes, another opens."

She groaned. "You're like a walking mantra. He closed that door in my face, and payback is a bitch. I'll walk through this new door, but I will find a way to get revenge on that guy. From now on, we all curse the ground he walks on. You got it?"

Maddox cringed. Lincoln Hendrix was his favorite player. He was a huge fan, and he'd been anxiously awaiting his announcement about where he would play next year.

"Done!" I shouted. "Lincoln Hendrix is enemy number one."

Maddox rolled his eyes before turning back toward the phone. "You need help to get packed up?"

"Nope. My apartment is small, and I can be out of there in a few days. I love you guys. I'll see you soon."

She ended the call, and I leaned against Maddox's shoulder. "Thanks for offering her the house. That was really sweet of you."

"Baby," he whispered. "How serious is she about us all hating Lincoln Hendrix?"

I turned in his arms to face him. "She's a bit of a grudge

holder. We still can't speak of Timmy Wilson because he kicked her bike over at the park when she was in third grade."

"Shit. Isn't Lincoln all three of your brothers' favorite player, too?" His voice was so concerned it was difficult not to laugh.

"Yep. They're big fans."

"And we all just hate him now?"

I shrugged. "It's sort of what we do. I won't tell on you if you keep your secret man crush private."

He moved so fast I didn't see him coming. He had me on my back on the couch as he hovered above me. "I only have one crush, and it's on my future wife."

"There you go again. Don't threaten me with a good time. Put your money where your mouth is, Bossman."

His mouth crashed into mine in response, and my lips parted in invitation.

Because I couldn't get enough of this man.

And I never would.

The End

Do you want to see Maddox propose to Georgia? Click here for an exclusive BONUS SCENE!

https://dl.bookfunnel.com/ktgk111av4

Are you excited for Brinkley Reynolds to find her happily ever after with Lincoln Hendrix? This small town, enemies-to-lovers, sports romance, ON THE SHORE, is available for pre-order now! Narrated by the amazing Erin Mallon and Joe Arden!

https://geni.us/ontheshore

acknowledgments

Greg, Chase & Hannah…you inspire me every day! I love you always!

Willow, Forever thankful for you! Your friendship, your support and the laughs that never end. So happy to be on this journey with you. Love you so much!

Catherine, thank you for your endless love and support. I'm endlessly thankful for your friendship. Love you always!

Kandi, I would not have gotten this book done without you! Thank you for your friendship and for all of your support! I love being on this journey with you and am so grateful for YOU! Love you!

Nina, thank you for guiding, listening and supporting me through this journey! Cheers to many more years together! Love you!!

Valentine Grinstead, I absolutely adore you! So thankful for YOU! Love you!

Kim Cermak, I honestly don't know what I would do without you. Thank you for keeping me on track, helping me with release stress, and being an amazing friend. I am forever THANKFUL for you!

Christine Miller, I can't begin to thank you for all that you do for me EVERY DAY!! I am SO THANKFUL for you!

Sarah Norris, thank you for the gorgeous graphics and always being willing to help even when I remember things at the last minute! LOL! I am incredibly grateful for YOU!

Meagan, my sweet, beautiful friend! Thank you for being an amazing beta reader and for creating the most beautiful reels and TikToks and for helping to get my books out there! Your support means the world to me!! Thank you so much!!

Kelley Beckham, thank you for setting up all the "lives" with people who have now become forever friends! Thank you so much for all that you do to help me get my books out there! I am truly so grateful!

Amy Dindia, thank you for creating absolutely perfect reels and TikToks. I am endlessly grateful!

Maren, Kat & the amazing Slack girls… thank you for the sprints, the laughs and the friendship!

Abi, Doo, Meagan, Annette, Jennifer, Pathi, Natalie, and Caroline, thank you for being the BEST beta readers EVER! Your feedback means the world to me. I am so thankful for you!!

Madison, Thank you for taking these gorgeous photos for the Cottonwood Cove Series. I am in love with this cover! Thank you so much!! Xo

Hang Le, thank you for bringing Maddox and Georgia's story to life so beautifully on this cover. I am so grateful for YOU!!

Sue Grimshaw (Edits by Sue), I would be completely lost without you and I am so grateful to be on this journey with you. Thank you for being the voice I rely on so much! Thank you for moving things around and doing what ever is needed to make the timeline work. I am FOREVER grateful for YOU!

Ellie (My Brothers Editor), So thankful for your friendship! I am so happy to be on this journey with you! Thank you for always making time for me no matter how challenging the timeline is! Love you!

Julie Deaton, thank you for helping me to put the best books out there possible. I am so grateful for you!

Jamie Ryter, I am so thankful for your feedback! Your comments are endlessly entertaining and they give me life when I need it most!! But this book took the cake! BEST COMMENTS EVER!! I am so thankful for you!!

Christine Estevez, thank you for all that you do to support me! I love when I get to work with you on projects. Your friendship truly means the world to me! Love you!

Crystal Eacker, I am so thankful for you! Thank you for doing whatever is needed! You are such an amazing support and I'm forever grateful!

Jennifer, thank you for being an endless support system. For rallying readers, posting, reviewing and doing whatever is needed for each release. Your friendship means the world to me! I can't wait to hug you SO SOON!! Love you!

Paige, my sweet, dancing, book recommending, fun, talented, amazing friend. Thank you for always making time for my books and for helping to get them out there in the world! I am so incredibly thankful for YOU! Love you!

Rachel Parker, I am so thankful for you! I love that I get to chat with you on every release day! I will keep Charlotte's swag coming for many years! Love you!

Sarah Sentz, thank you for making time for me on every release and helping spread the word about my books. I am forever grateful for you!!

Ashley Anastasio and Kayla Compton, I am so grateful for your endless support! I love the reels and TikToks that you make, and am so thankful for you both!

Mom, thank you for reading all of my words, and for the feedback and the love! I am so thankful that we share this love of books with one another! Ride or die!! Love you!

Dad, you really are the reason that I keep chasing my dreams!! Thank you for teaching me to never give up. Love you!

Sandy, thank you for reading and supporting me throughout this journey! Love you!

Pathi, I can't put into words how thankful I am for YOU! Thank you for believing in me and encouraging me to chase my dreams!! I love and appreciate you more than I can say!! Thank you for your friendship!! Love you FOREVER!

Natalie (Head in the Clouds, Nose in a Book), Thank you for all the support this year and always! I can't wait to see what the future holds, and I am so grateful to be on this journey with you! The countdown is on!! Love you!

Sammi, I am so thankful for your support and your friendship!! Love you!

Marni, I love you forever and I am endlessly thankful for your friendship!! Xo

To the JKL WILLOWS… I am forever grateful to you for your support and encouragement, my sweet friends!! I can't wait for us to all be together this year!! Love you!

To all the bloggers, bookstagrammers and ARC readers who have posted, shared, and supported me—I can't begin to tell you how much it means to me. I love seeing the graphics that you make and the gorgeous posts that you share. I am forever grateful for your support!

To all the readers who take the time to pick up my books and take a chance on my words…THANK YOU for helping to make my dreams come true!!

keep up on new releases

Linktree Laurapavlovauthor
Newsletter laurapavlov.com

other books by laura pavlov

Cottonwood Cove Series

Into the Tide

Under the Stars

On the Shore

Before the Sunset

After the Storm

Honey Mountain Series

Always Mine

Ever Mine

Make You Mine

Simply Mine

Only Mine

The Willow Springs Series

Frayed

Tangled

Charmed

Sealed

Claimed

Montgomery Brothers Series

Legacy

Peacekeeper

Rebel

A Love You More Rock Star Romance

More Jade
More of You
More of Us

The Shine Design Series
Beautifully Damaged
Beautifully Flawed

The G.D. Taylors Series with Willow Aster
Wanted Wed or Alive
The Bold and the Bullheaded
Another Motherfaker
Don't Cry Spilled MILF
Friends with Benefactors

follow me

Website laurapavlov.com
Goodreads @laurapavlov
Instagram @laurapavlovauthor
Facebook @laurapavlovauthor
Pav-Love's Readers @pav-love's readers
Amazon @laurapavlov
BookBub @laurapavlov
TikTok @laurapavlovauthor

Printed in the USA
CPSIA information can be obtained
at www.ICGtesting.com
LVHW091909110524
779688LV00019B/672